Last Dance
by
Earl T. Roske

Thank You:
Tim, Andrew, Erin
Trish, Megan
Andy
&
Wendy

For my wife and daughter.
&
Judy, my mom.
20 November 1943 – 14 March 2019

Other Work by Earl T. Roske

01

Acharon felt the barely perceptible slowing of the monorail carriages. With a force of will, he did not look up. This wouldn't be the first time that the carriages had slowed. Ever since they'd left Phoenix on the monorail track to Denver and then the detour via Cheyenne, Wyoming, Sovelet didn't hesitate to decelerate when she saw wildlife. She saw a lot of wildlife.

When it came down to it, Acharon was okay with not seeing animals. He had nothing against the fauna of the world rising to fill the gap humanity had slowly left. But it tended to remind him of San Francisco where an elk stampede had nearly trampled them to death. It especially reminded him of the wild dogs that had hunted him and Sovelet all throughout the city. The scars were physical and mental, and at 147 years of age, he could do without them.

Sovelet had nightmares over the San Francisco adventure more so than he did. Yet, she was still enamored with any living creature that came within even a binocular view of the carriages.

The carriages had been Sovelet's idea. Before this, they'd been spending days in a single carriage. All they could do was sit as it glided along the track over and through the Sierras, taking as direct a route as possible to Las Vegas. Granted, the trans-city carriages were larger and roomier than the city version. They even included a bathroom. But Acharon could only take just so much sitting. Once in Vegas, Acharon had spent a few days daisy-chaining three carriages together, creating flexible pass-throughs that allowed them to move freely between the carriages. The front carriage still had all the necessary controls and comfortable seating. The middle carriage housed a living room with a kitchenette Acharon had pulled out of a well-preserved motorhome, piece by piece.

The last carriage was the bedroom with a three-piece bathroom. It was here that Acharon had taken refuge with an old book, printed thirty-two years before he was born. He was trying to give it more attention than the carriages. Even though he was sure that Sovelet was slowing them down to gaze adoringly at some wild cows or deer, there was always the chance he was wrong.

"Ach!"

And this seemed to be that one chance.

Acharon stuck a torn wedge of paper into the book and slapped it shut. "On my way."

As he moved forward through the carriages, he briefly noted that it was still early in the day and that they were on a plain. There were animals, of course, but he didn't give them much attention. He grabbed a fruit bar from a basket in the kitchen as he passed through. Hopefully, they'd have fresh fruit or vegetables in New York. He hadn't thought to ask.

"What's wrong?" he asked as he stepped through the opening from living room carriage to control room carriage.

"Wrong?" She didn't even grace him with a furrowed-eyebrow look. "I wanted you to see this."

Which meant she wanted him to see some deer and admit they were cute.

"Alright." He grumbled his word as he moved next to her and looked out across the track slowly passing beneath them.

Acharon might not ever openly admit that Sovelet was right when she told him he had to see this. But this time, he was glad, and a little bit awed. As a child, in world history lessons on the events leading to the sterilization of all primate life, they always included pictures and videos of Africa. It was here that scientists confirmed that the chimpanzees and gorillas weren't reproducing. But even while addressing the GMO grain dust that covered the world, they showed the plains of Africa, dotted with herds of elephants, giraffe, and wildebeest. Sparse as those herds had been, they were still amazing to see.

Those herds had nothing on what currently grazed on the plains of Nebraska.

No matter which way Acharon looked, herds of native and non-native animals roamed and grazed. On one side, there were bison and zebras. Another area, cows and elephants moved alongside each other. The cows pulled at the grass while the elephants ate from bushes and stunted trees. Beyond the nearest herds, there were more. Different types of gazelle mingled together, moving aside as elephants and bison wandered through.

"It's amazing, Ach. Isn't it?"

"It's pretty impressive."

There had been a few zoos that tried sending all their wild animals to the countries of their biological origin. That project had turned out to be a colossal failure. Tens of generations had been bred in captivity, long before their progeny were returned to their native homes. Many of these animals failed to adapt to their once native environments. Those that did adjust quickly succumbed to diseases they'd never before encountered. So other zoos thought it more heroic and compassionate to euthanize the animals as their shrinking staff made it difficult to look after them. That resulted in protests and more violence. That was when they decided to release them onto the American plains. Give them a fighting chance as the angry slogan went.

But, as someone reminded them, the animals would overpopulate. Then, they'd overgraze and die of starvation while turning the plains into a dustbowl. That, too, had its solutions.

"There." Acharon pointed to a spot about a quarter-mile away. A herd of brown antelope-like creatures were running, clumped together, kicking up a cloud of dust and bits of grass. Behind them, close and moving closer to a lagging antelope, three female lions sprinted. Before Sovelet had a chance to gasp in surprise, the lionesses had taken down the slow-moving beast. They held it tight, one of them latching on to its throat, holding fast until all the life had drained from it. Within minutes of the assault, the rest of the lion pride, including a large and powerful looking male, trotted up and joined the feast.

"I did not need to see that," Sovelet said, turning away from the windows. She left the control carriage and slumped onto the couch covered with Navajo inspired blankets. They'd had the blankets for weeks, and still they smelled of mothballs from their original packaging.

"It's just nature, Sove," Acharon said. He was standing looking at the cupboards where they stored all the rations they'd scrounged at each major stop along the way. They were still less than halfway to New York, but they had enough rations for a return trip. Though, that wouldn't be necessary.

"Hungry?" The thought popped out as it occurred to him. Instantly he knew it was the wrong thought.

"Oh, Acharon!" Sovelet threw up her hands and then stood. There was a small smile on her lips that let him know that she wasn't really mad. "I'm going to go lie down until the ugly has passed."

"Could you bring me my book?"

Before Sovelet could respond with her feelings about fetching a book, they both found themselves staggering as the carriages slowed rapidly.

"That wasn't me," Sovelet said. She had braced herself against the couch, which had slid a half-meter across the floor. "Did we hit something?"

"A giraffe? I'll go look."

Even as Acharon moved forward, back into the control carriage, they continued to slow. By the time he was at the controls, the carriages had come to a complete stop. He leaned forward over the display and touchpads, to look at the track. The track appeared to be clear. He returned to the second carriage and reported to Sovelet.

"Nothing on the track. I'm going to go and take a look outside. Want to come?"

Sovelet looked a little shaken, but Acharon knew she'd come. If they could have put a balcony on the side of one of the carriages, Sovelet would have been thrilled. But that would have been impossible. Acharon knew this from experience.

"Okay, out we go."

Each carriage had an exit. Acharon had blocked the middle carriage door using a cupboard now filled with rations. Instead, they had to use the forward carriage door. The door creaked open slowly. It had been an awkward door from the beginning. Fresh air, infused with the smells of hundreds of thousands of wild beasts, their offal, and the kicked-up dust from their passing, washed through the opening. Acharon took a deep breath, surprised by the tens of smells he knew he could probably identify.

"Smells like a zoo," he said and got a gentle punch in the shoulder from Sovelet.

"Move over," she told him.

Acharon obliged by stepping down to the monorail base. He had to be careful because, unlike the cities, there wasn't a safety rail running the entire length of the track. That and the crusted guano made the initial step precarious. His right foot did slip once, but he already had a grip on the carriage's handrail when it happened.

"Should I stay here?" Sovelet asked.

"Good idea," Acharon said. There wasn't any need for both of them to risk themselves for a rail check. They certainly didn't both need to cake the soles of their shoes with guano. "Should just take a second."

He left her at the open door, breathing in the smells of nature and listening to the thousands of mouths chewing, the occasional lowing of one creature or another. There had even been one big cat roar which Acharon assumed was the male lion demanding to know what was for dessert.

At the front of the carriage, in the middle of the monorail base, the guano thinned, making Acharon's movements less precarious. He squatted and looked under the carriage. The rail looked in good shape. Nothing seemed to have interfered with the stabilizers on either side. There also didn't seem to be any animal or blood smeared across the rail or base. They hadn't hit anything.

"Nothing there," he told Sovelet. He sat on the floor inside the door and kicked off his shoes. They bounced off the base and then tumbled over, out of sight. "We might want to do a systems check."

There was no answer. Acharon turned around, concerned that Sovelet may have attempted to exit the carriage, too, and he hadn't heard her fall.

"Sovelet?"

"Right here." She appeared around the opening between the front two carriages, her favorite laptop cradled on one forearm. "System check is almost done. Nothing on the track?"

"Nothing." He climbed to his feet and went over to the control panels. The indicators for the solar panels were all green. He'd replaced and tested all of them before leaving Phoenix, knowing that enclaves were sparse across the middle of the country. In fact, after Denver, he didn't think they'd find one of any use until Des Moines. Batteries showed green as well. He'd kept all the battery banks from the three separate carriages and added a dozen more, just to be safe. Prepare for the worst had been his catchphrase since San Francisco.

So, the power system seemed to be working fine. That left the computers, which were Sovelet's bailiwick. He went looking and found her sitting on the bed, back to the headrest. Her fingers tapped rapidly across the keys. Even now, he knew not to interfere when she was working like this. He turned to leave.

"It's not the operating systems," she said.

He turned back. "Just a hiccup, then?"

"I guess." She pushed the laptop closed and turned, setting her feet on the floor. "What do you think?"

"Well, better safe than sorry. We'll move slowly and keep a watch on the systems for a couple of hours. See how that plays out."

Sovelet nodded. "Sounds like a plan."

"Good." Acharon started to turn and then stopped. "Have you gotten in touch with the New York Enclave?"

Their route had deviated twice, lengthening their time traveling to New York. Sometimes Sovelet was able to talk to someone in New York to keep them updated. Sometimes she had to resort to other measures.

"I left a message on their bulletin board back before we left Cheyenne. The network is spotty out here, so I'll try around Lincoln but probably nothing until Des Moines."

"Right, then. Guess I'll go watch the rail roll by."

At the front, Acharon overrode the motion controls and set the carriages moving. There was a gentle nudge as the carriages started forward, followed by a stuttering vibration that leveled out after ten or fifteen meters. He kept the speed down to twenty km/hr and scanned between the readouts and the track ahead. The engines drained the batteries a little faster, but they were on an incline, so that seemed within acceptable limits.

An hour passed, and Acharon hadn't seen anything wrong with the carriage systems. He'd slowly brought the speed up to 40 km/hr before walking away to grab something to eat. He'd found nothing wrong when he returned and was considering opening the throttle to bring them to 100 km/hr. That was when he noticed something odd about the track off in the distance.

Acharon dropped the energy bar he was eating onto a seat. He started tapping screen buttons, slowing the carriages down.

"Ach? We okay?" Sovelet was in the last carriage. Acharon assumed she was either watching the wildlife from the back or scanning through her hard drive of baby animal pictures. She'd had to abandon the hard drive with the human baby pictures when they left San Francisco and had been unable to build up her collection again.

"We're fine," Acharon said over his shoulder. "Track's not."

The carriages were crawling along by the time Sovelet had come forward.

"What?" Her voice faded away as she saw the track before them. "Oh."

When Sovelet had decided they should leave California to join the last twenty people in New York, she and some other savvy computer people had tested the tracks, mapping possible routes. They'd managed to locate any breaks in the track so that there weren't any surprises. That's why they'd come this way and not one of the other routes to the south.

"Why didn't our programs catch this?" Sovelet asked. The question was meant for herself as Acharon was a wiz engineer but not so much when it came to computer programs. "We tested every track."

"Not sure," Acharon said. He focused his attention on the controls and the track ahead. He was moving the carriages again, very slowly, approaching the damaged section.

The platform that held the monorail track, and doubled as a walkway in case of emergencies, was missing in the section just ahead. Some of the concrete and rebar that had been the platform could be seen dangling off the far end. The monorail itself was still intact, but it was sagging and twisted.

"I don't think we're going to make it across that," Acharon said.

He felt Sovelet push up next to him. He more heard than felt her hair moving as she scanned the area and the damage. Herds of animals still dotted the open prairie ahead of them, but not as much as they'd seen a couple of hours past when this whole new adventure had started.

"That might explain why the system hadn't registered the damage," Sovelet said. She pointed to the deformed track. "It's still connected. So any electric pulse shot through it would still read as green."

"But in other places, you got red, which meant the track was broken?"

"That's right."

"Which seems like a more normal situation than this." Acharon didn't like it. He couldn't say why. Maybe the damage went against what he would have expected as an engineer. He couldn't put a finger on it, but it was there.

"What?" Sovelet was grinning at him. "You think the lions did this?"

"You laugh." Acharon turned and moved over to the door. She was teasing, but then, maybe she'd forgotten what the dogs had almost accomplished when they were both in San Francisco. Yes, it was unlikely that lions managed to destroy the monorail line, doing just enough damage so that some unwary human might come zipping along and then crash, leaving themselves open to being devoured. But that didn't mean they should underestimate any creature capable of any semblance of reasoning.

He pushed the button, and the door slid open. The smells of nature wafted across their senses once again. Here, the guano wasn't so overpowering. It still meant the loss of another pair of shoes.

"Come on," he said, stepping down, careful not to lose his footing. "Let's go see how bad the damage is."

02

Acharon had made it safely to the broken edge of the monorail. From here, it curved over and down like a sculpture of a waterfall. Plenty of rebar was visible. They held chunks of concrete like a mad shishkabob. He ventured a little further, just enough to see the ground ten meters below. Here, he could see where the concrete that had broken away from the rebar had slapped deep turf-ripping dents into the earth. Nearby, a small herd of gazelle had been grazing but bolted as he'd approached the edge of the track's destruction.

"You going to fix it?" Sovelet had her mischievous grin on her face.

"I could, but I doubt we have the time."

She was teasing him, but he knew that she knew him very well. Repair solutions and other ideas had been trundling through his thoughts the moment he saw the damage. But the truth of it was that he didn't have the resources here to fix the track.

"Thoughts, then?"

Acharon stepped slowly back from his position near the edge. "Several. Can we go around? Take a different route?"

A sour grimace replaced Sovelet's mischievous grin. "There's two, but they'll both add months to the journey. We'd either have to go back to California and up to Seattle, then Vancouver. Or we go down to Austin, hit all the major cities along the southern coast before a zig-zag trip up to D.C., and then hope the subways are working."

"I could fix this faster."

"You could."

"If I had the tools."

"Yes, if."

Acharon looked at her and shrugged. "I don't have those kinds of tools."

"I didn't think you did." She smiled once more. "But you've never not planned for emergencies."

Acharon took a deep breath and a look around the open prairie. The herds of grazers had moved away from the track. They'd been pretty close when they'd first stopped. Maybe they thought he and Sovelet smelled funny. Maybe strange was different and best avoided. Not that any of them would have been much help. Well, a couple of elephants, if they were obliging.

"Of course I plan for the worst," he said. He started a cautious walk back toward the carriages.

"Never doubted you," Sovelet said. She took his arm and planted a kiss on his cheek.

Acharon leaned into the kiss, making it last a millisecond longer. "I've never given you a reason to doubt."

"Oh, off with you!" Sovelet gave him a gentle nudge, coated with laughter.

They both worked their way to the carriages. Acharon stopped to remove his shoes and quit again when Sovelet passed him, entering the carriage with her guano-stained shoes. She looked back at him, arching her eyebrows.

"Right," Acharon said. He climbed to his feet and entered the carriage. "It's not like we'll be staying here anyway."

Under the bed in the last carriage were all the parts of a small service carriage. It was bare-bones. There was a single set of rollers and stabilizers, a platform with controls, and a shade cover.

"We'll pull batteries from the carriages when we're ready," Acharon explained. "Probably nothing more than cushions to sit on. Should be okay until Lincoln."

"Should I pack anything?"

Acharon knew she wouldn't pack a lot, but most of what she picked would be burdensome. Several laptops, a box of external hard drives. They'd need food, too. That would add more weight. More weight meant Achron was going to have to make several trips.

"Pack the essentials," he finally said. "We can restock in Lincoln if they still have an intact warehouse."

He'd once had a map with all the warehouses across North America marked. But that had been in his toolshed, back on their Acharon-made island across the bay from San Francisco near the Sausalito marina. But every major city had at least two.

Sovelet retrieved a pack from a storage box in the middle carriage and started shutting down her computers.

While Sovelet worked on her stuff, Acharon unbolted all the parts for the service carriage. He then removed the rear window from the last carriage. With the way clear, he began pushing everything he was going to need through the opening. It took several hours to get everything onto the monorail base, and he only stopped for lunch when Sovelet insisted. She'd gone ahead and warmed up several pouches of chili that weren't half bad.

With a hearty lunch out of the way, Acharon started the next task, which was getting everything to the ground. For him and Sovelet, it wouldn't be problematic. It was only a short walk back to the last support. All supports had ladders on the outsides for emergencies.

To get the equipment and supplies down, Acharon rigged a pulley system with a winch. The winch was electrical since he had power here. The whir and whine of the winch and cable as it unwound and wound was a stark contrast to the quiet of the world around them. Even the ocean-like sound of thousands of herbivores munching as one was absent as everything with four legs seemed to have retreated from the land near the monorail track.

Despite his constant gazing and reflecting, it only took another hour to get everything down to the ground. Sovelet's stuff went last as she'd been anguishing over what to leave. Acharon finally relented and let her bring two bags of absolute necessities.

"Shall we?" Acharon asked once the last of their supplies were down.

They walked the fifty meters back to the last upright. Acharon tied them both off with rappelling harnesses and lines. Everything had been designed to survive until the last human had died. But many people had exceeded those expectations, and people like those waiting in New York were fifty to sixty years past the old expiration date. So, while the rungs going down the pillar might be just fine, they also might not, and better safe than painfully broken.

"I'll go first," Acharon said. He slid over the side and found the first rungs with his foot.

"Not very gentlemanly of you," Sovelet said. Despite her joke, there was a bit of worry around the edges of her smile. They'd both had some close scrapes over the last few years, each potentially life-ending.

Once his feet were on solid rungs that showed no sign of age, Acharon felt better about this particular part of their adventure. Even though she didn't need it, Acharon regularly acted in ways to protect Sovelet from any harm.

"Just wanted to dust off the cobwebs," he said from five rungs down.

He was ten meters down the ladder when Sovelet whispered loudly. "Acharon, stop. Please, stop."

Acharon shook his head. "The rungs are fine. You can start."

"The lions, Ach."

Acharon froze on the ladder. Slowly he turned, first just his neck and then at the waist, releasing one hand to allow for greater motion. He didn't see them at first and thought perhaps Sovelet had spooked at shadows. She wouldn't have played a prank, not in this situation. They both knew how deadly a determined animal could be.

When he finally thought he saw them, it turned out to be the remains of some other creature its remaining hide hanging loosely across its ribcage. Then he saw them. There was a little dip in the land, a wrinkle of terrain. In it, lined up like judges at some competition ready to raise their scorecards, six female lions lay as still as the Great Sphinx of Egypt. Further back, a couple of cubs chewing on his mane, the male lion also sprawled, watching and waiting. Their presence may have been the real reason the buffalo and other herd animals chose to dine elsewhere.

As much as he hated to do it, Acharon reversed direction and climbed back up to the top of the monorail base.

"Good eye," he told Sovelet.

"I almost didn't believe it when I first saw them. Maybe we should go back to Phoenix, reroute."

"No," Acharon said. "For this, too, I have planned. Well, maybe not lions specifically."

He returned to the carriages, Sovelet close behind. She slowly widened the gap between them as she frequently stopped to eye the lions. Acharon noticed her absence when he went to enter the carriage. He turned back to see her attention elsewhere.

"I doubt they're going anywhere, Sove." He climbed inside the carriage, reappearing at the open window. "They're curious and probably won't leave until they are satisfied. Mentally or gastronomically."

Sovelet had finally entered the carriage as he'd continued to speak. "What do you have?"

Under the bed, where he'd bolted the service carriage, was a gray metal box. He flipped the lid of it open.

"I got this."

What he referred to was an old M4 semi-automatic rifle with a black, corrugated tube beneath the barrel - an M203 grenade launcher. Acharon pulled the M4 out of the box along with a small case of 40mm grenades. He tapped the tube.

"This is a grenade launcher," he said.

Sovelet did not look pleased. "I know what it is."

Despite the cold fact that wild dogs in San Francisco had nearly killed each of them, she was still determined not to harm another living creature. Acharon had a slightly different philosophy now. He'd do his best not to kill anything, but he'd put a little harm on them if needed.

"They're the flashbang type of grenades," he explained, pointing to the markings on the case. "All bark, no bite. Well, maybe a nibble."

Acharon unpacked a shotgun for later, and they both returned to the ladder again. The lions did not appear to have changed positions, except for the cubs who had fallen asleep, one between the male lion's paws. Acharon pulled the grenade case open and tore through the plastic to retrieve the first one. It settled into the chamber with a metallic clink. He stepped forward and pulled the butt of the M4 to his shoulder.

Before he took aim, he turned to Sovelet. "I've never done this before."

"I know, I've been with you for nearly a hundred and fifty years."

"Then you'll know what to expect." He turned, aimed, and pulled the trigger. There was an unimpressive whomp noise. Acharon, being aligned with the grenade, saw it for a flash of a moment, and then he lost track of it.

"That was anticlimactic," Sovelet said. She'd moved forward as she spoke, one hand shading her eyes.

"Hold on." Acharon was loading the second round, doing it by feel so that he could watch for the flash when it landed.

The sound of the grenade exploding was sharp, the flash like concentrated lightning. Three of the female lions rose to their feet. The two cubs barely stirred. Acharon had shorted his target and not accounted for the breeze that had been picking up.

"Short," Sovelet said.

"Thank you." Acharon aimed and repeated the procedure.

Again, the whomp of launch and the sharp bang as it exploded on the ground. This time Acharon had aimed well. The grenade landed only a couple of meters from the lionesses. All six bolted from where they'd been watching Acharon and Sovelet. They sprinted past the male lion who was trotting away from the monorail line, the cubs tight behind.

Acharon rested the butt of the M4 on his hip as he watched the lions retreat. To his side, he could see Sovelet stepping up to join him. She was still holding one of the 40mm grenades in one hand.

"I'd like to say, 'That's, that,'" Acharon said, "but, according to previous experience, this isn't the end of it."

"We can still go back." Sovelet held out the grenade for Acharon to take.

"I'd still have to go down there to get your computers. Don't worry. We'll be fine."

Acharon turned back to the monorail track where he'd left the remaining grenades and added the one from Sovelet to the rest before closing the case. Sovelet didn't move, her gaze directed toward the lions' retreat. Not until Acharon started over the edge did she come out of whatever reverie had paralyzed her.

"You sure we shouldn't wait?"

Acharon paused on the ladder. "We're already into the afternoon. If we're lucky, we'll reach Lincoln before dark. That's if we don't dawdle."

He continued down the ladder. A few moments later, he could see Sovelet following.

When Acharon had planned for the possibility of using the service carriage, he hadn't planned on having to haul it a hundred meters after lowering it from the rail base, just to lift it again. So for the next couple hours, he trekked back and forth, dragging, pushing, or carrying everything to the next ladder past the broken span.

On his third trip through, pulling the stabilizers across the bumpy terrain, he stopped at the fallen concrete for a little breather. Even with all the gene correction and medical advances that made his 148-year-old body as healthy as a 21st century 50-year-old, it was still a lot of work he was doing. While he indulged in a short break, he let his gaze wander across the broken concrete.

"What do you see?" Sovelet asked. She was approaching with the shotgun over her shoulder and a thermos of water. She offered him the water. He took a long pull from the thermos.

"The concrete." He pointed at the jagged edges. "See how much brighter the broken edges and sides are? If this had happened even weeks ago, it would be more faded than it is right now.

"So, you're saying this happened recently?"

"Yes. Less than a week."

Sovelet took back the thermos and took a sip from it.

"I guess we were lucky to not be on it when it gave way."

"Something like that," Acharon said. He started pulling on the stabilizers again, bumping them across the prairie.

The stabilizers were the last of the heavy stuff. After that, the other pieces went quickly. It'd been an hour and a half of hoofing equipment. Now, Acharon had a pulley system rigged at the top of the monorail base with ropes run and ready to work.

He started with the heavy stuff first, hoping he'd still have the energy to put the service carriage together when he had everything topside. Fortunately, Sovelet was a big help, unlashing the things Acharon pulled up and shuttling them out of the way.

It was during one of those moments when Sovelet was out of sight, and Acharon was bent over, tying the next item on, that the lions attacked.

Acharon felt the itch of being watched and heard the rustle of prairie grass that hissed faster than the wind that swatted at it. He turned in time to see a female lion pounce. Her paws were stretched wide, the claws clear and sharp, wholly unsheathed.

There was little time to react, and Acharon barely had time to snatch up the thermos before she landed on him. As she went to crush his throat, Acharon shoved the thermos in her mouth, holding it in place even as her teeth and claws slashed at arms and shoulders. The lion kept trying to shake the thermos out of her mouth. Each time she did, Acharon shoved it in a little deeper. Finally, the lion back stepped several times, pulling the thermos out of Acharon's hand.

Acharon pedaled backward as the lion shook her head repeatedly to dislodge the thermos. Acharon could feel his clothes were wet and growing wetter. The fresh air across his shoulders hinted at the large tears in his clothes. His arm was also soaked, and he knew it wasn't from the lion drooling on him.

A hollow, metallic ting declared the lioness free of the thermos. Acharon could only watch as the growling lioness crouched. She was about to attack. Acharon needed another defense. But the pain in his arm numbed his brain, robbing him of ideas.

Then, the ground in front of the lion exploded, a flash of condensed lightning blinded Acharon. When he cleared his vision with rapid blinking, the lion was gone.

"Ach!"

He had to pause and regain his composure. "I'm here," he called back. He was doing his best to sound okay and safe. He would be surprised, though, if it fooled Sovelet. A small drawback of knowing someone for more than a century and a half.

"You need to get up the ladder," Sovelet said.

Her voice was sounding more distant. Was she moving down the track? Maybe she was trying to distract the lions? That'd be a good idea. Then he could rest.

"Acharon! They're all coming. You have to move!"

"Right." His voice was barely a whisper, which he found surprising. Where had all his energy gone? Maybe he did need a nap. A little rest. If only he didn't feel wet and sticky.

"Ach! Hang in there. I think someone's coming."

Acharon wanted to laugh. Yes, the lions were coming. There wasn't another human alive this side of 12th avenue in New York. Was there? He needed to rest. There was a roaring in his ears that just kept getting louder.

Yes, just a short nap.

03

The first thing that occurred to Acharon was how soft the ground now seemed to be. The second thing was the rain. He could hear it, and considering how out in the open he was when the lion attacked him, the rainwater should be washing over him.

Unless it had all been a dream.

After having been hunted through the streets of San Francisco and then finally attacked by the largest dog he'd ever seen, it was understandable that he would have nightmares about it. So maybe the lion hadn't attacked him. Maybe the track wasn't damaged. Maybe he was still back home on his self-made island near Sausalito, and no part of the last few months had ever happened.

There was one small problem with this great solution to his troubles. Acharon could feel a deep, slow throb of discomfort in his arm and his upper back. The very places the lion he'd dreamed of had attacked him.

So, not a dream.

He opened his eyes a fraction of a centimeter at a time. At first, the light flooding his vision faded out everything he might see. As he opened his eyes a little more, and they adapted to the brightness, which wasn't that bright after all, he found himself looking up at a cracked ceiling. Cobwebs hung like tired banners in corners.

On the edge of his vision, he could make out a wall covered in a blue and white pattern of wallpaper, a corner of it curled away. Several pictures hung crookedly on the wall, images of people and places that probably once had meaning.

With a slow turn of his head, Acharon could see a dresser and matching vanity of dark stained wood that would probably shine like glass after a good dusting and cleaning. A chair at the vanity was turned toward the bed. A pair of pants and a shirt hung across its back. On the seat, still in packaging, were socks and underwear. His old boots sat on the floor at the foot of the chair.

Past his head, where he couldn't quite see, had to be the window. He could hear the rain tapping frantically at the glass, occasionally urged on by a gust of wind. He was surprised by the sound. It hadn't rained once during the trip so far. Now that he thought about it, he hadn't seen rain in over ten years.

So, Acharon knew where he was. He just didn't know where 'where' was.

He moved to pull back the sheet and blanket that covered him, but his hand wouldn't cooperate. It was like trying to pick up a nail while wearing an oven mitt. He looked at his hand and saw why. Bandages and an easy-release cast held his arm from elbow to fingertips hostage. Acharon could have assumed that Sovelet had done some emergency first aid on his arm. However, the quality of the work, its characterless style, implied a medi-pod. It was not a last-generation pod. Not like the one that replaced his eye and later replaced Sovelet's lungs. This medi-pod was probably second or third generation.

Great. More scars.

With his left hand, he reached across and pulled the covers off. Slowly and awkwardly, he shifted his feet off the bed and rocked himself up to a sitting position. His feet touched down on a braided oval rug.

It occurred to Acharon that he'd been teleported two hundred and fifty years into the past. That or the only shelter Sovelet could find was in a museum. One of those old homes they used to preserve as examples of how people lived in the good old days.

Now that he was awake, the room took on the familiarity of a dream. He had a vague recollection of entering the room. But the memory was mixed with a hallucination because two people had helped him to bed. If they weren't in New York, and they weren't, then it was impossible and, therefore, a dream.

He turned from his musing to examining himself, now. His feet and legs looked okay. There were a couple dozen minor scratches but no stitches or bandages. His back felt tight. He pulled his shoulders forward and felt the pull. More bandages. If the dream of the lion attack had been real, he was lucky even to have shoulders. The memory of the attack shot a spike of adrenaline through Acharon. If he wasn't awake before, he was awake now, and with a pounding heart.

He stood and paced the adrenaline off for a few seconds. He kept looking at the window as he approached and turned away. The outside of the glass had broad waves of rainwater running down it, punctuated by little dots where more rain threw itself at the collective. He finally stopped directly in front of the window and focused beyond the rain-slicked glass. He found himself looking down from a second-floor window onto a street of small brick houses with overgrown lawns. Rusted mailboxes sat balanced atop posts that had become backbones to ivy and thistle.

His voice cracked as he spoke to no one. "Where am I?"

Receiving no answer, Acharon turned to the business of getting dressed. The cast made getting the shirt on a bit awkward, and he hadn't had this much trouble tying a shoe or buttoning a button since he was a child. But, when finally dressed, he opened the door to the room and stepped out into a hallway.

There was a door directly across from where he stood. A third door was down the hall on the right. To the left, he could see the first hint of a stairwell leading down.

"Hello!"

No answer.

Acharon knew he shouldn't worry, but he found himself starting to do precisely that. With all the speed of a battered old man, he made his way down the stairs to an entryway. He had that brief sense that he'd come through here, but he'd been sluggish of mind and hallucinating. Even now, he wondered why there were two people in his memories. Seeing double in a hallucination? He supposed that was likely. Suvelet would sort it all out. All he had to do was find her.

He searched the house. Not for Sovelet but for the kitchen . He reasoned that if she put him here, she would have also left him some food. Or at least he hoped so. He had to cross an old-fashioned dining room where a mirror over a mantled fireplace on the opposite wall reflected the rain still washing the windows.

The kitchen was through an arch. It was full of linoleum, dusty chrome, and an apple pie. Acharon approached the counter, one slow step after another. He wanted to say it was a plastic pie, a decoration. The scent of apple and cinnamon, however, was impossible to deny. There was also a fork and a plate. Without any further hesitation, he scooped a slice onto the plate and dug in.

After leaving San Francisco, they'd stopped a few places where the auto-diners still worked. It was good to have a hot meal prepared and served, even if everything was dehydrated or freeze-dried to start. Psychologically, it was better than ripping open a dull-looking plastic packet and spooning out whatever was in it. All of it, the auto-dinner food, the ready-to-eat meals, were wet sawdust compared to the pie. He'd hadn't had real pie since before they'd left their home. And that thought made him pause again.

This was a real pie. Where did Sovelet find it?

Acharon had a second piece before he left the kitchen, still licking a bit of the filling off one finger. The rain had slowed, which was a good thing. Maybe now he could find Sovelet.

On the covered porch, he took a seat for a few minutes. The rain was barely a sprinkle. The sky, looking like cracked concrete, leaked rays of sunlight. Places where water had pooled, and sunlight touched, released lazy tendrils of steam. Moss, grass, overgrown ornamental bushes, trees, all had grown with abandon. The roadway was merely a suggestion under a blanket of grass and dirt.

He was of two minds. On the one hand, he wished that it would rain harder so he'd be forced to sit a little longer. On the other, he wished that it would stop so that he could go looking for Sovelet.

Very quickly, the choice was made for him. The last droplets of rain had fallen, the sun had forced more of the clouds apart. The ground steamed like some primordial landscape.

The primordial landscape brought the thought of lions to mind. How far were they from the monorail track? Was it far enough? Acharon stood. What if they'd gotten Sovelet? He winced his way down the stairs and toward the grass-covered roadway. His boots sloshed in the soaked earth, squelching with each step.

On the road, he stopped and looked up one side and down the other. To his left, the street seemed to run off into the distance, finally lost among thick trees and rain steam. The other way, there appeared to be two more blocks of the same and then squat, square buildings of brick and glass. It was a small-town main street. He went that way, toward the buildings. If she were there, she'd either be looking for more food, or internet access, or even new clothes like what was laid out for him.

The more he moved, the more loose he felt. The more loose he began to feel, the quicker he walked. Soon enough, he was on the corner of the street he'd walked down and that of the main thoroughfare that was once the heart of the town.

The heart seemed to be doing just fine.

He and Sovelet had coasted through many places on the monorail. At first, they'd taken the occasional stop to look around. Each time there'd been overgrown streets, trees and bushes and tall grass taking over everything. It had become so consistent and monotonous that they'd quit stopping except when necessary for food and water resupply.

This town was not like all those others. The sidewalk was clear and clean for a block in either direction. The road itself, though cracked and potholed, was clear of dirt and grass for several blocks in both directions. There were benches, street lamps, and street signs. The fronts of the stores were clear of vines and other destructive growth. No wayward trees were sprouting in the middle of the sidewalk or against the buildings.

And the buildings. The windows were clear of dirt and bird droppings. The signage above them was faded but also clean. Acharon walked to the barbershop that was just to his right. The old-fashioned barber pole was attached to the wall next to the door. It shone, free of dust. Covering his eyes, Acharon took a peek through the glass. He jerked back so fast he almost fell over.

Inside the shop, a man was sitting in the barber chair. The barber stood over him, comb and scissors in hand. Acharon recovered and stared in disbelief. No one was supposed to be alive through the heart of the continent. Every known living being had been on the east and west coast and soon just the east. So who were these people?

Acharon put decency aside and stared at the two men in the barbershop. He stared long enough to realize they weren't moving. They weren't paused in surprise, looking back at him.

"What the hell." Acharon's voice was a whisper.

He moved back to the window and peeked through once again. Now that he wasn't backpedaling, Acharon was able to study the two men a little better. They still weren't moving, but at least he now knew why. They were mannequins.

"Doubly, what the hell," Acharon said.

The entire shop inside looked clean enough actually to open up for business. There was a light layer of dust, but that was it. Something you might see in any shop too busy to dust every morning. Acharon stepped back and looked down the street. The next shop was a hardware store.

He walked down to the windows and looked inside past the stacks of paint cans and ladder display. This time he wasn't shocked to see several people at the counter. The proprietor was at the register, and a young couple was standing with a full red basket sitting on the counter, waiting for its contents to be rung up.

Curious, Acharon went over and tried the door. It was unlocked. He slowly opened the door, cringing as the bell overhead jangled his presence.

"Hello?" he called out.

There was no answer, and that didn't surprise him at all. He was very much tempted to enter the shop and wander around, but he still had to find Sovelet. He shut the door soft enough to avoid the jangling bell and moved on.

The next storefront was a dentist's office. There were no mannequins here. He crossed the street to a small clothing store where a mannequin with its baby in the stroller was accepting a package from a young, female mannequin behind the counter.

Now back near the corner where he started, but on the opposite side of the street, Acharon saw a diner. For Acharon, a diner meant an automat that turned freeze-dried or dehydrated foodstuffs into meals. It was doubtful that this diner was the same.

The big, unlit neon sign over the door read, Claire's Eats. Despite the two generous servings of pie he'd had, Acharon's stomach grumbled. He patted it. Find Sovelet first, then eat. He shaded his eyes and looked through the window of the diner.

It was much busier than the other shops. A mannequin behind the counter was serving coffee to two other mannequins sitting on counter stools. Several booths had pairs of mannequins sitting over empty plates. Two more occupied a table in the middle of the room.

One of them turned.

Acharon stepped back. It wasn't his imagination. There'd been no trick of the light here or in any other store. He stepped back to the window and looked again.

"Sovelet."

She was waving for him to come inside.

Acharon found the door and turned the knob. Inside, the place was as clean as all the other shops. Chrome glistened, wood glowed. Sovelet smiled as she came up to him.

"I didn't expect you to be awake so soon." She hugged him, her arms gentle on his shoulders.

Acharon hugged her back, a little more securely. "There wasn't a note," he said.

She stepped back, her hands still gently on his shoulders. "I went out for a bite to eat, Ach. I was coming right back."

He nodded. There was no doubt to Sovelet telling the truth. In her place, he would have done the same thing.

"Sovie," he said, his gaze still wandering around the diner. "How did we get here?"

Sovelet laughed. It raised a smile on Acharon's face, as it always did.

"That's a long story," she said. "But, let's start here."

She turned to his side, and Acharon's knees went weak. One of the mannequins was standing.

"Acharon, I'd like you to meet Katuva."

04

Katuva had a soft smile on her face, as if unsure about what a smile was. She waved a single swipe, moving at the wrist only. "Hello."

Acharon looked at Sovelet and then to Katuva. He looked back at Sovelet, who was grinning.

"I don't know," Acharon said. "I'm confused."

Sovelet hooked her arm in his and guided him to the table. There were three coffee cups. Two were half-filled, the third was empty.

"I was confused, too," Sovelet said. "I couldn't get the stupid grenade into the gun and started throwing stuff down at the lions. Then I heard this terrible noise."

She poured him a cup of coffee. The steam rose, carrying the smell of the coffee to his nose, awakening the hunger he just tried to put to sleep.

"Diesel engine running on syn-fuel," Acharon said. The memory of the roaring noise just before he'd tried to take a permanent nap played across his mind. "Problem with compression in one of the piston chambers."

"It's been like that for a long time," Katuva said. She offered him the ceramic box with the creams and sugars, pulling it back when he shook his head. "I only use it when I have to move fast. Which isn't often."

"The synthetic fuel deteriorates the engine over time." Acharon looked around again. "How did you know we were in trouble?"

"I didn't," Katuva said. "I heard several booming noises. Knew they weren't natural noises. So I jumped in the truck and started heading in the direction I thought they might be coming from."

"I know, Ach," Sovelet said. "It seems a bit of a long shot, guessing where the sound was coming. But there's more."

"There's always more." Acharon drained his cup and helped himself from the carafe.

"It wasn't all a guess. I told Sovelet that I knew you were crossing the country. I haven't been able to do much on the internet, not since the fire at the post office."

"The post office?" Acharon grinned. "You were expecting mail?"

Katuva smiled. Her head seemed to pull further into her shoulders. "That's where the town's internet and phone systems were consolidated. People tended to interact more when they had to come to the post office to send an email or check on a chat board."

"So she knew we were out there, somewhere," Sovelet said. "She just didn't know if we'd be coming by way of Lincoln."

"But the explosions. Had to be human-made, and the only people I could think of that might be nearby, was you and Sovelet."

"Well, in that case." Acharon raised his coffee cup in salute. "I thank you for saving my life. Our lives."

"I'm just sorry we didn't have a more advanced medi-pod."

Sovelet gently touched Acharon's shoulder. "You're going to have some real he-man scars, dear."

"I'll miss my baby-skin softness." Acharon paused and looked around. "I don't suppose there's anything to eat here?"

"Of course." Katuva stood up. "Give me just a second."

When she left, Acharon picked up the coffee cup, almost too hot to touch, and took a sip of the dark liquid. They'd been down to the last granules of coffee on the monorail carriages. Along the way, they'd found chicory and black tea. Neither of which was Acharon a fan of.

"This is real coffee?"

"Hermetically sealed in the Last Wave canisters." Sovelet topped up his cup even though he'd only taken a sip.

"In the future," Acharon said, pausing for a sip of the steaming coffee. "In the future, some other species is going to find Last Wave canisters, and everything inside will still be edible. Or drinkable."

"I know."

Acharon sat the cup down and looked toward the diner's kitchen. He could see the other woman moving back and forth past the service window.

"Who is she?" He asked. He kept his voice low, not wanting her to hear him.

"Her name's Katuva," Sovelet said.

"I got that part," Acharon said. "But who is she? How'd she get here?"

Sovelet patted his arm and looked toward the kitchen. "That's her story. She'll tell you."

The pat on the hand and the looking away meant that there was something he wasn't going to like. Fortunately, he liked the coffee and continued to sip at it for several minutes. When he heard the kitchen door squeak, he looked up.

The woman, Katuva, was carrying two plates, one large and one small, across the diner, toward him. Her smile still seemed awkward. But her eyes revealed an inner happiness.

"Sovelet told me you don't eat meat." She set the plates down in front of Acharon. "But, eggs were okay?"

Sovelet nodded.

Acharon looked down and almost forgot to breathe. Scrambled eggs with a side of toast.

"I wasn't good with the cows," Katuva said. She sat back down and poured more coffee into Acharon's cup. "So they eventually died, or the lions and wolves got to them. The chickens, though, have fared well and learned to get into the coop as the sun begins to set. I've got plenty of eggs, just no milk or butter."

"Wheat?" Acharon asked. He indicated the toast. It had a light smear of jam across it that tasted fresh.

"The canisters." She made a vague wave past her shoulder toward the back of the dinner. "There's still a dozen or so storage units back there. Lots of staple items."

"She made the jam herself," Sovelet said. She had a proud smile on her face as if she'd somehow had something to do with it. "Sweetened with honey that she harvested."

Katuva seemed to blush.

"Well, it tastes delicious," Acharon said. He paused, looking at the two women, and then set the toast down, wiping the crumbs from the corners of his mouth with his fingers. "The food is delicious. The coffee is wonderful. But what I don't understand is how you are here. In the middle of Nebraska. Are you even real?"

He watched as Katuva looked to Sovelet and then down at the table. Sovelet reached out and patted Katuva's hand.

"Sovie?"

"It's awkward, Acharon. You need to understand that first."

"You didn't know she was here? Did you?" Acharon was starting to feel a bit alarmed. Sovelet rarely beat around the bush. She liked things direct. He'd taken so long to tell her he'd loved her, back when they were in their thirties, that when he did, she rolled her eyes. As far as she'd been concerned, it was common knowledge. She hadn't waited for him to ask for her hand in marriage. She took care of that.

"I didn't know," Sovelet said. She busied herself, topping off her coffee cup. "There'd been hints that I didn't put together until we started talking. Downloads from websites from a computer address I didn't recognize. Anonymous entrances into chat rooms. I'd originally thought it was someone from the San Francisco enclave who'd been ignoring Thyme's orders to not communicate outside the enclave. Turns out, it was Katuva."

"How long have you been here?" Acharon asked.

Katuva finally looked up but avoided eye contact with Acharon.

"Alone? Forty-three years."

"Jeezus," Acharon said. That was a long time alone. He knew there had been, still might be, isolated individuals in places like Japan, Australia, South Africa. But they were in contact with each other over the internet, and up until recently, with Sovelet. He couldn't imagine being alone. Which was the very reason he'd worked so hard to get Sovelet to San Francisco for new lungs.

Another thought occurred to Acharon that might explain her isolation. "Have you lived here all your life?"

If she had, then that might explain how she adapted so well.

"No. I moved here about fifty? No, fifty-two years." She was talking to him, but she gave the table all her eye contact.

"So you moved here? Why would you move into the middle of nowhere? You don't even have a complete medi-fac." He held up his arm, showing the cast and bandages.

This time the silence went longer than Acharon would have liked. The only place that Katuva bothered to look, besides the table, was to Sovelet. Sovelet's only response was to raise her eyebrows in response to Katuva's look.

Finally, Katuva spoke. But it was mumbled.

"Sorry?" Acharon asked.

Then, in a slightly louder whisper, she said, "Traiectus e mortem."

Acharon was confused. "Traiectus?" He looked to Sovelet for some help, but she was avoiding eye contact as well. He'd heard the word. He'd heard the phrase, but where? He sipped the coffee while the women stewed in silence, and then, like the clouds just a few hours ago, his ignorance cracked, and the truth shone through. It was an ugly truth.

"Shit." He said. He set the coffee cup down. "Passage by death. You came here to join a suicide cult."

"Ach," Sovelet said. Her voice was a mixture of pleading and warning.

Her concern was a fair enough issue with Acharon. He didn't have much compassion or patience for the suicide cults. Hundreds of thousands of Last Wavers had taken the passage as they liked to say. As far as Acharon was concerned, you could paint it pretty and put some cute labels to it, but it was still suicide.

He and Sovelet had gone around in circles, debating the issue. Even after their last friend in California, Murphy, had taken his own life, Acharon still was unsympathetic. Even after having it pointed out to him that they were all just waiting for the inevitable end of the species, he still had no sympathies for those who wanted to rush to the end. He had a life to live, and he was going to live it.

His hard-edged opinion on the matter was tempered by Sovelet's empathy for those that did take their own life or considered taking it. So while he would have liked to have gotten up and stormed out, he remained. But the eggs went cold as his appetite had left without him.

"If you belonged to a suicide cult, why are you still here?" He turned to face Sovelet. "Do you know why she is still here?"

"I didn't ask," Sovelet said. "And Katuva hadn't any reason to tell her story."

"Because you didn't question her," Acharon said.

"Because I didn't judge her."

A three-way pause ran for a dozen heartbeats.

"Fair enough," Acharon finally said. "Katuva?"

She looked up, met his gaze briefly, then darted back to the tabletop. "Yes?"

"I've met people in suicide cults before. But that was before they all took their passage. Their traiectus e mortem." Acharon had to work hard to keep the sarcasm out of his voice. " But I've never met anyone who belonged and was still around after the passage. I'm curious as to why? If you'd share."

Acharon felt Sovelet's hand squeeze his. Apparently, he was doing okay.

Katuva laughed. It was small and sounded like what an eye roll looked like. She took a deep breath and let it out slowly.

"It was my husband's doing," she said. "Carter. We'd come here from Washington State. There'd been other groups, closer to where we lived, but some of them just seemed a little hysterical."

Acharon snorted in agreement.

"So when we heard this group was gathering and that there wasn't anything mystical or dogmatic, I told Carter I wanted to come. He understood. I used to have terrible nightmares of waking up alone. All alone. And though it's not possible, in my dreams, I'd been alone on Earth for hundreds of years. That frightened me. Sometimes I would wake up crying and couldn't go back to sleep for hours. I just lay there, crying and feeling abandoned, even with Carter there, holding me close. I didn't want to be the last person alive.

"So, we packed up a few things and moved here. Allan Reece, he's the one who put it together, got permission to take over the town. Most of the townsfolk had already moved into Lincoln. A few remained, refusing to leave. A few others remained, wanting to join the group.

"We shared a house with others. We had communal gatherings and individual therapy with a couple of psychologists who had joined the group."

"Seems a bit insincere," Acharon said. "Taking advice about suicide from someone intent on committing suicide."

"They didn't give advice," Katuva said. She poured the last dribbles of coffee from the carafe into her cup and took a slow sip before continuing. "They just listened and helped some of us talk our way through our fears."

"You were afraid?" Sovelet asked.

"Yeah. I mean, I was going to take my own life. It wasn't like dying of old age or in an accident. I was going to take the little pink pill with two thousand other people. The end wasn't a mystery. It was a date on the calendar. So, yes, a little afraid. But not as fearful as I was about being left alone forever.

"Anyway. When no one new arrived for several weeks, Allen said it was time. We planned a big party with lots of food and drinks. A couple of people played instruments, so we had some dancing. I drank a lot. I didn't realize it at the time, but Carter kept feeding me drinks until I was on the edge of passing out, drunk.

"He told me we needed to go home, sleep it off, so we had clear heads for tomorrow. I don't remember how we got home. It seemed, then, that walking was taking forever. Then he rolled me into bed, took off my shoes, and I was asleep.

"I woke the next day, well past morning. The sun was throwing squares of light on the floor, close enough to the window to let me know we were on toward noon. It was supposed to be a morning passage. I jumped out of bed, confused. Someone should have come and woken us. Why didn't they come and get us?

"When I left the room, I knew something was wrong. I had to go downstairs. That didn't make sense, because we didn't have an upstairs bedroom. And the layout of the house was all wrong.

"Carter was on the front stoop when I opened the door. He just sat there when I asked him what time it was. I hit him on the shoulder and yelled at him, 'What time is it?'

"He said, 'It's too late.' Then he told me what he'd done. He'd gotten me drunk and then took me to a house on the far side of the town where no one was living, where no one would look for us. He said that he'd tricked me out of my passage because he was scared to do it, and he was afraid to live alone, knowing that I'd gone without him."

Katuva shook her head and laughed. "I didn't speak to him for six months. Slept in a different house and everything."

"I don't understand," Acharon said. "If you wanted to die, to take the passage, why didn't you just do it then, even if it was too late."

This time she looked at Acharon for a long time. She looked until Acharon looked away.

"I couldn't. That was the point of the group. That's why so many of us were there. We didn't have the courage to do it alone. But with friends, in a large group, together? We had a shared courage. Carter stole that courage from me."

"Katuva," Sovelet said. "What happened to Carter?"

"He died. A year and two months later. He was fixing a connection on the water tower and slipped. He hadn't bothered with the safety harness because he was in a hurry. All that talk about not wanting to live alone and yet, that's what he did to me. I was so angry I just left him for the crows."

"Oh, Katuva." Sovelet reached out to squeeze her hand.

Katuva pulled back. "Anyone else like more coffee? I could use more coffee."

She stood and snatched the carafe before hurrying back to the kitchen.

"I upset her," Acharon said. He was watching Katuva as she rushed toward the diner kitchen.

"She just needs a minute." Sovelet pulled Acharon's plate of uneaten eggs over in front of herself and picked up the fork. "It's one thing to remember in your head. It's another thing sharing those memories out loud. To other people."

Acharon looked down at the table. "Those were my eggs."

"You lost your appetite. I'm just making sure they don't go to waste."

"Fair enough." Acharon tipped his cup and looked at the bottom where a small droplet of coffee rolled with gravity before he set it back on the table. "Murphy at least had us nearby. He wasn't completely alone. I can't imagine so many years without any contact. Why didn't she reach out?"

Sovelet caught a rebellious piece of egg on her fork as it slid onto her chin. She tucked it safely in her mouth before speaking. "She never said. Maybe she felt guilty for not making the passage, and this was her way of punishing herself."

"That's just silly."

"Or," Sovelet looked hard at Acharon as she spoke, "maybe she felt people wouldn't understand her and would distrust her."

Acharon got the hint and nodded as Katuva exited the kitchen. She came to the table with the carafe and a plate. She set the plate in front of Acharon.

"You said you liked the pie."

He waited until Katuva had poured coffee for each and then said, "Indeed I do. Thank you."

His appetite was slowly recovering, and the pie encouraged it along. He took several bites and gave Katuva a nod to let her know it was good eating.

"When you're done," Katuva said, "I could give you a tour of the town."

Acharon was inclined to say no. Then he felt the pressure of Sovelet's foot on his and changed his mind. "That'd be great. Thanks."

05

A tour of a small town was, in Acharon's words and to Sovelet's dismay, a short tour. He got to see the damaged post office with its centralized communications. There was the fire engine house that held all the town's working vehicles, electrical and synthetic diesel. He enjoyed that part of the tour the most. The Five and Dime store had been staged like the other shops. But in the back, was an entire town block of long term storage containers. Many of them were still hermetically sealed.

As they'd walked down the main street, Katuva explained how once a year she hitched the snowplow to the truck and scraped most of the dirt off the main street.

"I'm not very good at it," she'd said. "But between the snow, rain, and my minimal efforts, it keeps fairly clean."

"Why bother?" Acharon had asked. And then, because he'd been dying to understand. "And why stage the storefronts as you have?"

They'd stopped outside the dry cleaners. It was one of the shops past the diner that Acharon hadn't seen. A man behind the counter was holding a dress, draped over his arms. A woman was pointing to a specific place on the dress. Her other hand held a leash that ended at the collar of a stuffed dog. Acharon was glad to see that it was a child's toy dog and not an actual taxidermied animal.

Katuva stared at the tableau for several quiet moments before she started talking.

"It wasn't intentional," she said. She emitted a short, breathy laugh before continuing. "Well, not intentional at first. I had been in the lady's fashion shop for the first time since everyone else had made the passage. I'd ducked in there because I saw Carter coming out of the hardware store, and I was still upset with him.

"I was looking at the dresses and noticed the mannequins. Then, for what I thought was merely a lark, I posed them like employees and customers. I even put one in the left changing room. I just moved them. I didn't pose them or change their clothes. Not right away.

"But the more I moved them, the more entertained I became. Only later did it occur to me that I hadn't thought once about Carter or my situation while I was working with the mannequins. Then it was like I was looking at a giant dollhouse. They kept me entertained and busy. Fortunately, there were enough of them stored in the back of the Five and Dime and the clothing shops.

"Though there aren't enough to really fill the place. I tried a couple on the benches outside, but the weather, it either bleached them or cracked them. So only in the shops."

Acharon had looked around. He looked past the shops where he could see some of the homes. "You didn't put any of them in the houses, did you? I want to know if I should prepare myself for a surprise."

"No, not in the houses," Katuva had answered.

Acharon had expected her to laugh at the suggestion of the houses holding mannequins. But she was as serious about that as she had been about everything else.

Shortly after, Katuva pleaded a headache. Probably from too much excitement, she'd suggested. She excused herself and went to her house, which was several streets from where she and Sovelet had put Acharon after the medi-pod had released him.

"The house has hot water," Sovelet had said. They were walking the grassy lawn of the street.

"Yeah? Why's that important?"

Sovelet had grinned happily. "I haven't had a bath in too long. Showers are okay, but I want to soak."

There was a clawfoot tub in the bathroom on the second floor at the end of the hall. Acharon gave it a quick one-handed cleaning while Sovelet had rounded up some towels. She'd even managed to discover a half-dozen candles and a working lighter. It wasn't quite dark as the water filled the tub, but Acharon wasn't going to question any of it.

"Are we going back to the diner for dinner?" he'd asked as Sovelet settled into the tub.

"No." She'd paused long enough to sigh with pleasure as she sank into the suds covered water. "I told her you'd probably need some time to process. We'll join her for breakfast. French toast, I think, is what Katuva said."

"Right then." Acharon had rubbed his hands together. "I guess I'll see if there's anything in the house to eat."

"Got your appetite back?"

"Seems like it."

Now, as he searched through the kitchen, he found plenty of the long-term storage foods, still sealed tight. They were good for centuries of storage under ideal conditions. Under any conditions, some were not very tasty. Still, it was food, and he was hungry.

Acharon found a container with packets of dried fruits and nuts. That was a passable choice. He found and opened a package of dates. They were still moist, and he nodded approvingly as he continued to poke through the cupboards.

"Well, well." In the narrow pantry, covered in dust and laying on their sides, were two bottles of red wine. He pulled one out and dusted it off. The date was faded but visible enough that Acharon could quickly do the calculation in his head. He came up with one hundred and fifty years.

The wine had been bottled shortly after he and Sovelet had been born.

"Do I dare?" Acharon asked the room.

There wasn't an answer, which he took for a yes. He set the bottle on the counter and searched again. This time he was looking for a bottle opener, which was quicker to locate than something to eat.

The wine gurgled friendly enough into a freshly washed glass. Acharon took a sip while leaning over the sink, ready to spit and rinse if it tasted like vinegar. Or worse. The sip lay nicely across his tongue as he swirled it about, still prepared to abandon the wine if it turned on him. But, it kept its friendliness, so Acharon had a second sip.

A hundred and fifty years, and it still tasted good. Acharon washed a second class and carried everything upstairs. He tapped gently on the door frame outside the bathroom.

Acharon heard a quiet laugh and then, "Enter."

Acharon stepped over the threshold and presented the wine. "I come bearing gifts."

Sovelet looked at the wine. Her eyes narrowed. "Gifts?"

"Safe to drink." Acharon poured Sovelet a glass and added to his own. "I've already taste-tested it. And as you can see, I'm still standing."

Sovelet accepted the glass. Acharon watched as she took a tentative sip. Her eyebrows slowly rose, matched by her smile and a nod of her head.

"That's not bad."

"Considering." They tapped their glasses together.

"Yes, considering." She took another sip and settled back into the tub. "When's the last time we had wine?"

"Las Vegas, several weeks ago."

She looked at him sideways. "Wine that wasn't a powder mix from an automat."

"Ah, that kind of wine." Acharon stalled with a sip of the wine. "I think that was the night before I lost my eye."

"Oh, right. Sorry, dear."

There'd been lots of wine during those days. Many of the more libertarian and anarchist minded members of the San Francisco enclave had retreated to one of the old apartment buildings. There, they kept each other's good company while allowing Thyme to continue exerting his power and control over the rest of the enclave's population. When Acharon had finally stood up against Thyme and his power hoarding, there'd been the fight. He'd taken a penknife to the eye, and the trip to the off-site medi-fac to get a new one made.

How many years had that been?

"More than forty years," he said.

"So long," said Sovelet. She sipped from the glass and then looked at the filled volume. She held it out over the edge of the tub. Acharon dutifully, gladly, poured more into her glass. Acharon knew that she didn't know precisely what he was thinking, but she always had a pretty good idea.

"In all that time," he said, as he moved the towels to the sink., "we were never alone."

"Yes?" It was an invitation to continue.

"Katuva. She's been alone that long." He sat on the toilet lid, which allowed him to face Sovelet and relax against the porcelain tank. It was cool against the heat of his healing wounds.

Sovelet sloshed water and suds with her left foot. They both watched her swirl circles for several long moments.

"You're suggesting something," she finally said.

"If she's so intent on this passage garbage, why is she still alive?"

"She's not suicidal, Ach." She terminated her sentence with another sip of wine.

"Joined a suicide cult. Could have fooled me."

Sovelet sat up sharply enough that the water sloshed to the edge of the tub. It splashed a few drops of water and suds onto Acharon's lap.

"Joining one of these groups doesn't mean a person is suicidal." She held out her glass. Acharon topped it off. "There's more to all this than wanting to be dead. And you know this because we've talked about this. Often."

Acharon nodded, but shrugged, too. "But we've never talked about someone who's been in a cult and then alone for forty years."

"So, she should have killed herself?"

"No." He pointed at Sovelet with the edge of his glass. "I'm saying it's surprising that she didn't."

Sovelet settled back into the tub, poking her toes up through the suds several times. Acharon wasn't sure if she was thinking of something new or chewing on what he'd said.

"Should I apologize?" he asked. If he was in the dog house, he wanted to apologize and move on to a different conversation.

Instead of hearing a yes, he received a smile. "You are not in the dog house."

"Good."

"But."

Acharon groaned, which made Sovelet laugh. When she stopped, her eyes still shone with mirth.

"Did you listen to her when she told you what happened? She talked about the collective will of the community. They didn't want to die, but they didn't want to be the last to live either. They were able to take their lives because they had the support of others who were making the same journey."

Acharon snorted and tried to cover it up with a cough. Sovelet merely rolled her eyes.

"Yes, it's a euphemism, Ach," she said. "But it's also part of the psychology that helped them."

"And I've always said it's not a journey, but the end of one."

Sovelet's focus shifted for a moment. Not until Acharon heard the clang of a metal lever and the muted sound of rushing water, did he realize Sovelet had used her foot to push the bathtub lever that started the tub draining.

"Then you know what my response is to that." She set the wine glass on the floor and held out one hand.

Acharon handed Sovelet a towel. Yes, he knew her response. The journey wasn't the being dead part. It was the communal part. The taking of the pill together. That was the standard response that came up in the arguments. No, not arguments, discussions. Discussions that came up whenever Sovelet would report on someone else in the world that had gotten tired of waiting. Back then, the conversations had happened on their self-made island with the fairy lights strung overhead and cups of tea steaming in their hands.

Now, it was soap suds and wine.

He waited while she toweled dry and wrapped one around her hair. When she left for the bedroom, he followed with the wine bottle. The lights glowed small but bright. The room mixed the aromas of the musk of time and the bright cheer of flower-scented bath soap.

Sovelet pulled open a dresser drawer and removed a set of pajamas still pressed flat from their time in air-tight storage. While Acharon had been sleeping off his encounter with the lion and the medi-pod, Sovelet had gone shopping with Katuva. They'd found both her and him some new clothes. He waited while she dressed. Something he could say he'd seen thousands of times.

"We can't stay here, Sove," he said as she made herself comfortable on the bed, her legs crossed, and began rubbing her hair in the towel.

"I never said we should."

"But you also haven't mentioned anything about getting out of here."

Sovelet paused in the process of drying her hair.

"We've time, Acharon. Try and relax."

As an example of the opposite of relaxing, Acharon stood and paced the four-meter distance between door and window. He went back and forth twice before stopping to pause and look out the window. The rain clouds had worn themselves out earlier in the day and left the sky to the stars and the moon. A night time glow lit the town, highlighting the edges of trees and the corners of buildings. It was quiet and maybe a bit magical. If only there weren't the taint of suicide spoiling it all.

"People are waiting for us." He turned and found that Sovelet had shifted on the bed. She could now see him as he paced. She had the soft smile of patience.

"We'll get there, Acharon." She patted the bed. Acharon went and sat next to her. "It'd be rude to leave as quickly as we got here. And considering as how she saved our lives? Doesn't that deserve a little consideration?"

"It was all rather convenient," Acharon said. He'd been mulling on it since he'd met Katuva and learned how she'd played at cavalry, arriving in the nick of time. "She just happened to have enough synthesized diesel ready when we needed her to appear? That broken span was fresh, Sovelet."

"Are you suggesting she somehow knocked that span down?"

Acharon was up again. He about-faced on the threshold and walked back to the window. Every once in a while, he missed their little island with their gardens and Adirondack chairs. Sitting there during the sunset, watching the stars slowly appear as if waking up from a long day's nap. This was one of those moments. He really did want to get to New York, but at the same time, he'd like for all of this to not ever have happened. He had control when they were in Sausalito. He'd had very little of it since then.

"Ach?"

"I don't know." He turned from the window. "No. Clearly, she didn't just knock it down. But, you have to admit, it's pretty convenient."

"I think the word is 'coincidence'?" She slid off the bed and came over to the window where he stood. She wrapped an arm around him and joined him, looking out on a world nearly free of the shackles of humanity. "It's late, dear. We've been drinking wine, and you only just recovered from the whole getting eaten by a lion thing. You need to sleep. I could use some sleep, too."

Acharon returned the hug. "It won't make things go away."

"No, it won't." She hugged him hard with both arms and then planted a kiss on his cheek. "But the light will make things easier to look at."

She released him and started walking toward the door.

"Where are you going?" He'd thought she wasn't mad at him, but now he wasn't sure.

"Wine, Acharon," she said as she continued out of the bedroom. "I have to pee."

06

In the morning, with his skull aching just enough to remind him how out of practice he was with drinking, Acharon and Sovelet made their way downtown. It had rained while they'd slept. The ground squelched and gurgled under their feet as they walked to Main Street. A haze brought the walls of the world in close.

Many of the lights over the shop doors were still on. The streetlights glowed as well with halos of mist. The street here complained less as they walked across it than had the road in front of their house. Their borrowed house, Acharon reminded himself. This town was not their home. They were not like the mannequins in the windows, frozen for decades in one place. He and Sovelet were not permanent.

Acharon held the door to the diner open so that Sovelet could precede him. They both stepped into a room warmed with the aromas of coffee, baked bread, and skillet cooked food.

"I'm back here." Acharon saw a spatula waving through the door window that blocked the kitchen from view.

"Does she ever sleep?"

"Probably when she's tired." Sovelet sat as Acharon moved the chair in for her. "Her sleep patterns are probably all out of whack. She doesn't have anyone with whom to share a schedule. No one to remind her when it's time to sleep, time to eat."

"Doesn't answer the question, Sove," Acharon said as he sat.

Sovelet had the coffee carafe in hand and poured for both of them. "She probably slept better before we arrived. She's most likely all kinds of excited and nervous."

"Anyone like pancakes?" Katuva was leaning past the edge of the kitchen door.

"Who in this town doesn't?" Acharon grinned at his joke. He could see Sovelet shake her head.

"We'd love some pancakes, dear," Sovelet said.

"Great." Katuva disappeared behind the door.

"When are we leaving?" Acharon asked in a soft voice as he lifted his coffee cup.

"How are we leaving, you mean."

The coffee was hot and smooth. It distracted Acharon for several moments as he had a second and third sip.

"I was thinking we could borrow one of the vehicles in the firehouse."

Sovelet looked at him with a look of curiosity. "'Borrow'? And how will you return it?"

"What do you mean? Set the onboard nav-system to return home." Acharon set his coffee cup down and sat back, shoulders sagging. "They probably don't have automatic navigation."

"Mhm," Sovelet said. She'd just taken a sip of coffee. "Besides, maybe that's not the best solution."

"You can't be thinking of staying here." There was just a hint of panic in his voice.

"No. That's not what I meant. Drink your coffee."

Only slightly mollified, Acharon picked up his cup and had several more sips before topping off the contents and starting again.

Moments like this were how it had been before, back on their island. Mornings spent together, drinking tea in silent company. Sometimes they wouldn't say a word for several hours. Even then, it was something gentle, innocuous, like, "Oh, look, the sea otters got into the garden, again." Their day would ramp up slowly. There'd never been a need to hurry. Not until they made their last trip into San Francisco.

Since then, it seemed to be a constant movement forward. The silent moments were rarer than the years before.

"Ach? You okay?"

"Me? Oh, yeah." He added more coffee to his cup that had somehow drained itself halfway. "Just thinking backward."

"Regret leaving the island?" She put her hand on his forearm and gave it a soft, slow squeeze.

"No. No regret. But I do miss the simplicity of it all."

"Would pancakes help?"

Sovelet smoothed her placemat. "Yes, they would. Thank you."

Katuva's appearance startled Acharon. He hadn't heard her coming. Sovelet, who had a direct view of the kitchen, hadn't given any indication that Katuva and the pancakes were arriving.

"Smells great," Acharon added. He watched as Katuva set a plate in the middle of the table. A small mountain of pancakes tickled the air with steamy tendrils. Acharon breathed in slow, savoring the aroma with his olfactory senses.

"Sourdough pancakes," Acharon said.

Katuva nodded.

"Yep, they are. The same starter since I've been here. I've eaten a lot of bread keeping it going." She put down a small pitcher filled with a dark fluid. "Syrup's reconstituted, but it still tastes good. Tastes real good if you haven't had any in a few decades."

"Then it should taste great." Acharon forked several pancakes and laid them on Sovelet's plate. He added pancakes to Katuva's plate, despite her protestation, and then to his plate.

There was a short pause in the conversation at the table as they reduced the stack of pancakes to nothing. The talk, when there was any, was merely about the weather and the night's rest.

When the final piece of pancake made a run through the last smear of syrup on Acharon's plate, the conversation turned to more important things.

"So," Acharon said. He wiped the paper napkin across the corner of his lips. "I was hoping we could talk about borrowing one of your vehicles."

"Borrow?" Katuva looked confused.

"What Acharon means is that we need one."

"To get to Lincoln," Acharon said. "Our friends in New York are probably going to get worried about our absence."

"You're going today?" Katuva looked at Acharon and Sovelet, switching between the two several times. "Right now?"

Acharon laughed, slightly embarrassed by Katuva's concern. "Well, not right now. It'd take a few hours to prep a vehicle, and then, if you don't mind, load some supplies."

"Oh, well, sure. I guess."

"Great. Thank you." Acharon looked at Sovelet, feeling a bit triumphant. His high spirits were quelled by the look Sovelet flashed him.

Sovelet reached out and put a hand on Katuva's. "Honey? Are you okay?"

Katuva, whose head had tilted down, moving her eyes out of Acharon and Sovelet's view, slowly looked up to them, once more. "I wanted to cook you a nice homemade dinner. Not here in the diner, but my place. Like real friends would."

"There's no need to go through the trouble," said Acharon. He was itching to get back on the road. He wanted to get to New York, but he also wanted to get away from this town.

"Nonsense," Sovelet said. She flashed the same look that blunted his triumphant feeling seconds ago. "We'd love to stay for dinner."

Katuva's face brightened. A smile slowly faded into existence. "Thank you."

Both women seemed to be pleased with the arrangement. Acharon had more than a century during which he'd learned that when Sovelet set her mind, his attempts to change it would fail as surely as science's attempt to clone humans.

"Sure, we'll stay for dinner. But tomorrow we have to get moving."

"Of course," Katuva said.

"The window for crossing the Atlantic is closing."

"I understand."

"Thank you, Acharon, for the update," said Sovelet. They were just a few words, but the unsubtle hint to shut up was evident. "Now, if you don't mind, I'd like to have a look at your communications center? Maybe I can salvage enough to send a message to New York. Let them know we're okay."

"Oh, I don't know." Katuva shook her head. "The fire after the lightning hit was pretty bad. I haven't gone in there since I saw what a mess it made."

"You'd be surprised what Sovelet can do when it comes to computers," Acharon said. His words were rote. He was more interested in the nervous actions in Katuva's face and hands.

"And Acharon is a mechanical genius," Sovelet said. "I haven't seen anything he can't fix."

"Really?"

She looked like she was about to panic in Acharon's opinion. "Don't worry, if it's already damaged, our efforts won't do anything worse."

"It's not that," Katuva said. "It's just that I, um, hate to see you waste your time. It's not worth the effort, I promise you. The fire was really bad. I'm surprised the building is still standing."

Acharon felt Sovelet looking at him. He looked back at her but didn't see a reprimand in Sovelet's eyes. Instead, she seemed curious and was looking at Acharon as if he might have the answer. He didn't.

"If it's that bad inside, we won't mess with it," Acharon said. "But we have to do something at least, so we don't feel like we've let our friends down."

"That's right," Sovelet said. "If it looks unsafe, we'll keep out."

Katuva looked at each of them again. Sovelet had the same smile she'd had for kittens when Acharon found one and brought it back for her to raise. It was soft and reassuring and eased even the most feral and frightened baby cat set before her.

"I can't stop you," Katuva said.

"But it is your home, your town," Sovelet said. "So, we don't want to assume."

Katuva's shoulders, which had risen to hide her neck during the conversation, slowly lowered with an accompanying sigh. "Okay. If that's what you want to do."

"You want to come with us?" Sovelet asked.

"No, can't," Katuva said. She was up on her feet as she spoke, grabbing plates and utensils. The plates clattered against each other, and Acharon realized her hands were shaking. "I have to take care of all this. Besides, I need to start preparing dinner."

She gathered up as much as she could carry and made her way to the diner kitchen door. She turned and said, "I'll see you for dinner. Six? At my house?"

"Six at your house would be lovely, Katuva," Sovelet said. "Thank you."

Katuva's response was hidden in the kitchen as she pushed past the door.

"She doesn't want us to go to the post office," Acharon said.

"Yep." Sovelet drank down the last of the coffee in her cup and then stood. "Let's go find out why."

Sovelet led the way out of the diner. She moved with determination, and Acharon had to take a couple of run-steps to catch up with her. They walked in silence across the scraped road, past the shops with their mannequin clients, to the post office.

Acharon had taken several more steps before he realized Sovelet had stopped. He turned around. Sovelet was standing with her feet planted shoulder-width apart, her hands on her hips. Her eyes were scanning the area behind Acharon.

"I thought you wanted to go in?" he asked.

She answered without looking. "I do. And I want to see where the lightning hit the building."

Acharon was about to suggest walking around the post office when Sovelet started moving. Again, her actions caught Acharon off guard.

Sovelet went counterclockwise around the post office. She stumbled several times as she focused on the building's exterior and not where she was stepping. Acharon moved up next to her, ready to assist the next time she stumbled.

In the back, near the roll-up receiving door, Sovelet stopped. Acharon side-stepped to avoid running into her.

"There," she said. She pointed to a ragged V cut into the brick exterior, along the flat roof. It was charred, and several bricks still seemed to cling precariously to their previous positions in the wall. Running down from the V to the ground was a blackened and rusted metal conduit.

"That's old," Acharon said as he noticed the conduit.

"Everything's old," Sovelet said. She gave him a wink.

"I mean," he said, "that the conduit is not the work of Last Wavers. That wasn't intended to last a century. We would have run it inside to protect from the weather and then encased it in the fire-retardant conduit that new builds required."

"Could that have brought the fire inside?" Sovelet asked. She'd stepped closer and was looking at the conduit as if the answer was engraved on it.

"Maybe," said Acharon. "But I'd have to go up and look. Inside, too, to see if this was how they were running power to the communication equipment."

"But," Sovelet said. She looked over her shoulder at Acharon.

"But, it looks like the energy from the lightning went straight to the ground from here."

"Let's go inside," Sovelet said.

This time, Acharon moved the moment Sovelet started talking and was with her when she started walking rather than having to hurry to catch up. They went back around to the front door. Sovelet turned the knob and slowly pushed the door open. Her nose wrinkled with the first whiff of the interior of the post office.

"Smells burnt," she said.

Acharon followed her inside. The walls inside were covered in swirls of gray soot. The ash-coated windows let in a hazy light. The counter that crossed most of the room was blackened and charred, burnt down in several places. The air smelled like a combination between a forest fire and a factory fire, reeking with a blend of burnt wood and plastic.

Along the wall with the door were four computer terminals. The fire had melted the keyboards. Cracks spiderwebbed several monitor screens. Their frames had melted, sliding down their fronts like wax on a candle.

"Here," Sovelet said. She'd found the counter section that doubled as a door and had pushed her way through. The palms of her hands were now dark grey with ash.

On the other side of the counter was the rest of the communication equipment. Some of it was charred, but some of it looked untouched except for the blanket of ash.

"Kind of random," Acharon said.

"I know. And look. The fire doesn't seem to have come from where the lightning hit."

Acharon looked up to the approximate spot of the lightning strike. There was a bit of charring there, but then it was clear of anything else but the soot.

"It looks like the fire came upwards in some places and then jumped around. Do fires jump around?"

"They can if they're hot enough and have a wind pushing them."

Sovelet nodded longer than required to agree. Acharon knew she was thinking about the fire. So was he. He wasn't an expert, but he was confident that the person who'd set it wasn't an expert on fires, either.

"Do you think Katuva could have done this?"

Acharon wasn't sure what Katuva was capable of doing. "I couldn't say for sure. Maybe someone in the cult did it to keep people from calling out for rescue."

"No one was being held captive, Acharon," Sovelet said. She was looking closely, without touching, at some of the equipment not burned by the fire. "People were free to leave. Some people did leave."

Acharon might have been tempted to say that all the information was suspect. Still, he knew that Sovelet had talked to thousands of people as the population wound down. He'd heard some of their stories relayed to him from Sovelet while they sat in their Adirondack chairs on their island, watching the sky change with the sunsets. She'd never talked about the people who had gone to join a suicide cult or those that left them. She probably didn't because she knew his feelings on the subject. Arguing with her about it would only get him in hot water.

"Someone could have done it on the last morning to destroy information?"

"What information?"

Acharon raised his arms. "I have no idea. It was just a suggestion. Maybe Katuva did it to keep us from communicating with our friends in New York."

Sovelet looked over her shoulder at Acharon. "Doesn't that seem a bit crazy?"

The question wasn't rhetorical. Acharon could tell by her voice that it was an acknowledgment. Had Katuva tried to burn down all the equipment in the post office to keep them from calling their friends?

"Why would she do that?"

"I don't know about that," Sovelet said. "But I know that if you can fetch my bag from the house and get me some power in here, I think I can get us access to the satellites and then the internet."

Acharon smiled. "You've asked the right man."

Sovelet rolled her eyes. "I've asked the only man. And he's still standing here."

Acharon laughed and started moving towards the door. "I'm on it."

07

Acharon spent most of the day on the post office roof. He'd cleaned and rewired the solar panels that hadn't been damaged by the electrical surge from the lightning strike. He also discovered that there was power coming in from a wind turbine. There was a small farm of wind turbines in one corner of the town. Fortunately, it was inside the fence. The mere thought of going outside the fence made his arm tingle.

When he wasn't repairing the power sources for the post office communication equipment, he was running errands for Sovelet.

Sovelet looked like an old fashioned chimney sweep. Her hair was tied up in a bun, held in place by two tablet styluses that had escaped the fire. Ash and soot coated her clothes. There were several streaks of it across her face. The knees of her slacks were blackened from kneeling in the debris while she scavenged for useful equipment and parts.

The only part of Sovelet that was meticulously clean was her hands. When Acharon had returned with her bag, she'd immediately sent him out to find some wipes to keep her hands clean. Acharon had opened all but three of the storage containers behind the store before he finally found a plastic case, still sealed tight, filled with handy wipes.

She'd asked for one pack, but Acharon knew better and brought three. He'd gone back once more to reload before Sovelet was done.

"That should get us started," Sovelet said. She'd pushed several power buttons, and the station she'd pieced together began to whir to life.

The screen flickered several times before finally agreeing to cooperate. Between the flickers, which they'd both been watching, Acharon saw the light reflection of the front door opening. A human silhouette was framed by the light.

Acharon turned. "Hey, Katuva."

"Hi."

Sovelet smiled and waved Katuva over. "Hello. Look. We got it working. Some of it anyways."

Katuva looked at the computer, the screen with its desktop display glowing brightly. Acharon thought she looked more upset than pleased.

"You've already talked to your friends in New York?""

"Hardly," Sovelet said. "I've still got programs to run. Then I've got to find a satellite to bounce off of. Most are still operational, but there's a couple that don't want to cooperate."

"It's three o'clock," Katuva said.

Acharon had the feeling she would be pleased if they stopped work for the day. He also wondered if they did stop, would there be another accidental fire in the night?

"Is it?" Sovelet turned to Acharon for confirmation, which he gave. Sovelet turned back to the computer and quickly tapped several lines in the command window. This sent more lines scrolling upward too fast to read. "Well, that shouldn't be a problem as long as the systems cooperate, and I latch onto a working satellite in the first couple of tries."

"She's very good at this," Acharon said.

"I can see," Katuva said. She still looked disappointed. "So you'll do all that, then talk to people in New York?"

"I'll leave messages, most likely," Sovelet said. She paused to enter more commands that once more sent the lines whizzing up inside the computer screen window. "Someone would have to be monitoring the system on their end, or someone would have to be looking at one of the discussion boards when I sent my update."

Katuva looked at the monitor with its open command window spewing lines from the bottom of the frame and gobbling them up in the top edge. Her left hand was massaging her right. She chewed on her lower lip.

"You okay?" Acharon asked. He had his opinion on that, but Sovelet would be displeased if he ever said it out loud.

"Are you going to mention me?" Katuva said. She was looking at Sovelet and seemingly ignoring Acharon.

Sovelet looked confused. "Mention you? Sure I was. Everyone will be excited to know there's still someone else out here. You'll have nearly two dozen new friends by this time tomorrow."

Again, Katuva stared at the monitor before she spoke. This time her voice was quiet, reluctant. "Please, don't tell them about me."

Acharon realized that Sovelet was looking at him. He shrugged. He had no idea why she wouldn't want people to know she was alive or why she wouldn't want to have non-mannequin friends to talk to.

Getting no good answer from Acharon, Sovelet turned back to Katuva. "Why do you want that?"

Katuva's neck had again taken refuge in her shoulders. "It makes me uncomfortable. You can do it, though? You can tell them where you are and that you're safe without telling them about me?"

Sovelet looked lost. Acharon felt lost.

"I can do that, yes," Sovelet said. "If that's what you really want."

"I do." Katuva spoke resolutely. Her hands had stopped clutching at each other and started smoothing the sides of her dress. "Dinner is still at six. Unless you need me to change it?"

"No, dear," Sovelet said. "We'll be there."

"Good."

She turned and left. Acharon watched her go before turning to make a comment to Sovelet. He bit it back when he saw that she was already in another program.

Acharon recognized the program as one that was used to find and connect to satellites.

"I'm assuming you checked the dish for damage?"

Acharon shook his head in disbelief. "Of course I did. Do I need to adjust its angle?"

"Not sure yet." Her voice sounded detached as she tapped keys and scanned the monitor screen. "I'll let you know in a couple more minutes."

Acharon stepped back and let Sovelet tackle her task. He knew when she focused like this, he could tapdance or drop an armful of pots and pans, and she would likely not even be aware of it. Instead, he wandered to the door and looked out on the street.

It was unsurprisingly empty and still. He noticed that the moss and weeds were beginning to regrow in the streaks of dirt marking the street. Back home, in San Francisco, and in most major cities, automated street cleaners would have cleaned the most used streets regularly. Several times, Sovelet had hacked into the program for Sausalito to keep Bridgeway, the main thoroughfare, clear. They'd abandoned that over time, eventually allowing the street to grow over with grass and dandelions.

San Francisco had looked like someone with a green fetish had laid green carpet on every street by the time they'd made their last visit there. Thoughts of San Francisco made Acharon's arm ache. He chuckled at the effect. It seemed that every place they'd visited since leaving their island made his arm ache.

A giggle inside the post office pulled Acharon's attention back to Sovelet. He turned, absentmindedly rubbing his arm.

"You sound happy," he said.

"I am. I found two good satellites, and someone is on the international discussion board."

"Someone from New York?" Acharon asked.

"Nope. Paris. Clara was on. Good luck, that." She stood up and started to put her hands on her hips. She stopped and then checked her hands for ash. "I need a bath. Well, a shower. I want a bath, but I'll settle for a shower."

"What about New York?" Acharon pointed at the screen. "You still trying to contact them?"

"Don't have to." Sovelet started packing up her equipment, slipping them all back into their proper places inside the bag. "I left messages. Clara will confirm we communicated. I'll check back in the morning."

"Assuming the post office is still standing."

Sovelet stopped packing her bag and looked at Acharon for a long time. He wasn't sure if he was in trouble. And if he was, how bad.

"If she did it before," Sovelet said. Her voice was just above a whisper. "I don't think she'll do it again. Not now that we've made contact with other people."

"I'll take your word for it," Acharon said, though he was thinking about stockpiling fire extinguishers.

"Good. Now," Sovelet said, handing her bag to Acharon. "I need a shower. Come to think of it, so do you."

It was fifteen minutes before six when Sovelet emerged from the bedroom. She'd kicked Acharon out, leaving him to settle for getting dressed in one of the other rooms. He'd been ready to knock on the bedroom door, to remind Sovelet of the time, when the knob had turned.

"Well?" she asked. "Like it?"

She was wearing a dress with a hem ending just below the knees. It was a flora print with short sleeves and no collar. Acharon was the last person to ask for fashion advice. He knew nothing about what went with what and stayed with khakis and jeans, depending on the season. Always paired with a long-sleeved shirt, because you can make a long sleeve short, but you can't make a short sleeve long.

"You look lovely," he finally said.

"And if I'd come out here in a burlap bag?" Her hands were safely on her hips now that everything was clean to touch.

"You'd look lovely," Acharon said without hesitation.

"That's what I thought." She stuck her tongue out at him and sashayed her way to the stairs. "Coming?"

Acharon trotted past her and led the way down the stairs. In the foyer, he held the door open for her. They left the house, arm in arm, and made their way down the street. They had to cross Main Street to reach Katuva's home and arrived with three minutes to spare. Katuva was waiting on the porch.

"Hi." She spoke in the same shy tone she'd used when first introduced to Acharon.

"Hi," Sovelet responded. She gave Katuva a hug and a buss on the right cheek. "Thank you for inviting us."

Sovelet released Katuva and turned so the two women were facing Acharon. He suddenly felt self-conscious.

"Katuva," he said with a single nod.

"Acharon." A brief pause then, "Won't you both come in? I have some hors d'oeuvres, and the meatloaf is just about ready."

Sovelet looked taken aback. "Meatloaf? Like 'meat' loaf?"

Katuva covered her mouth. "Oh, no. Goodness, no. I remembered. It's chickpeas and vital wheat gluten and vegetables from the garden."

"Oh, good." Sovelet smiled and gave Katuva another hug before she turned to Acharon. "You going to stand there or are you going to come inside?"

Acharon started up the stairs. "I'm coming."

As he took the five stairs to the front porch, Acharon noticed that everything was neat and orderly. There were two plastic wicker chairs with a little table between them. A floral wreath hung on the wooden door, which was stained and rubbed often enough that it had an inner glow. But it was the big things that Acharon noticed that said a different story. One of the four pillars was cracked and showed signs of rot. The paint on the pillars and frame around the door was chipped and faded.

There was only so much one person could do alone. Especially if they were busy keeping up the facade on Main Street.

Inside, the house was warm and inviting. The living room to the left had two claw-footed sofas parallel to each other and bracketing the fireplace. The fireplace crackled with a small fire on its hearth. A piano was on the same wall as the entry from the foyer. Pictures hung on the walls, everywhere.

Acharon noticed that most were paintings of landscapes. None of them were portraits.

"Is this the house you and Carter shared?" Acharon asked. He had to raise his voice. Both women were on the far side of the formal dining room, disappearing through a door on the right.

"No," Katuva called back.

Acharon wandered into the dining room. The square table was set for three. There was a low bowl of flowers in the center. The three settings were each on their own side. The empty side was against the back wall. The plates and bowls were all of a set and gleamed like only brand new dishes could gleam.

"This is the house Carter brought me to after I passed out," Katuva said. She was carrying a platter into the room. She set it at the empty place on the table. "I refused to go back home after what he'd done. He never slept in this house after I woke up. It was a year before I even let him through the door. Still had to go back and sleep in his own bed, though."

She left again, moving through what looked like a pantry between the kitchen and dining room. The hors d'oeuvres were little squares of toast with something creamy and decorated with thin slices of bell peppers. Tentatively, Acharon tasted one of them.

"Yummy," he said through a mouthful of the cream cheese-like substance and toasted bread. He swallowed and said it louder.

"You're welcome." Katuva had reappeared with a pitcher of water. She poured a glass and offered it to him.

She disappeared again before Acharon could finish his mouth-clearing sip of water.

"Where's Sovelet?"

Sovelet's voice drifted through the pantry. "Working on a salad."

"Oh," Acharon said more to himself than anyone. When Katuva appeared with a basket that smelled like freshly baked bread, Acharon asked, "Can I help with anything?"

Katuva smiled a rare smile. "We've got it. Thank you."

"If you're going to eat, sit."

Acharon turned to find Sovelet standing behind him with a small bowl of green salad highlighted with tomato wedges and carrot shavings. Automatically, Acharon took the bowl from her and set it on the table.

Again, Acharon found himself alone in the dining room as both women disappeared. He started to follow but found himself backpedaling just as quickly.

"Stand aside, buster," Sovelet said. She was carrying a bowl of steaming potatoes and root vegetables. She threatened Acharon, playfully poking in his direction with the bowl.

He managed to step aside as Sovelet reached the table. Right behind her, Katuva arrived with a medium-sized platter holding the not-meat meatloaf. She set the platter on the table and adjusted the placement of the meatloaf, salad, and roasted potatoes and vegetables before stepping back to look at the entire setting.

"I haven't cooked for more than one in so long," she said. She spoke less declaratively and more in surprise. "I hope I did okay."

"You did great," Sovelet said.

Acharon agreed and said, "It looks very delicious."

Katuva turned to both of them. "There's only one way to find out. Sit. Eat."

Acharon moved to where Katuva was standing and held out a seat for her. She thanked him and sat. Acharon repeated the process for Sovelet. By the time he'd gotten around to his place, Sovelet had already served him up helpings of everything.

"Thank you," he said. He waited until both women had their plates full before he started.

They all began to eat in silence. It stayed that way for several minutes. Acharon was glad for the absence of table talk as it allowed him to enjoy the flavors. The food was delicious. A quick glance at Sovelet and Katuva showed that they were both pleased as well.

When his plate was half empty, and he wasn't sure he could get any more in, Acharon set his fork and knife down, helping himself to his glass of water.

"It's delicious, Katuva, thank you."

"It's wonderful," Sovelet said. She still had a lot on her plate. Acharon knew she was generally a light eater, so she wasn't just being polite.

Katuva set her utensils aside. She continued to look down at a spot about a half-meter in front of her plate. She offered back a quiet thank you and then seemed to fold her hands into her lap.

"Katuva?" Sovelet asked. "It really is excellent food."

"I know," Katuva said a little louder. "I just realized that this will be the only dinner we'll have like this. When everyone was here, before they took the journey, there were big meals every night. If people weren't eating together in someone's home, they were out having barbecues in the park or pushing tables together in the diner. I didn't realize I missed it until now."

Acharon looked at Sovelet, who'd turned to catch his eye. He didn't know what to say and, it seemed, neither did Sovelet.

Katuva seemed to be unaware of their dilemma. "I'd been so busy punishing Carter by ignoring him and doing things on my own, it became automatic. I don't think I ever really stopped to think about it. And by the time I might have, I got fixated with the mannequins.

"Then you guys came. I started thinking of what it was like when everyone was here. So much laughter. The dancing in the evenings. Just being with so many people who loved life."

"I'm sorry," Acharon said. "If they loved life, why did they end it?"

"Acharon." Sovelet's voice was a harsh whisper.

"It's okay, Sovelet," Katuva said. "I know it's difficult to understand. I think we all loved life as much as you, Acharon. I think what no one liked was the idea of passing alone. Here, they all went together."

"Honey, you don't have to talk about it." Sovelet reached out and took Katuva's hand.

"Is that why you didn't take your own life, later?" Acharon asked. "You didn't want to pass alone?"

Acharon could feel the heat of Sovelet glaring at him, but he was already on the path, and Katuva seemed willing to talk.

"It is. I thought maybe with Carter, I could do it. Two of us, that's still a journey together. But he kept refusing. After a while, I stopped asking. Then he died by accident, and I was on my own. Then you and Sovelet arrived."

"I don't know if 'arrived' is the right word for it."

Katuva smiled. "True. But you're here. That got me to hoping."

A shiver ran down Acharon's back. "Hoping for what?"

Katuva pulled her hand out of Sovelet's gentle grip and reached down to her waist. Slowly, as if afraid to share a personal secret, she placed her hand back on the table. Underneath her palm was a small, metal box. She pinched the sides of it, popping the lid loose, and removed it to reveal seven little pills, purple with red spots.

"I was hoping three could make the journey."

08

"Shit," Acharon said. He pushed the plate away. He pushed his chair back and stood.

"Acharon?" Sovelet asked.

"No." He held out a hand which kept Sovelet from talking. He started pacing, a panic begging to rise and be set free. He didn't feel funny. Not dizzy or queasy. Sweating? Yes, but that was from nervous energy. Was there an antidote? He turned to Katuva, who'd pulled back into her chair, eyes wide. "What did you do?"

"Nothing," Katuva said. Her voice was fearful, timid.

"Acharon, stop."

"Stop?" He jabbed in the direction of the little pillbox. "She's poisoned us."

"I haven't!" Katuva was on her feet. "I wouldn't."

"No? You're so eager to be shot of this life – this only life! – that you'll do anything to get out of it."

Katuva broke into tears, sinking back into her seat. Through her tears and her hands, she said, "I would never."

"You need to stop, Acharon," Sovelet said. Her words were hard enough to pause Acharon in his tracks. "You've missed the point. You've let your personal feelings get in the way, again, of a discussion."

"What did I miss?" This was an argument, not a discussion, and Acharon hated arguing with Sovelet. It made him feel like he was letting her down, but his back was up. He had no problem admitting to himself that he was scared. "I can see them quite clearly. Right there."

"Exactly, Acharon. Exactly." She waved him with slow hand motions to return to his chair.

Acharon's legs were shaking. It wasn't from being poisoned. He knew it was his body reacting to the burst of adrenaline that he'd scared into himself. He sat, slowly, his knees quivering and threatening to give way. When he finally settled into his chair, hiding his shaking hands beneath the tabletop, Sovelet gave him a look that required an acknowledgment.

"Okay," he said. His voice vibrated with restraint. "I'm okay."

"You will be," said Sovelet. "Now, if we can discuss this rationally?"

Acharon barked a laugh and instantly regretted it. "Sorry," he said.

"I'll let it slide. This time." Sovelet turned her attention to Katuva. "Honey? Are you going to be okay?"

Acharon found it frustrating that Sovelet would concern herself with how Katuva was feeling. She was feeling suicidal in Acharon's opinion.

Katuva, in response to Sovelet's query, nodded her head. She slowly sat up, lifting her head from her hands. Her face was red and wet with tears. She rubbed a ribbon of snot from her lip with the back of her hand.

"I would never."

"I believe you," Sovelet said. "Now we just have to convince Acharon of it. He's heard it all before, so it's just a matter of knocking it out of the attic of his thick skull."

"It's not that thick," Acharon said in his own defense.

"Then stop acting like it." She turned her attention once more to Katuva. "Tell me, so Acharon can learn, how many people were forced to make passage?"

Katuva looked shocked. "What? No! No one. That was always the point. Passage was for those who accepted the end and embraced it. People left. People were allowed to leave. People were encouraged to leave if they had even the slightest doubt."

"What about Carter?" Acharon asked. "Doesn't seem like he was allowed to choose for himself."

"That's not how it was," Katuva said. "I mean, it was his idea to come. He said that maybe this was the best idea. I didn't fight it. When he suggested it, it was like a great weight taken off my shoulders. Finally, I had an answer to the meaning of my life."

"And yet," Acharon said, despite Sovelet's subtle shake of her head. "When it came time, Carter had to trick you so he wouldn't have to go through with it."

"Maybe we shouldn't have this discussion," Sovelet said.

Katuva put a hand on Sovelet's. "No, it's okay. I always did wonder why he didn't just say something."

"Well, maybe he didn't know until those last hours," Sovelet said. "Maybe he didn't know how to ask you. So, he acted in a way he thought was best. People can be irrational."

"No kidding," Acharon said.

"All right, smart guy," Sovelet said. "Give it a rest or you're sleeping on the porch tonight."

Acharon pressed his lips together even though he felt he had a lot more to say.

"Tell us about the pills," Sovelet said to Katuva.

"These were the ones everyone took that morning." She picked up the lid and slowly set it over the pills. She pressed down until the cover clicked into place. "I've saved them. I didn't think I'd ever be able to use them. Not once Carter died."

She looked at Acharon, defiance in her eyes. "And I would never trick someone. No matter what you think."

"What did you intend, dear?" Sovelet asked.

"Just what you saw here," Katuva said. She waved her hand over the meal and the pill case. "A meal. And an offer. Once I realized you might be leaving, I thought I should ask. It couldn't hurt to ask."

Acharon felt he could argue a counterpoint to that. She about gave him a heart attack as far as he was concerned.

Sovelet took Katuva's hand in both of hers. "Katuva, dear. If you want to make the passage, we'll sit here with you. You won't be alone."

Acharon was on his feet. "Oh, no. No no no. I won't sit here and watch someone kill themselves. Even if it's not messy, I'm not a part of this."

Katuva put up her hand, a pleading gesture to Acharon. "Please don't go. I'm not. I mean, I don't want to go alone. If you – and I know you don't – were to go, too, then I think I would have the courage. But not by myself. I'm tired of doing things by myself."

Acharon sat down. He could really use a cup of coffee but thought better of asking for one. Not now, anyway.

Across the table, Sovelet was rubbing Katuva's hand. Katuva had her head tilted back, probably feeling as exhausted as Acharon felt.

"Katuva."

Katuva and Acharon both turned their attention to Sovelet.

"Yes?"

"Why don't you come with us to New York?"

"Seriously?" Acharon said.

Sovelet shrugged. "Why not? Katuva doesn't want to do the passage alone. She's tired of doing things alone. If she stays, it'll be just that until she dies alone."

"I don't know," Katuva said. She'd slipped her hand free of Sovelet's.

"Acharon?" Sovelet asked. The tone of her voice implied she wanted him to chime in, supportively. It was a rare tone, but familiar even after many years without it.

"If she wants to stay," he said. Sovelet's look after he began to speak suggested he rethink his words. "However, Katuva, Sovelet is correct. This is no place to be alone. There's a variety of people waiting for us in New York."

"You might find some other people there who'd help you to keep finding reasons to live," Sovelet said. She'd turned so the back of her shoulder was toward Acharon. He nodded his head in acceptance of the trouble he was likely going to be in later.

"I can't say." Katuva stood and fussed with her plate and glass, moving them a couple centimeters to one side and then back again. "I don't know. Not right now. I need to think. Please don't clean up. I'll need to do something later. Good night."

She gave Sovelet a peck on the cheek and walked into the living room and then the foyer. Acharon could hear her on the stairs up to the second floor. He and Sovelet sat in the silence that followed a door closing overhead. Acharon noticed the pillbox still on the table.

"We should destroy that," he said.

"It's not ours, Acharon." Sovelet wiped her lips with her napkin and laid it on the table. "I'm going home."

Acharon avoided expressing his feelings of the word "home" and followed Sovelet to the door.

"May I walk with you?"

"Just keep your hands to yourself."

The sun had set, but the sky still glowed with the deep blue of a sunless sky. Stars were sparkling in the east. Somewhere, Acharon thought, way over there, people who wanted to live were waiting for him and Sovelet. Yet, here they were with someone who thought the best way to live life was to give it up.

"I'm sorry," he said instead of voice his other thoughts. "The pills really threw me."

"I know," Sovelet said. She shoulder-bumped him, which was a good sign in Acharon's eyes. "I figured it might happen. I should have warned you."

"Well, it's done. Do you think she'll come with us?"

Sovelet was quiet for a few minutes. "I'm not sure. She should, but I can understand why she might not want to."

"I don't know how anyone in New York will react when they learn what she was a part of."

"No one has to tell them," Sovelet said. She moved over and hooked her arm around his, hugging it.

Acharon squeezed her arm between his and his body. "Someone will work it out. They'll put two and two together. Or someone will ask, and she'll answer honestly."

Sovelet stopped and stepped back a step to look at Acharon. Her face was filled with mock shock. "What? No subterfuge?"

Acharon's head wobbled with the weary expression of one oft put upon. "I overreacted. I apologized."

"Not to Katuva." Sovelet retook Acharon's arm as they stepped onto Main street.

Streetlights and lights in the shops gave the place a warm and surreal feeling.

"I'll apologize tomorrow?"

"That sounds like a good idea." Sovelet pointed to the diner. "We never got dessert. You want something?"

"Sure," Acharon said. He led the way, holding the door open.

Sovelet stopped on the threshold and put her hand on his chest.

"And tomorrow, you'll apologize."

"Tomorrow, I'll apologize."

Sovelet smiled. "Then the pie's on me."

Acharon woke to a tapping sound. At first, he thought it was a woodpecker. He laid still, listening to it. Slowly it dawned on him that woodpeckers don't peck on glass.

"We have company," he said. He sat up and reached for his pants.

"You're dreaming," Sovelet said and pulled the covers higher over her head.

Acharon stood, buttoning and zipping his pants. "If we weren't the only ones in town, I'd agree with you."

Sovelet pushed the covers off her face, turning enough so that Acharon could see her tired eyes looking in his direction. "Katuva?"

"That or a polite lion. I'll check and let you know."

"If it's a lion, tell it we gave at the monorail." She flashed a tired smile.

Acharon stopped at the door long enough to say, "You mean, I gave at the monorail."

Sovelet's retort was lost amongst the rustling of the comforter as she flipped it back over her head.

Acharon took the stairs slowly, listening to the tapping on the glass. While he didn't expect it to be a lion, it could still be something wild and dangerous. At the last stair, he peeked around the corner. He relaxed when he saw Katuva's face, turned slightly away, courteously not looking through the door's window.

When Acharon turned the doorknob, Katuva turned her attention to him and the opening door.

"Cinnamon roll?" She held out a plate with a metal cover over the top.

"I haven't made coffee yet," Acharon said.

Katuva looked down, drawing Acharon's gaze with hers. A gray carafe had been set on the bench by the door.

"In that case," Acharon said, pulling the door open further, "why don't you come in."

"Thank you," Katuva said. Her voice was soft, reluctant.

"Go on in, I'll get the coffee." Acharon expected Katuva to make her way to the dining room on her own, but when he turned from grabbing the carafe, she was still in the entryway.

"Is Sovelet awake?"

Acharon waved Katuva forward, into the hall that led to the dining room and kitchen. "She's half-awake. I'm sure she'll be down in a moment. Did you sleep at all?"

"For a bit," Katuva said over her shoulder as she turned left off the hall into the dining room. "But then I started working on these."

"It took all night?"

Katuva set the plate and lid on the empty tabletop. "I had to start over a couple of times. It's been a while."

"Sure, sure," Acharon said. "I'll get cups and stuff."

He left Katuva and went to the kitchen. When he returned with a collection of plates, mugs, and forks, Katuva had taken a seat. Sovelet still had not come downstairs.

Acharon set the plates out and poured coffee. Katuva dug out several rolls and placed them on the plates.

"Listen, Katuva," Acharon said. Katuva stopped and looked at him. "I wanted to apologize for my actions last night. I overreacted a little. Well, a lot if you trust Sovelet's opinion. So, yeah, a lot. I'm sorry."

She smiled at him. "Thank you. I appreciate it, but I can't say I blame you. I don't think I'd want anyone to make that decision for me, either. And if I didn't know that person very well, I can understand the concern."

"Nicely done, dear." Sovelet came into the dining room through the kitchen. She had an oversized robe wrapped around her, and her hair was still disheveled. She stopped and gave him a kiss on the cheek before circling the table and doing the same for Katuva. "Oh, cinnamon rolls. They smell wonderful."

"Thank you."

Sovelet sat. Acharon poured her a cup of coffee. They again lapsed into silence as they ate the food that Katuva had made. Acharon paused for a guilty second and then took a large forkful of the cinnamon roll. He decided after two bites that if he had to die, death by handmade cinnamon rolls wasn't a bad way to do it.

"These are very good," he finally got around to saying. "I don't think I've had better."

"You haven't," Sovelet said. She scraped the last of the sugar frosting off her plate with her fork and stuck it in her mouth. "Have you thought about my suggestion? About coming with us to New York."

Katuva nodded and set her fork down. She reached for her coffee mug and then pulled her hand back. She took a deep breath and let it out slowly. "Do you think they'd accept me?"

Sovelet looked at Acharon.

"There's really no reason why they wouldn't," Acharon said. He knew there were probably exceptions. He'd met a few, but he didn't think Katuva, despite her history, would be one of them. "You'll be a celebrity. Someone that none of them know anything about. Unlike the rest of us."

"You probably know a lot about them, and us," Sovelet said. She picked up her mug.

Katuva looked guilty. "I wouldn't say I know a lot."

"But you do know some," said Acharon as Sovelet was mid sip.

As Sovelet set her mug down, she added, "The point is that you already sort of know everyone in the New York enclave. Might as well go visit them in person."

Katuva looked at Acharon and then Sovelet. She slowly nodded her head.

"You'll come?"

"Yes, I'll come," Katuva said in response to Sovelet's question.

"Hurray," Sovelet said.

They both looked at Acharon. What did they want? A celebratory speech? There was only one thing on his mind. "We've got a lot of work to do."

09

The gas station and garage were a block past the quainter parts of Main street. From his earlier tour, Acharon knew that the old fuel pumps were now for show. The 35,000-liter tanks had been removed around the same period as the discovery that there would be no more children born. But not all vehicles ran on electricity alone. Especially in places far from urban centers. Places where people were more resistant to change.

That was where the synthetic fuel came in. The nickname, syn-fuel, humored a lot of people. Acharon found the syn-fuel equipment inside the garage.

The fuel synthesizer machines had been installed along the wall of the last garage bay. The bay had roll-up doors in the front and back. Acharon would have to guess, but he had a feeling that this allowed a vehicle to drive in and park while fuel was synthesized and pumped directly into the gas tank of the waiting vehicle. The syn-fuel could be made in advance and stored in a tank, but it had a very limited shelf life.

Syn-fuel was far from perfect as it tended to eat through rings and gaskets. It also deteriorated quickly. A person had to plan ahead for its use. And it also never fully combusted. The syn-fuel burning vehicles were noisy and smelly, and right now, they were all Acharon had to work with.

The truck Katuva used for clearing Main street and for emergencies, like saving random passersby from lions, sat in the syn-fuel bay. It was sturdy enough, but the abuse over the decades made him leery. Perhaps one of the other vehicles would work better.

Before investigating his options, Acharon took a moment to start the syn-fuel system going. It was going to take a while to synthesize enough fuel to get them to Lincoln.

After that, he spent several minutes climbing around the engines of a short school bus, an emergency medical wagon that was missing most of its medical equipment, and a soft-top sedan that looked like it had been resurrected from a time centuries ago.

The sedan was interesting. Someone had put a lot of energy and time into that one. The engine wasn't original, though, which was a good thing. The metal of the old engine block wouldn't have held up to the aggressive corrosion of syn-fuel. Its new engine would handle the fuel well and would undoubtedly get them to Lincoln. But, Acharon thought as he rubbed his one arm with the other, it had a roof of cloth. It was like a candy wrapper for a hungry lion. Maybe as a last resort, but the sedan was going to have to sit here until something else evolved far enough to appreciate it.

The emergency vehicle was sturdy and made of metal but had two regular seats and one uncomfortable looking fold-down jump seat. While it might be good for emergencies, it didn't look like anyone would enjoy the three-hour ride over rough terrain and broken roads. If he suggested Katuva sit there, Sovelet would turn him to ice with one cold stare. But like hell if he'd put Sovelet on that seat.

That left Acharon with the school bus. Half the seats had been torn out. In their place, tie downs had been bolted in. If he had to guess, once again that was the only way he was getting an answer here, he would say that this was the vehicle they'd used to bring in new members of the cult. Perhaps there was a small airfield nearby. Or maybe they just pulled an emergency stop on a carriage and did like he and Sovelet and climbed down the rail pillar.

All but the driver's seat looked uncomfortable. At least Sovelet couldn't say he was being unfair to Katuva.

Whoever had been in charge of the vehicles had been smart. All of the syn-fuel had been drained from the vehicles. It wasn't allowed to sit and focus its attention on ruining the rings and gaskets. That was at least one good thing in Acharon's favor.

The syn-fuel synthesizer was still slowly making fuel. It would take several hours to make enough for the trip. He wanted to have about twice what he needed, just in case. He wanted a few jerry cans of extra fuel, just to be prepared for emergencies.

There was a lot of mechanical equipment stored inside the station. Parts for the air turbines, spools of cable and wires of different gauges. Three plow blades for the truck were backed up to each other behind Katuva's truck. Acharon could tell which one Katuva was using by its blade, shortened by decades of scraping debris off Main Street.

Unsurprisingly, there were no jerrycans in the garage. In times gone by, there would have at least been the bright-red plastic variation. Acharon wasn't dismayed by their absence. It only meant he'd have to go hunting inside the four long-term storage containers behind the garage.

There was a manifest on a computer, somewhere. But as he had hours to spare, Acharon was looking forward to rummaging through the containers. He was confident he'd find the jerrycans easily enough. The fun part would be seeing all the other things people around here thought would be important enough to keep extras of for the future. Back in Berkeley, while searching through a container for electrical equipment, he'd found a thousand yoga mats.

So, with a crowbar, flashlight, and a sharp knife, Acharon stepped out behind the garage, ready to break the seals of the containers and begin foraging for jerrycans. The first container had been open a while, based on the rust on the edges of the wide-swinging doors. Here were mostly parts for the synthesizer and the raw chemicals that were combined for the syn-fuel. The reservoirs in the synthesizer had been nearly full when Acharon checked. They held more than enough to do the job he required them to do. It was unlikely he'd need any more, but it was nice to know where to go.

He was surprised, however, that there weren't any jerrycans in the container. Maybe the people who'd stocked these containers didn't feel they would need jerrycans. Someone else had thought a thousand yoga mats was essential, so who knew what logic people were engaged in.

Surprisingly, the second container had also been opened. Based on the faint beginnings of rust on the edges where someone had scraped away paint while opening the doors, it was pretty recent. Acharon didn't have to guess at who that had been. Maybe there were parts in here for the truck Katuva drove. Though, she did say she didn't have the mechanical knowledge to perform maintenance. Maybe headlamps?

Acharon didn't have an answer, but he did have an easy-to-open container. That was always nice. The doors swung open without complaint allowing sunlight to poke its way into the darkness. There was a narrow aisle down the center of the container. Nothing large, like an intact vehicle, blocked the line-of-sight to the back wall.

With slight turns at the waist to accommodate his shoulders, Acharon began to make his way down the aisle. As he moved, he read the labels on large boxes, hoping to see 'fuel cans' or 'jerrycans.' He didn't find a container of them, but he did hit paydirt about three-quarters of the way back. On a pallet to his right, he found them stacked on each other with a thin sheet of plastic between layers. They were held in place by heat-lock plastic strips that peeled away with only a little effort. Now he had all the jerrycans he needed, and a surplus.

He only had two hands, though, and he wanted six cans. Leaving his scavenging equipment behind, he toted the first two cans to the front of the container and set them on a box just inside the door. Three more trips and he had six cans and his crowbar and flashlight.

Even then, he still only had two hands to carry things back to the garage. Acharon pocketed the flashlight, and with the use of the crowbar, he managed to get three jerrycans back to the garage. When he came back for the other three, he saw something that caught his attention.

When he'd first entered the container, he'd seen that the lid of a wood box to his right was slightly ajar. He'd paid it no mind while he parked the jerry cans there until he had all six. It was only as he lifted the last one that he noticed what the box's contents were.

Yoga mats made sense if someone wanted to have a lot of yoga classes. Woodworking tools made sense if someone planned on doing a lot of stuff involving wood. Occasionally things needed to be demolished. So Acharon wasn't surprised to see a case of C-4 in a container. It was pretty stable as far as explosives went. They'd used it occasionally to break up concrete from a collapsed building.

So the C-4 wasn't a concern. What concerned Acharon was that the case had been opened. Inside, there were three neat rows of C-4 bricks where there should have been four. Half of the fourth row was missing. Even that wouldn't have been much of a concern except that everything pointed to the storage container having been opened recently. There was only one person who could have taken the C-4.

Question was, why did she take it? Acharon chewed on that question just long enough to return to the first container where he'd seen earlier, and now quickly relocated, a metal box with individually wrapped detonators. The box's seal was already broken. Acharon would have to count them, but he was pretty sure at least one detonator was missing. And he also knew what Katuva had done with the C-4 and detonator. He and Sovelet would never have stopped here if the monorail was still intact.

Frustrated, Acharon retrieved a brick of C-4 and took it back to the garage. He checked the fuel synthesizer and started running diagnostics on the bus. He was distracted with thoughts and several times managed to bang knuckles or an elbow when normally he'd be more cautious.

He was just connecting the syn-fuel hose to the tank's filler neck on the bus when distance-muted conversation caught his attention. He left the syn-fuel off and grabbed the C-4. Sovelet and Katuva were just stepping onto the nearby sidewalk when Acharon cut them off.

"Oh! Acharon," Sovelet said. "You surprised us. How's everything coming along?"

"Just great, thank you." He turned to Katuva, who seemed to sense Acharon's anger and took a step back. "That must make you unhappy."

"Acharon?" Sovelet looked confused and troubled with Acharon's behavior.

"Why would I be unhappy?"

Acharon tossed the C-4 to the ground in front of Katuva. It thumped onto the concrete, deforming its straight brick shape as it landed. "Unhappy that I got a vehicle working. Unhappy that your little plan to stop us here and make us kill ourselves just so you wouldn't have to do it alone. That plan."

"Ach, we've been through this," Sovelet said. He didn't want to upset her, but she needed to see who they were dealing with, once the veneer of simple-woman was removed.

"We haven't been through it all, Sove." Acharon kept most of his focus on Katuva. She was still looking at the deformed brick of C-4. Acharon continued speaking. "I found an open box of that stuff. It might not seem a big deal at first, but it wasn't opened that long ago. And then we have the situation with the monorail track being damaged. Though, now I'd use the word 'demolished' or maybe even 'sabotaged.' Would you like to convince me otherwise, Katuva?"

She looked even more unsure than the first time Acharon had met her in the diner.

"I can't," she said.

"Ach," Sovelet said. "This isn't necessary."

"It is necessary," Acharon said. "She destroyed the track on purpose. That's why we had to stop. She had to know we were coming. You know what that means, right?"

Sovelet nodded. Acharon was sure she'd figured that part out the moment they walked into the post office.

"You burned the communication equipment." Sovelet wasn't looking at Katuva, but Katuva appeared to be aware of who Sovelet was speaking to.

"I did," said Katuva.

Her face had gone ashy pale. Acharon was torn between his normal reaction to find her a seat and his anger that said to just let her fall where she stood. Then, Katuva straightened her shoulders and looked straight at Acharon. There was a tremble that seemed to connect her fingers to her lips.

"I did do those things. I did hope you would stay and would make the passage with me. But you aren't, and you didn't, and I see how things can be different."

"You got that, Sovelet?" Acharon asked. "You said they never forced anyone. Maybe she didn't hold a gun to our head, but she did try to compel us towards it by removing our hope for a new future."

"There is no future," Katuva said. "There's just now. Then, there's nothing. There's no community to remember us when we die. No family to mourn us. No children to carry on after we're dead. There is no future."

Acharon pointed a finger at her. "You don't get to make that decision for me."

"Stop!" Sovelet didn't scream her command, but her voice was raised high enough and loud enough that it was successful in achieving the result intended. When they both looked at her, she spoke in a tone and volume close to her usual self. "That's behind us. Katuva knows, now, that we wouldn't – that we aren't interested in passage. That we have no intention of taking our own lives. Am I right, Katuva?"

Katuva was silent, but she didn't hesitate in nodding her head in agreement. Her gaze rose towards Acharon's but slipped away at the last moment.

"And she's agreed to come with us, to explore and see that there's more than sitting and waiting to die. Is that right, Katuva?"

This time she found her voice. "Yes."

"What guarantee?" Acharon asked. "How can I be sure that she won't try and urge us every chance she gets to take her damn pills?"

Without a word, Katuva moved. She walked into the garage. Acharon went to stop her. He was concerned that she would suddenly sabotage the fuel synthesizer. Sovelet's hand on his arm stopped him. He turned to complain but stopped when he saw the sad smile on her face. It was like the time she'd had to tell him that the last kitten he'd ever found her had died during the night. She'd been sad, but appreciative of his efforts.

"She could do something," Acharon said. His voice was lowered so as not to give Katuva any ideas.

"Wait." Sovelet gently squeezed his arm. "Let's see."

Katuva returned before Acharon could put any real consideration into ignoring Sovelet's request. In her right hand, she carried a hammer. Acharon took a step back. Katuva tilted her head a few degrees. Her eyebrows rose as she caught his movement, and her expression shifted to a bunched-lip look of annoyance.

A few feet from Sovelet and Acharon, Katuva stopped. She reached into the left pocket of her skirt and removed the tin she'd presented the night before. With an ease that had to have come from practice, she popped the lid off. She locked eyes with Acharon while she held out the tin, the pills still present, and turned it over.

The pills dropped to the ground, tapping it like small hail. One of them broke, but the others bounced random patterns for several bounces and then stopped. A lone pill had rolled rather than bounce. Katuva stopped it with her foot, all of it while staring at Acharon.

When the pills had settled, Katuva casually tossed the pill tin to the side. She squatted in front of Acharon and Sovelet. With one last look at Acharon, she turned her attention to the pills. She started with the one her foot had stopped, smashing it with several whacks of the hammer. She continued to the next and then the next. She pummeled each pill until all of them were dust, mingled with the dirt already on the ground.

Katuva stood and held the hammer out, handle first, in Acharon's direction. After a nudge by Sovelet, he reached and took the hammer. He held it close to his stomach, unsure what he was supposed to do. Make a speech? Apologize?

"If you're thinking what I'm thinking you are," Katuva said, "no, there aren't anymore. I can't prove it to you, though. So now it's up to you, I guess."

"He believes you," Sovelet said.

Katuva shook her head. "I don't think so, Sovelet. I don't think he'll ever believe me. Maybe I should just stay here. Maybe I deserve all this."

Acharon would have liked that. One less worry. Fewer chances that her willingness to end her own life might infect Sovelet's thinking. She wasn't susceptible to persuasion, but she had voiced her own willingness to stop trying to live. He wasn't going to let that happen.

He also knew that Sovelet wouldn't leave Katuva alone. That didn't mean she would refuse to leave, too. What it meant was that there'd be a lot of verbal pressure by her until he did what he nearly always did. She argued well, but that wouldn't be the reason. He'd finally agree because he wanted to make her happy.

So, if bringing along a passenger with suicidal thoughts was going to make Sovelet happy, he would do it.

"No," he said aloud. "If you say those are the only pills, I'll take your word."

"And you are still invited to come with us," said Sovelet. Her face was the only one smiling.

Acharon realized that Katuva was now looking at him. It was his response she was waiting for.

"Yes, you are still invited to come." Acharon looked at the sky. It was still blue, but darker to the east. The day was more than half over. "We'll leave in the morning."

An impish smile flitted across Katuva's face. "You want me to make breakfast before we go?"

He knew she was teasing, but it still made his stomach flop with dread. The always reassuring squeeze of Sovelet's hand on his arm provided reassurance.

"Wouldn't want to travel on an empty stomach."

10

In the morning, while Sovelet and Katuva packed the last of the supplies for the trip to Lincoln, Acharon went to the garage. It took time to unlock all the padlocks he'd secured the building with. There was the old axiom, trust but verify, that he'd found useful through much of his life. Though, keeping honest people honest worked in this instance, too.

Dinner with Sovelet had been a mostly silent affair with just the two of them present. Katuva had begged off with the headache excuse, which suited Acharon just fine. Sovelet had politely inquired about the readiness of the bus. Acharon had responded with just enough detail to satisfy the question.

During the night, as they'd laid in bed, Sovelet had scooted across the mattress, filling the gap between them. She'd draped an arm over Acharon's waist and fell back asleep. Acharon had lain awake a little longer, pleased with the pressure of her arm around him. His mind began spooling out memories of their long life together. Somewhere in the good thoughts, he'd finally fallen back asleep.

First light had roused him and Sovelet. Katuva was already making omelets when they entered the diner. She'd seemed in better spirits now. Acharon did his best not to hurt the mood.

He was glad, however, when breakfast was done and he could finally get the bus out of the garage. The delay with the locks was only a few minutes. Still, when he brought the bus to a stop outside the house he and Sovelet were using, she was sitting on the front porch like a mother waiting for a tardy child.

"Took you long enough," she said.

"Battery didn't hold a charge like I thought it would," Acharon said. He helped her load two boxes of foodstuffs and a third box with clothes still in their hermetically sealed bags. "I had to switch with the one in Katuva's truck."

"Speaking of," Sovelet said. She settled onto the bench seat behind the driver's. "Let's get a move on."

Acharon set the bus in motion. It slid several times on the dirt and grass layered road. Unbidden images of their last trip to San Francisco seeped into his consciousness, distracting him. In that misadventure, they skidded to avoid the pack of wild dogs. They skidded to avoid a brown bear. And finally, they skidded on the side of the jeep they drove after nearly being trampled by a herd of stampeding elk. San Francisco sure had changed.

A sheepish grin that Acharon could just make out in the window reflection pushed at his cheeks. With a slow shake of his head, he managed to shake it loose and focus on the road as he turned the bus to the right on Main Street. It was fascinating to him how disconnected events seemed to so easily draw together.

Even driving down this street with its windowed tableaus of normalcy stirred memories. Here there were mannequins behind windows, acting out normal lives as he paraded down the street in the short bus. In his memories, they paraded down the streets of San Francisco atop an automated street sweeper, a pack of angry dogs surrounding them, intent on killing them. So different, and yet they clung to each other.

"You missed it."

"Missed what?" Acharon asked. He took his foot off the accelerator. Had she been reading his thoughts?

"The turn, Acharon." She was leaning over his shoulder, pointing to the left.

"Right," Acharon said. He put the stubborn gearbox into reverse and slowly backed down the street. When he had enough clearance for a turn, he shifted back into drive and slowly turned onto the street where Katuva lived.

Katuva was standing on the curb, or at least where the curb would be if not buried under a hillock of decades of amassed dirt and debris. There was a look of relief on her face that surprised Acharon.

He stopped the bus where she stood and pulled on the big lever, opening the doors. "All aboard."

Sovelet must have seen the look on Katuva's face, too. She was already on the stairs as the door slapped open.

"Honey? You okay?" she asked Katuva.

Sovelet had exited the bus and put a hand on Katuva's shoulder. Katuva had immediately made it an embrace by stepping into the curve Sovelet's arm had made. Sovelet didn't hesitate to return the hug, but Acharon knew how compassionate she was.

"Katuva?" she asked. "What's wrong?"

Acharon had put the bus into park and belatedly followed Sovelet. Instead of attempting to comfort Katuva, he'd picked up several of the boxes that were on the ground behind her.

"Maybe she's going to miss this place," he said.

"I thought you were going to leave me," Katuva said. Her face was buried in Sovelet's shoulder so that Acharon almost missed what she said.

"Leave you?" he asked. Not that it hadn't occurred to him. However, he also knew he wouldn't have been allowed to do such a thing.

Katuva stepped back. She opened a gap between her and Sovelet, who still had hands on her shoulders. Katuva wiped the tears from her face with a sleeve.

"I heard the bus coming," she said. Her head moved to point the direction with her chin. "And then I watched you go right by the street. I thought maybe you were leaving. Then I realized what it would mean to be alone again."

"That's the wrong direction," Acharon said. He'd gotten two of the boxes onto the bus. "Lincoln's the other way."

"You're not helping," Sovelet said.

Acharon wondered if she missed the irony of her statement as he carried the last two boxes onto the bus.

Sovelet had turned her attention back to Katuva. "We didn't leave you, see? Now we can all go to New York together."

"Lincoln," Acharon said. He was sitting down in the driver's seat.

Sovelet rolled her eyes and shook her head. Katuva, much to Acharon's surprise, laughed. Perhaps things would work out.

Two hours en route to Lincoln and Acharon was already of a mind to call it a day. The drive was exhausting. Keeping to the road had become a guessing game a half kilometer past the gate of the town. A gate Katuva begged him to close and lock.

The dirt layer over the road had been stirred up into a bumpy terrain by the passing of thousands of creatures in hundreds of herds. The bus, in hindsight a poor choice for off-roading, bounced constantly and irregularly with short, rapid bounces that rattled the teeth. Sovelet's usually warm demeanor had filled the time with conversation, filling in Katuva with all she knew about everyone still alive. But even she had ceased talking, more intent on staying in her seat, as the first hour jostled into the second.

"Maybe a break," Acharon suggested.

"Yes, please," Sovelet said.

"Katuva?"

Her response had been to shrug and say, "Sure, I guess."

Acharon gladly brought the bus to a stop and turned off the motor. The sudden silence was like a glass of fresh, cold water after working hours on a hot day.

Sovelet had slowly gotten to her feet and stretched first one side and then the others.

"Is it like this the entire way?" she asked Katuva.

"I've never been this way," Katuva said. She'd turned and was watching Sovelet opening a box. "I've rarely left the town. Except a couple times when I went to the rail to pick up new members of the group."

And to blow it up, Acharon thought but didn't say aloud. No need to go picking at that scab. Instead, he contented himself with a trip around the bus to check for damage and to relieve himself. There was a portable toilet he'd found and brought on board. That was meant for the women, just in case. How they hadn't had to go after all the jostling and bouncing was a testament to their strength.

The bus still looked resilient. There were some minor dents along the bottom edges of the body. Dirt had already stained most of the lower half and caked inside the wheels. There'd been no differences in the sounds of the engine and gears along the two-hour drive. As much as it felt like the bus was going to shake itself apart, Acharon was confident they'd get to Lincoln before it did.

"Acharon?" Sovelet called.

"Outside," he called back.

"Where?"

What did that matter? "Just coming around the front. Hang on."

"Don't panic," she said. "But be quick."

What had happened, he wondered as he walked faster around the last corner and started up the stairs into the bus. Katuva was standing by the driver seat, both hands on the door lever. Both of Acharon's feet had barely cleared the threshold when she yanked on the lever. The doors snapped shut, just brushing against Acharon's backside.

"Hey!"

Her actions surprised him. Was she trying to trap him outside the bus but was too slow? He looked for Sovelet to get an answer. He found her kneeling on the seat nearest the door, shotgun poking out the open window. He looked back at Katuva, confused.

"Company," Katuva said. She pointed in the direction behind Acharon.

Acharon turned around and looked through the door's windows. It took a few heartbeats, looking around the center of the door, but he finally saw the lions.

He counted four of them, but he was sure more were present. They were head and shoulders above the tall grass, about thirty meters away.

"How long have they been there?"

"Don't know," Sovelet said. She'd pulled the shotgun back in and was lifting the window up to shut it. "Katuva saw them first."

"Well, thank you," Acharon said with a head nod to Katuva. "Thank you both."

Acharon took another look back at the lions. So much for calling it a day.

The trip into Lincoln was the longest four-hour drive Acharon had ever undertaken. His original calculation of three hours had been based on a time scale that included a clean and open highway. Instead, it was nearly eight hours of relentless jostling and fighting the steering wheel to reach their goal. Only twice since the send-off with the lions had they stopped. Both times had been the result of collapsed overpasses. Each time, with Katuva taking a role, they'd found paths through the debris to drive the bus forward. Acharon had to admit, for all her suicidal faults, she had a good eye.

Now, after one final undulation of the open Nebraska prairie, Lincoln was in sight. However, the view was fading fast as the sun was already tapping on the horizon. No matter how hard Acharon pushed the bus, they weren't going to make it into the city before complete darkness fell.

When they did make it into Lincoln, it was as tricky as the plains outside the city limits. Each intersection, like a gentle rise of the prairie, never seemed to be the last. There was always one more to cross, then still one more.

Even when they'd finally found the location of the Haymarket monorail station, they still had to go several blocks beyond. They'd been using State Route 6, which was elevated. They had to take a right on 9th Street and then a right on N Street. They followed the street in a darkness exacerbated by an overcast night sky that blocked the quarter moon, and only one headlight to guide them.

"Can't say I'm charmed," Sovelet said. She shoved her fist against her mouth. A yawn escaped anyway. "Of course, I can't say I can see anything either."

"The postcards always looked lovely," said Katuva. She looked more tired to Acharon than Sovelet did. But she also wasn't used to traveling.

N Street bent to the right and became Pinnacle Street. To the right, as they passed under State Route 6, which they also learned was O Street, a series of parking garages stood. They were dusty and empty, looming weakly on the edges of the single cone of light the bus provided.

The closer they got to the Haymarket station, the more Acharon could discern the parts of the monorail track and platform. Every city and large town that had a station also had a service yard. Some service yards were smaller than others. Places like New York, Chicago, Seattle, San Francisco, had facilities that took city blocks. Places like Colorado Springs had what Lincoln probably had. There'd be enough to run maintenance on the carriages and even minor track repair. If there'd been significant problems, like a section of the track wholly destroyed, maintenance would have come out from a major hub.

Of course, that was the way it all worked when there were still millions of people who needed to use the system. The fact that there were two dozen people left in the western hemisphere meant that no one was running maintenance or repairs. Hadn't been for decades. Not even Acharon.

Fortunately, he'd been involved with the monorail system from his first years at university. He was sure he could overcome any small obstacle. As long as no one blew anything up before the sun rose, he'd have them on the way to Des Moines and then Chicago.

"It's dark," Katuva said. She had the outside edge of her right hand pressed against the window. Her forehead rested in the V between fingers and thumb. Small plumes of her breath would condense on the window, expanding and contracting with each breath, with each word.

Sovelet was looking out the windows on the left side of the bus. The pillars of the elevated tracks, like ribs of a giant beast long dead, were ghostly in the weak light of the thin, shielded moon.

"You aren't planning on working tonight, are you?"

Acharon could hear the concern in her voice. "No," he said. "I'll definitely be waiting until it's light enough to see."

If he'd had light enough to find power for the station, he'd have started working. But Lincoln was unknown territory for him. He knew San Francisco because he'd spent most of his time in the area before the enclave came into being. When the population had slipped below a thousand, he, Sovelet, and a few friends would wander the city, seeing the sights, staying in way stations or long-abandoned homes.

If Lincoln had way stations, Acharon didn't know where they were. He wasn't even sure that anything worked in the city. He definitely wasn't going to drive around in the dark, looking for something he might not find, inviting curious company he didn't want to deal with. He rubbed at his arm as he thought about what wild animals could be living in Lincoln. They didn't even know where the medi-fac was.

No, he wasn't going to play with his life that loosely.

Acharon turned off the engine and stood, stretching as best he could with the ceiling so close.

"Try to get comfy," he said. "The fun begins at sunrise."

11

No one was awake at sunrise. It wasn't until the sun had cleared the parking structures near the station and was able to poke its bright business into the bus did anyone stir.

Acharon groaned with discomfort as he switched positions from where he'd slept most of the night. He'd slept sitting, legs stretched out across the bench seat, his head insulated with a jacket against the cold window glass.

Across from him, Katuva had managed to curl up on her side, one of the blankets they'd brought wrapped around her. A corner of the blanket draped her face, shielding her eyes from the indifferent sunlight.

Behind Acharon's seat, in the storage space, Sovelet had made a rough bed over the boxes of supplies. Acharon recalled waking several times to the sounds of Sovelet muttering about mattresses and pillows as she shifted positions. Only when they'd decided to bed down for the night in the bus, did Acharon realize and regret that they hadn't planned for it and brought a couple mattresses, blankets, and pillows.

But it was only supposed to be a four-hour drive to get here.

Acharon emitted a two-beat chuckle of chagrin.

"If there's something funny in all this, dear, I'd love to know what it is."

"Not funny." Acharon turned and sat facing forward. He rocked at the waist, feeling his muscles complain. "Just hindsight."

Sounds of boxes bumping against each other and quiet grumbles pulled Acharon's attention to where Sovelet was slowly pushing herself to a sitting position.

"Any chance we can look for a way station?" She rubbed at her eyes with the heels of her hands. Her hair was all pressed over to the left side of her head. "Coffee? Maybe a shower?"

Acharon stood, much slower than usual, using the bench backs for an assist.

"I'll look and see if there's a map in the station." He sidestepped into the aisle. "Maybe I can get power on. Or find a map, at least."

Sovelet yawned. "I'll try searching for satellites. Check in with everyone in New York."

"Sounds good."

He walked to the front of the bus, arching his back, rolling his shoulders as he went. He briefly wondered if this was how people his age in the 21st century felt like all the time. Then he remembered that no one had lived this long in the 21st century.

"Take the shotgun, please," Sovelet said. She was sitting hunched over, a laptop pulled onto her lap, a blanket wrapped around her.

Who wouldn't feel old, sleeping on boxes or school bus benches, Acharon wondered. He went back to his seat and claimed the shotgun. "Come shut the door after me. I'll try and be quick."

"Not so quick you hurt yourself," Sovelet said. She followed him to the front of the bus, reclosing the door once he stepped outside.

Acharon rarely rushed into anything. There were too many animals about and too many animals who'd lost their fear of humans. In fact, Acharon was tired of having encounters with large wild animals. So, yes, he'd be quick enough, just not foolish about it.

Leaving Sovelet and Katuva on the bus, Acharon walked around it to the stairs he'd seen in the gloom of the bus's one headlight the night before. There was a set of metal stairs that went up to the platform. They were thick with debris and moss. Next to the stairs was an elevator, but Acharon wasn't betting anything that it was working.

With one hand on the rail, also sporting a coating of moss, Acharon made his way safely to the platform. The sight was encouraging. The station was covered, and most of the glass was still intact. Acharon quickly counted twenty-one carriages. Most of them seemed in good shape. If their batteries were still good, if the solar panels still worked, a few of them might even have a charge.

"Something's going my way," Acharon mumbled as he looked around for the station office. "That's never a good sign."

The station offices were locked, which was unusual. It took Acharon several minutes of feeling around before he got lucky and found the key behind the panel of a relay box. The key, and now Acharon's hands, were covered in muck and decaying plant life. But the key worked, which Acharon chalked up as another bad omen.

The good luck kept coming. Clearly, the locked door had kept out any animal that might have played with the doorknob long enough. The only thing covering the workstations and other furnishings in the office was a nice thick layer of dust. Acharon wiped a seat clean and pulled it up to one of the workstations and pressed the switch to power it up.

He paused long enough to ascertain that his luck wasn't a hundred percent. No power to the workstation. That didn't mean it would never turn on. It just meant Acharon had to find the problem and solve it. He set to work and quickly regained his lucky streak.

There was a central power switch for the station. He found it in a small electrical closet ten meters down the platform. The meters showed there was a charge. While it wasn't operating at full capacity, it was enough for a few things like powering a workstation.

Back in the station office, the workstation powered on. It had been offline for a while and was sluggish. Not wanting to waste any more time than necessary, Acharon used the time to visit the carriages on the tracks.

There used to be an old saying about being so lucky a person should buy lottery tickets. That always seemed like pushing luck too far in Acharon's opinion. However, if there was still a lottery, he'd have to buy a ticket, considering the luck he was having.

The first two carriages opened easily. They had working electrical systems and relatively clean solar panels on top. They were also of the same generation as the ones he and Sovelet had ridden out of Las Vegas. That meant he shouldn't have much difficulty in modifying them to suit the needs of three travelers heading to New York.

Acharon closed up the carriages. No need to tempt fate. He then went back into the office, where the workstation was on and ready to do his bidding. Fortunately for Acharon, workstations weren't designed exclusively for people of Sovelet's skill level. If they had been, he'd have never found the maps folder.

After the maps, Acharon surveyed the systems for the station. He was able to connect with and run a diagnostic on more than half of the carriages parked at the platform. The luck that was starting to worry him provided another surprise in a service carriage in its carriage house about a kilometer away. It was functional, too.

He was certain that no one would ever believe how lucky he was getting.

"You're right," Sovelet said when Acharon returned to the bus. "I don't believe you. You want me to pinch you? Maybe you're dreaming."

Acharon laughed. "Nice try, but no, it's not a dream. Now, do you want coffee and a shower?"

"You found a way station?" Katuva asked.

It hadn't gone unnoticed by Acharon how Katuva seemed intent on shrinking into the background as much as possible. It had to have taken an enormous effort for her to speak up and try to be part of the conversation. He didn't know how he felt about that right now.

"Several," Acharon said. He turned the ignition key for the bus. It coughed and rattled but slowly came to life. "The closest one wasn't sending any data back on a ping. There's another one in the middle of the university campus."

The way station was to one side of a building with "Coliseum" carved in the stone over the main entrance. The M and several supporting columns beneath it had collapsed long ago. The rest of it was dark with age and dirt. The door to the way station was held in place by moss and leaf loam. Acharon had to retrieve a shovel from the bus to scrape away the debris.

He led the way inside. Lights winked on after a ten-count.

"It's like déjà vu," he said.

"You've been here before?" asked Katuva.

Sovelet laughed and patted Katuva on the arm. "They pretty much all look the same wherever you are. But, no, we've never been here. Still, I can show you where the showers are."

"I'll see to the coffee," Acharon said. "Let me know if there's a problem with the showers."

As it turned out, Acharon's luck was fifty-fifty. The showers worked fine. There were towels, soaps, and shampoos in dispensers that still worked. The coffee machine and food dispensers weren't working. It was a physical problem rather than a computer problem. Acharon had to remove a panel and climb in behind the machines to find out what was wrong.

Rodents had been nesting for decades, it seemed. They'd long deserted the place, but their nests and their dead were still there. Acharon knocked most of it free, using a stick to pry off the more stubborn bits of hair and bone.

When he finally climbed out and tested the machines, gratefully accepting the first cup of steaming coffee the machine presented, he found he wasn't alone. The fact was made apparent by several amused giggles and a whisper.

"What was that?" Acharon asked before blowing several times on the coffee.

"I said you look like you took an anti-shower," said Sovelet. "How'd you manage to get so dirty in the short time we were gone?"

Acharon used the coffee cup to point at the wall of machines. "By making that work," he said. "They'll make scrambled eggs, protein patties, rehydrated fruit, coffee, anything else still available on the menu. Now, if you'll excuse me, it's my turn for the shower."

Several hours later, clean and with warm food in their bellies, they returned to the monorail depot via a Last Wave warehouse built under the bleachers of the old university stadium. They transferred their food and personal items up to the platform. Then, while Sovelet worked on her computers, checking for problems down the line and making plans with people in New York, Acharon and Katuva moved three carriages into position.

Acharon hadn't wanted Katuva's assistance. First of all, he was used to working by himself with a little help from Sovelet when a third hand was needed. Secondly, he still didn't trust Katuva. While he didn't think it likely she would attempt to kill him, which would make it easier to talk Sovelet into taking passage, he didn't want to tempt fate. And as his luck was going so well this day, the last thing he wanted to do was scare it away.

Sovelet felt differently. She hadn't said it with words, but after nearly a century and a half together, Acharon knew she could communicate her feelings with a single look. The look was explicit: don't be a jerk. Help Katuva feel like she's wanted.

So, begrudgingly at first, Acharon utilized Katuva's assistance in connecting carriages. They removed windows to create crawl-throughs to access all of the carriages without having to stop them. They removed as much of the interior as they could, replacing it with items lifted from the warehouse.

When Acharon got to the minutiae of the job, the electrical and welding, Katuva excused herself. Acharon would have been pleased if even Sovelet had been there and done the same thing. This was the kind of work that Acharon lost himself in. It was his version of mediation where he could allow his thoughts to go where they would while his body focused on the physical details. He often became lost in the work and his thoughts, so it was no surprise when he recognized a forceful tapping on his shoulder.

Lifting the welding mask that he'd dropped in place when he'd begun making the passage between carriage one and two, he turned to see Sovelet smiling down at him.

"Yes?"

"Hungry?" Sovelet asked. "We made some sandwiches and lemonade."

Acharon looked past Sovelet, where Katuva was arranging some boxes as seats. A fourth box had a tray with a plastic pitcher and plates stacked with sandwiches. He looked back up at Sovelet, arching an eyebrow.

Sovelet slapped his shoulder. "You need to stop that. They're not poisoned."

"I never said they were," Acharon replied as he turned off the welding machine and set the helmet next to it.

"I know you well enough," Sovelet said. "Now, come and eat. I'll take the first bite."

"Maybe she should," suggested Acharon. He sidestepped a swat from Sovelet.

While they ate, Sovelet updated Acharon on the New York enclave. They were appreciative of the check-ins that Sovelet was once more giving them. They looked forward to the arrival of Acharon and Sovelet.

In his turn, Acharon apprised Sovelet on the status of the carriages. "If my luck holds," Acharon said, "we'll be ready to roll in three hours. Give or take a half-hour."

Four hours later, the carriages rolled out of the station. They slowed long enough for the service carriage to precede them on the track.

"This way, if there are problems," Acharon said with an introductory wave to the service carriage, "we'll have some extra help."

The extra help was needed the next day. A little more than ten kilometers east of Des Moines, Iowa, the front axle of the middle carriage seized. It filled the air with squeals of metallic anguish and the scent of overheated metal. Without the service carriage present, Acharon was positive they would have had to continue into Chicago with only the front carriage. Three people and a host of supplies would have made for cramped quarters.

As it was, Sovelet and Katuva redistributed the supplies to the forward and rear carriage, as well as the service carriage. While they shuffled supplies around, Acharon had to unhook the center carriage. Then, using the service crane, he lifted the middle carriage up and out, slowly lowering it to the ground and releasing it.

Acharon paused and looked down at the carriage. He could already visualize it being lost in weeds and vines in the coming years. Perhaps an animal would make its home there, too. Maybe they'd raise their young inside it year after year, completely unaware of the creatures that had been here long before. In time, though, the carriage would collapse as its metal rusted away. Then, not only would the animals on the plain not have it for a home, one more marker of the existence of humans would be erased.

"You going to brood in there all day?"

Acharon blinked and looked at Sovelet, standing just outside the crane cab.

"Not all day," he said.

"Then let's get going." Sovelet waved for him to follow. "I've made a hot lunch. Don't worry, Katuva stayed back."

Acharon followed. "I didn't say anything."

"You don't have to. She knows."

"Oh," said Acharon. He knew he should feel embarrassed at the least, but he was also happy to know that Katuva hadn't touched the food, and he wouldn't be poisoned. It was illogical. He knew it. Still, he couldn't help himself, not after the dinner at Katuva's home.

While Acharon ate, Sovelet got onto her laptops and reloaded the route into Chicago.

"Where do we go after Chicago?" Katuva asked. She had her own bowl of stew and sat closer to Sovelet than Acharon.

"Cleveland," said Sovelet with a distracted voice. Her fingers were tapping rapidly at the keyboard. "Then it's a straight shot to New York."

"Unless things go wrong," Acharon said around a bite of brown bread.

Sovelet closed the laptop and looked at him. "Do you think things will go wrong?"

"I don't know." Acharon shrugged and took a second bite of the bread. "We've been pretty lucky so far."

"So we keep getting lucky."

Katuva seemed to agree with Sovelet and nodded in agreement.

"Luck never lasts," Acharon said. It was why he had a reconstructed eye in his skull and scars on his arm. Luck had its limits.

"Well, maybe it'll last until New York, at least. Now, why don't you make all of this go so we can get to Chicago."

"And Cleveland," said Katuva.

"That's right," Sovelet said with a grin. "And then New York."

"As long as our luck holds," Acharon said. Still, he rose from his seat, bread in hand, and sat at the forward console. "So let's see if we can get to New York."

12

Six days later and three stops, one of them to park the service carriage, they arrived at the Hudson River. The bridge over the river looked a little sketchy to Acharon. He'd directed the carriages to stop as he eyed it, wondering if there was any more luck in the barrel. When he couldn't decide for himself, he asked Sovelet to do her thing.

Sovelet had quickly opened up one of the laptops she'd cobbled together along the way. She'd been using it to update the New York enclave, so it wasn't much more to test the monorail systems in the area.

While Sovelet ran the tests, Acharon did the override on the door to the front carriage. He stepped out onto the rail's narrow footpath and edged his way around to the front. Moss and ivy embraced the rail line, reaching up from the ground supports.

They'd come down what had once been a turnpike. It was now a jumble of concrete and steel. Much of it had been pushed aside by young trees and determined bushes. The shifting had affected the rail as they rolled through, making for a shaky ride. If the track had failed then, it wasn't too far down. They'd have probably escaped with a few cuts and bruises, a broken bone at the worst.

If the rail failed halfway across the Hudson, the outcome would be different.

Acharon wasn't rash. He liked things planned out and orderly. He liked it when things went as he'd planned. Granted, lately, things had not gone in the ways he'd planned. He hadn't planned on finding anyone in the middle of nowhere, for instance. And if he had planned it, it wouldn't have been Katuva in his plans. And the lions. Acharon was sure he'd never forget that poorly made plan.

Acharon looked over his shoulder. Inside the carriage, he could see Sovelet in the carriage, hunkered over her laptop. Katuva was near Sovelet. He was okay with Katuva being away from him, but he was still reluctant to leave Sovelet alone with her. He couldn't help but fear Katuva poisoning Sovelet's mind. Even after a thousand reassurances by Sovelet.

He went back to the carriage door and leaned in. He gave a passing glance to Katuva, who looked away, and then focused on Sovelet.

"How we doing?"

"Almost." Sovelet didn't even look up.

"Can I get you something?"

"No, thank you," Acharon said. He really didn't want Katuva to handle anything he ate.

Sovelet looked up now. She had the same look she always had when he acted this way.

"Seriously," he said. "I don't need anything." He went back to the rail in front of the carriages.

They'd slowly pushed through an overgrown park. The tree limbs had scraped along the sides of the carriages, like fingernails on a chalkboard, until they were reduced to wiping gently and finally disappearing as they emerged at the shoreline. The maps said it had been the Fort Lee Historic Park. Now, it was an overgrown forest. There were some signs that a forest fire had burned through not too many years ago. Black spears of dead tree trunks, hugged by creeper vines, jutted upward partially hidden by the younger trees.

He could see where the monorail line arced gently over the river before diving into the building canyons of Manhattan. The bridge that had run alongside collapsed decades ago. Birds had turned several surviving sections into bird paradises, free from all the predators except those that could also fly.

He'd heard it somewhere that nature finds a way. Whether it's to survive and reproduce or to hunt and kill, nature found a way. Mankind, of course, stubborn as always, found their own way. Now he, Sovelet, Katuva, and fifty other people were all that was left of that hubris.

Acharon still found it difficult to absorb. Even after decades of living in the dwindling population. Even after so much time like this, it felt like it had always been so. Then he would see a scene like Manhattan. Empty buildings that had once held millions and now held less than thirty. Soon it would hold zero. Instead of being one of the first to step onto a brand new continent, he'd be one of the last to step off it.

"Ach?"

"What?" He turned to find Sovelet reaching out to touch his shoulder. Katuva stood back by the carriage door. "Everything okay?"

Sovelet barked a short laugh. "I should ask you. I've been calling your name. I would have sent Katuva, but I didn't want to scare you."

He smiled at her spear-point joke and then turned back to the panorama. He wiped his hand across the scene. "I was just looking at this. And thinking."

She stepped up next to him, wrapping her arms around him. She squeezed gently before releasing. "Time for action," she said. "All the line tests indicate safe passage."

"But?"

Sovelet laughed and shook her head as she turned back to the carriages. "But, take it slow. There's a few warps in the track."

There were warps in just living, Acharon thought as he followed Katuva and then Sovelet into the carriage.

Inside, he tapped the override to shut the carriage door. He brought the control panel to life with a few taps and cleared the destination to green. He reduced the power to the carriages to half and tapped the 'go' button.

There was a mild lurch, and the carriages settled into a slow, steady ride out across the Hudson. The rail, as they moved further out over the river, showed the pockmarks of age and disuse. It had been designed, like so much else for the Last Wavers, to last a lifetime. Of course, no one had anticipated that the last of the Last Wave would live this long.

The trip across the river was more vibration than actual potential for disaster. Acharon kept his hand hovering over the emergency stop button on the panel. When his arm began to shake from holding it out so long, he had to switch hands. This required him to sit in an awkward position so that when they finally rumbled and screeched off the bridge, not only did both his shoulders hurt, but he had a stitch in his side.

"You're getting old," Sovelet said. She rubbed his shoulders as the carriage shifted rails carrying it over the Manhattan remains of the bridge.

"Had to happen eventually." He patted Sovelet's hand with his. "Thank you."

There was a lot more vibration here than there had been out across the midwest. The carriage growled its discontent as it rolled into a switching line. The system knew that they wanted to go to the station at 5th Ave and 59th. Without that bit of information, the carriage might just run on over into the Bronx.

As it was, the carriage still started slowing down. Acharon had been watching, so he was already making plans.

"What's going on?" Sovelet had returned to his side.

"Switch issues," Acharon said. "I think it's corroded shut. Though, it might just be debris build-up. I'll go look."

He gave Sovelet a peck on the cheek and then went to the midpoint between the two carriages where he'd stationed his toolbox. He grabbed gloves and several tools. He used the override on the door just as Sovelet turned her attention back to him.

"A sledgehammer?"

Acharon looked at the tools nested in the crook of his arm. "As a last resort," he said. "Sometimes, things just need a little more convincing. Shouldn't be long."

"Right. Should I start dinner? Just in case?"

"It won't take that long." Acharon stepped onto the walkway. "But, maybe a snack? Keep my strength up."

"Of course," Sovelet said. Her voice held a tone of disbelief that her smile proved to be a lie. Or, at least partially a lie. Acharon would take that.

The switch was twenty meters ahead. There were three the carriages had to roll through, but it was the second one that wasn't moving. Just to be sure, though, he gave the first switch a visual. There was a little dirt and moss smashed between the rail and switch rail, but the carriages would negotiate that with little difficulty.

The second switch had barely moved. There was a large amount of debris. Much more than the first switch. Judging from what he could see of the third, more than that one, too.

Acharon set the handpick, sledgehammer, and trowel aside. He kept the crowbar and used it to prod the debris. He pushed, turned, and flipped a layer. Just as quickly, he stepped back. Bones.

He allowed himself an embarrassed laugh at his reaction. He'd uncovered plenty of bones over the decades. He'd found friends in states of death and decay and helped to bury many of them. He had a pretty good familiarity with dead things. Enough so to know, after chastising himself, that these bones weren't human.

These were a small mammal. Raccoon or skunk, most likely. He moved in and began prying more of the bone-littered debris, breaking it loose. He didn't used to be this jumpy. He was sure of that. And it wasn't hard for him to decide on when things changed. It wasn't the life or death battle with the alpha dog in San Francisco. No, it was directly related to his encounter with Katuva.

Before her, suicide cults had just been a distant, unreal thing. Something that was debated over in the San Francisco enclave without any serious consideration that people were a part of it. That, despite the reports of tens of thousands of people every month across the globe taking their lives as a group.

There had been suicides. Murphy had been the last one. Not the last discovered, but the last one committed that Acharon was acquainted with. But that was a person. The idea of a thousand or more people gathering and purposefully choosing to die together didn't click. For him, it was too alien a concept. Then they'd met Katuva.

Her presence was like a bucket of cold water on the face of his ignorance. Without being aware of it, she'd made him confront his own fears. Not the fears that he might give in and take his own life, but that Sovelet might finally give in to the temptation.

"Stop it, stop it," Acharon muttered to himself as he grabbed the garden trowel and dug at the dirt, decay, and bones.

Katuva claimed she wouldn't force anyone to commit suicide along with her. But taking away someone's option by destroying the monorail track, forcing them to stop, was as much a force as was gunpoint. Now she was with them. And he was bringing her to the last enclave of humanity in the Americas. Sovelet hated the analogy, but he did feel like he was carrying a snake into the garden.

How was he to trust her? After they rejected her offer of a group death, she'd agreed to join them and come to New York. Since then, she'd withdrawn into herself. Achron was okay with that, but Sovelet kept dragging her into conversations.

Sovelet had pressured him and chastised him for his actions. But, it was challenging to take food from a person who was so willing to cajole others into joining her in death.

"Acharon?"

He jumped at the sound of his name. His toes caught on a section of rail. He pitched forward, catching himself on his hands and a knee. Concrete and steel were unforgiving. The impact raised a well-deserved explicative. Especially since it wasn't Sovelet who'd said his name. He turned onto his butt and nursed his bruised knee to hide his bruised ego.

"Katuva," he said. "Maybe an earlier warning, next time."

She looked at him with what he had come to accept as her sullen look. After a long pause where he rubbed his knee and tried not to look uncomfortable, Katuva held out a plastic shopping basket.

"Sovelet thought you might need something to eat." She set the basket on the ground. "It's a sealed food packet. You're welcome."

She turned and walked back to the carriages, high-stepping over the tracks.

Acharon pulled the basket closer and peeked inside. There was a sealed package of energy bars and a glass bottle of water from the reservoir he'd added to the front carriage when they'd passed through Iowa City. He'd bolted the reservoir shut so no one could access it but him. But he hadn't been there when this bottle was filled.

He held the bottle up to the sky. If it was poisoned, he'd likely have no way to know for sure.

"Acharon!" Sovelet's shout drew his attention past the bottle to the carriages where she stood, hands firmly planted on her hips. "Just drink the water!"

He rarely did anything sheepishly. However, having been caught being paranoid, he sheepishly opened the bottle and drank. Since it was too late now, he drank half the bottle before opening the packet of energy bars.

With his paranoia put to the test, he decided to relax for a few minutes. He sat on the rail, his hurt knee stretched out, and chewed on an energy bar. Around him, the sounds a person would not associate with city life played. There was the low din of countless chirping birds. Squirrels chittered, not too far away. They bounced from tree to tree, and it felt to Acharon that they were watching him, trying to figure out what he was.

"I'm nothing of importance," Acharon said.

He climbed to his feet, testing his knee. The only medi-pod he knew of was at the New York enclave. Some research might locate one closer. Not that he was going to look. Not when he could limp along for a couple more hours.

Despite the knee and his mild fear of poisoning, he was able to turn his focus back to the track. A small skull and some rocks were all that was left to clear. He considered the sledgehammer, purely for a way to burn off some nervous energy. The noise would attract Sovelet's attention, though. He'd likely get a laser-sharp glare for it. So, he found the trowel and dug a little harder.

The skull broke and came away in pieces. Acharon pulled the jawbone free with his gloved hand, pausing to examine the canine teeth. He hadn't really given much attention to biology a hundred plus years ago. He'd been too busy with engineering. He was sure, though, that this wasn't a dog or wolf, so he stuck with his original thought of raccoon or skunk.

"Sorry, little guy." He tossed the jaw to the side and dug the last rocks from the switch.

He dropped the trowel into the basket with the bottle and energy bar wrappers. He carried it with the other tools back to the carriages. Inside the first carriage, he found Sovelet on her laptop. Katuva was nowhere visible.

"Look who's still alive," Sovelet said. She'd looked up from the computer screen for a brief glance. She added, "I let Boone and the others know we're running late."

Acharon mumbled a quick acknowledgment. No need to get Sovelet started with a silly comment. He stowed the tools and basket, put the wrappers in a box for waste, and put the water bottle back in its rack. In the process, he caught a quick glimpse of Katuva, sitting on the backbench. She looked his way once and then turned again to the rear window.

He didn't like it when Sovelet was disappointed with him. He could care less if Katuva was.

"Shall we get going, then?" he asked no one in particular. He tapped on the system screen, waking it up.

"Please," Sovelet said. She snapped her laptop shut and left the front carriage.

Acharon watched her leave and then turned back to the panel. The trip was almost over. Then Katuva could be someone else's problem. He swiped the screen until he reached the panel for the override and released the carriage to continue.

"Almost there." He whispered his comment to the city they were once again in motion toward.

The carriages rattled their way through the switches. They growled unhappily on the second switch, causing a twist in Acharon's stomach until the sound faded.

The track smoothed out after the switches put them on Broadway, heading south. The carriages rolled along through a low canyon of buildings. The buildings were slowly disappearing behind a forest that had shoved its way up through the concrete and asphalt. Despite having been a busy hub of existence long after San Francisco had gone to sleep, it was ahead in the return-to-nature phase.

As the carriage crossed a switch, putting it onto St Nicholas Avenue, Acharon overrode the carriage door lock. He stood in the doorway, mindful of Katuva's location, and watched the Bronx forest slide past.

"You sure that's safe?"

Acharon looked over his shoulder at Sovelet.

"I can shut it."

She shook her head. "Just wondering."

"It's a nice view. Smells nothing like you'd expect New York to smell like."

Sovelet smiled and then walked over to join him. Acharon was glad to see the smile.

"It hasn't been a city in fifty years at least," she said. She put a hand on his shoulder and leaned forward to peek out in their direction of travel. "Central Park coming up?"

Acharon looked forward. "Hard to tell, everything's a park now."

"It smells nice." Katuva had moved close enough to see out the open door. She had a hand pressed against the doorframe, leaning sideways enough to see out.

Acharon could feel Sovelet's eyes boring into the side of his face. She expected him to say something pleasant. He took a deep breath and a pause before saying, "Yes, it does smell nice. Let's see where we're at."

He left the doorway and moved to the front of the carriage. The monitor showed their location to be several blocks north of the park. St. Nicholas Ave was going to bear right in another block. Several more would put them on the 5th Ave side of the park.

"Almost there."

13

There were a couple false stops along the last two hundred meters. The carriages slowed and jerked forward, almost knocking Acharon off his feet. After feeling like the carriages were about to run off the monorail track, they settled down before coasting into the station, stopping like a feather touching the ground.

"Everyone ready?" Acharon was shutting down the carriage's computer.

"Yes." Sovelet had her bag by her feet, standing in the gap between the carriages.

"No."

Acharon looked past Sovelet, who was turning to look towards the back of the second carriage. Katuva was a shadow against the back window.

"Katuva?" Sovelet stepped further into the second carriage. "You okay?"

"No."

She sounded like a broken record to Acharon. He sort of understood what she was feeling. He had butterflies in his stomach. He'd spent decades with the enclave in San Francisco before spending decades alone with Sovelet. There was Murphy, but that was a different story altogether. Now he was going to immerse himself in a group of people he knew mostly from conversations with Sovelet, sometimes along with images she'd point to on one of her laptops.

From conversations, he knew that Katuva had spent even more time alone. And she hadn't talked to anyone. Except maybe the mannequins she'd played dolls with. That, and the unavoidable fact that she was the sole survivor of a suicide cult, meant he could understand her reluctance.

"Do you want to go back home?"

"Acharon!"

"Sorry." Though he wasn't. And based on the smile he could see lurking in the shadow of Katuva's face, she saw the humor too. He looked away to keep from saying something else to get in trouble with, or worse, laughing. There was movement outside. "The greeting party is here."

"We'll be few minutes," Sovelet said. "Stall."

Acharon tapped the button for the doors. "Yes, ma'am."

The doors opened. On the platform, five people waved hello. If he remembered correctly, the taller man was Boone. Not the designated leader, but the most respected in the enclave. Like Acharon had once been.

"Boone?" He stepped out, offering his hand in a general way. In case he was wrong.

The man he suspected to be Boone stepped forward and shook his hand. "Acharon. Good to see you. Is everything okay?"

"Yep. Just great. Why?" He let go of Boone's hand and followed his gaze to the empty entrance to the carriage.

"Is Sovelet okay?"

Acharon turned his attention to the woman who asked. "Yes. I'm sorry, I'm at a bit of a loss with names."

"Oh, right. Sorry." Boone stepped to the side and began to point. "That's Asher, Green, Jaina, and Sena."

Acharon looked at each and repeated their names. Then, "Jaina, I think Sovelet spoke about you a lot. She's fine. She just needs a minute."

"A minute?" the man that had been identified as Green asked. "What's she need a minute for?"

"Stagefright?"

"Acharon."

Acharon looked back to the carriage and then to the waiting New Yorkers. "Just a second."

He went back into the carriage. "What's going on?"

Sovelet and Katuva were sitting on the bed. Sovelet was holding Katuva's hand in hers. "She's still a little concerned. She was hoping you wouldn't mention that she belonged to a passage group."

Passage group. Acharon schooled his actions and kept his eyes from rolling. Call it what you want, it was still a suicide cult.

"Don't they have a right to know who's coming into their home?"

"I knew this was a bad idea." Katuva's head was bent, and her whispered words barely made it to Acharon's ears. But he heard them.

"You could have stayed in Nebraska," Acharon said.

"Everything okay in there?"

"Just a moment, Boone," said Acharon. He turned back to find Sovelet glaring at him. "What did she - what did you, Katuva - expect to happen when you got here? That no one would notice her presence? Your presence?"

"At least for a little while? Acharon?" Sovelet's voice was soft. He knew she was pleading with him. He hated to ever let her down. "At least until they get to know her?"

"Fine. But I don't think this will fly well when they learn about what kind of people she used to run with. We may get tarred with the same brush."

"Just for a while?"

Acharon spun on his heels, throwing his hands up in defeat. "Fine. But if they figure it out before you tell them, it is not my fault."

"I'm sorry," Katuva said.

"No, honey," Sovelet said. She put an arm around Katuva and pulled her close. "You don't have to be sorry. Acharon and I will look out for you."

She gave Acharon a wide-eyed, raised-eyebrow look. Acharon nodded once in understanding. There would be no getting out of this. He gave Sovelet a half-hearted smile and left the carriage. He ran into Boone, who had started to enter the front carriage.

"Sorry," said Boone. He backed up. "We were getting concerned. Everything is okay, right?

With a smile and a hand on Boone's shoulder, Acharon guided him back to the other four people. "Everything is great. There's just one little thing. It's crazy."

"She's not--." Jaina looked at the others, then back at Acharon, and continued. "She's not pregnant, is she?"

Without a thought, Acharon started laughing. That would have been crazy. How many decades had the world's scientists tried in vitro, cloning, a half-dozen other things he didn't understand before they finally admitted that it wasn't going to happen? And now Sovelet should be pregnant?

When he realized he was the only one laughing, he stopped.

"Sorry," he said. "Don't know what came over me."

"Ach?" Sovelet's voice was muffled by distance and corners.

He turned and raised his voice. "Everything's okay. Just a second."

"Then what's going on?" It was the guy named Green.

Acharon's hands came up in a placating manner. "It's this: we found someone else still alive."

"Wait. Someone living?" The woman, Sena, looked at Acharon then over his shoulder at the carriage. "Where?"

"Nebraska."

A chorus of voices responded. "Nebraska?"

"I know. We were as surprised as you are. We had problems with the monorail."

"Right," Boone said. "Sovelet told us about that. But she didn't mention another person."

"Why would she keep that a secret?" asked Jaina.

"We didn't want to," said Acharon. "But she asked us not to say anything. She's nervous."

Asher asked, "Why would she be nervous?"

"That's something you should ask her." Acharon became aware that they'd pressed close to him, which had caused him to back up. They'd continued to press, and he was now a meter from the carriage entrance. He pushed his hands toward the group. They stopped. "She hadn't seen anyone in something like forty years. Hadn't talked to anyone after her husband died. Not until we happened along."

"Can we meet her?" Sena asked. She'd started to move around Acharon. He raised an arm to stop her.

"Yes. You will. She just needs a little time."

"She's ready," Sovelet said.

Acharon turned to see Sovelet standing in the doorway.

"I guess that time is now," Acharon said.

He stepped aside, joining the five New Yorkers. Sovelet stepped aside, staying in the carriage. Katuva appeared, taking short steps and long pauses, her neck bent, her face hidden until she was in the center of the doorway.

"Everyone," Sovelet said. "This is Katuva. Acharon? Can you do the honors?"

"Right." He took a step forward and started pointing out each person and identifying them by name even though he was sure Katuva didn't see any of this. "And eighteen more people to meet."

"Hi," Sena said. She waved a short wave. "It's wonderful to meet you."

Katuva raised her head until her eyes were visible. "Thank you."

"We don't bite," Asher said. His comment drew a mild chuckle.

Green elbowed him, saying, "Yes, you do."

While they forced jokes and had a laugh, Sovelet had stepped off the carriage and offered her hand to Katuva. "Coming, dear?"

The dear was typically reserved for Acharon. While he didn't feel a sting of jealousy, he did feel a bit resentful at losing his private moniker.

In the meantime, Katuva had taken Sovelet's hand and made the short step across the gap, onto the platform. The New Yorkers stepped forward, offering a handshake and reintroducing themselves.

"You were in Nebraska, eh?" Green said as he released Katuva's hand. She nodded an affirmative, and he continued with, "What's it like? In Nebraska?"

"Flat." A half-smile flitted across Katuva's face as the others around her laughed.

"We'd love to hear more about flatland," Boone said. "But I think Katuva should save it for the dinner party we've got ready for you all."

"Dinner party?" Katuva's nervousness seemed to shake her whole body. Sovelet was instantly by her side, a hand on one shoulder, the other on Katuva's upper arm.

"I don't know," Sovelet said. "Maybe after a few day's rest?"

"No," Katuva said. Her shoulders rose to her ears and then slowly drifted back to their normal position. "I'll be okay."

"You're sure?" Jaina asked.

"If you want to wait," Green said.

Katuva shook her head. "No, not if everyone's gone through the trouble for Sovelet and Acharon. I don't want to be the one to interfere."

"Darling, you are not interfering," Asher said. He stepped up and offered his arm to Katuva. "Contrary to what you're thinking, Acharon may be the one interfering with the fun, tonight."

"Hey, now."

There was good-natured laughter all around. Acharon thought it was a bit unfair, but was mollified by Sovelet's arm linking through his.

"There, there," she said in a whisper.

"We have a bus waiting downstairs," Boone said.

They'd reached the stairs that led down to street level. Acharon noticed the buildup of dirt and weeds that likely covered the stairs had been scraped up and shoveled to the sides. It left a meter wide path down to the street. The bus was waiting, and it caught Acharon by surprise. He'd assumed that they were speaking broadly, maybe with humor. This was not what he expected.

"That's a real bus," he said.

"Yep," someone ahead of him said.

"I want to ride up top," Sovelet said. "I hope it's clean."

The bus that Boone had mentioned, and they were now standing next to, was an old tour bus. It was a double-decker with an open-air top deck. Along its side, someone had taped old musical placards. The bus was bright red, but Acharon noticed the bubbling of rust under the paint around the wheel wells and the bottom edge of the body panels.

"Where'd you find it?"

Green had turned at Acharon's question. He looked at Asher and then to Boone, and then turned back to Katuva. He handed her up the bus stairs.

"We were doing some scavenging," Boone said. "Found it in one of the waterfront warehouses."

"Had an old diesel engine," Sena added. She spoke as she entered the bus. "Took a while to find an electric engine big enough."

"Last Wave warehouse," Acharon said.

"You'd think," Boone said. "But we found it in another warehouse over in Brooklyn."

"Was this just a random scavenging?" Acharon and some of the others from the San Francisco enclave used to do random searches. Sometimes they had a shopping list, sometimes it was just for fun.

"We were just looking around," Green said. His voice was loud, his words quick.

Boone's eyes flickered in Green's direction before he answered Acharon's question. "Yeah, we were just looking around."

As they boarded the bus, Acharon caught Sovelet's eye. He hoped she saw the curiosity in his eyes. Her response was a shrug, which was open to interpretation.

Boone seated himself in the driver's seat while everyone else took the spiral staircase to the observation deck.

"You want company?"

"It's all good, Acharon," Boone said. He'd turned the start key. The lights on the dash winked to life. "Go on up and enjoy the sights. Such that they are."

Acharon nodded and followed Jaina as the last one up. The observation deck was clean, the dirt and debris of the decades had been scoured clear up here. The plastic on the chairs was faded in places, cracked in others, and duct-taped in a few places, too.

He looked around for Sovelet, finding her near the back. Jaina had made her way there, sitting in the seat ahead of Sovelet's. Across the aisle, Sena had taken her place, sitting sideways, her feet dangling in the aisle. Green and Asher were at the very front with Katuva between them.

"You've never been to a big city?" Green was asking her.

Acharon turned and walked to the back of the bus, missing any comment that Katuva might have made.

"Ladies and Gentlemen." Boone's voice squawked through several small speakers at the front and rear of the bus. "If you aren't holding tight, please do so now."

Jaina and Sena laughed. Sena waved at Acharon to sit. "You don't want to be standing for this."

Acharon took the hint and sat. His butt wasn't on the seat before the bus lurched forward. Katuva and Sovelet both shrieked in surprise. Acharon's exclamation was pushed out of him as he was thrown against the seat's backrest.

"You okay?" Sena had scooted to the aisle edge of her seat.

"I'm good," Acharon said. "Just wasn't ready for that."

"You should have been on board for the maiden voyage," Jaina said. She had a rueful smile on her face as she shook her head. "Four people got stitches, and two people had broken noses. I got away with a minor concussion."

"How?" Sovelet had leaned forward, placing a hand on Jaina's forearm.

"Wrong engine size for the bus?" Acharon asked.

Sena and Jaina both nodded.

Sena said, "Everything else they found was too small. No one expected it to be like riding the mechanical bull. Boone was one of those who got the broken nose when the bus threw him over the steering wheel."

"He's much more cautious now," Jaina said.

Both of the women laughed again. Sovelet joined in.

Acharon turned to look forward. Katuva was still sandwiched between the two men, but they were having some sort of hushed argument over her head. Katuva looked like she'd managed to shrink as small as she could.

"Excuse me," Acharon said to the three women. He stood, and with his hands for safety lines, moved to the front of the bus. "Everything okay up here?"

"What?" Green had turned in surprise. "Why? Yes, everything's fine."

"Just enjoying the sights," Asher added. "Giving Katuva the ten cent tour."

Katuva looked over her shoulder at Acharon. It was only his opinion, but he didn't think she was having a good time.

"Well, I do hate to intrude on the fun," Acharon said. He slid into the seat behind theirs. "But the other women were hoping Katuva would join them for a bit. Women things. Above my pay grade."

Green opened his mouth. Before he could get a word out, which Acharon was sure wasn't going to be acquiescence, Katuva was up and moving.

"I'll be back," she said in her hushed tone.

"We'll be here," Acharon said. He watched Katuva hurry back to the other women.

She moved in next to Sovelet, her head bent. Acharon couldn't hear, but he knew she was saying something. Her head came up, confusion on her face. She looked in his direction at the same time Sovelet did. He shrugged. Sovelet shook her head, but Katuva mouthed, thank you, and then turned to a question Jaina was asking.

Acharon turned back to Green and Asher, who were shooting eye daggers at each other. "How about that tour?"

The ten-cent tour wasn't worth one cent. By the time the bus turned onto 9th, Acharon had only learned that the enclave was at 25 Central Park West and that they shared an apartment on the tenth floor where someone, who Green wouldn't call out by name, had left a light on.

"Company." Boone's voice startled everyone. "Small herd, dead ahead."

Twenty deer, mostly does and a couple young bucks, were tearing at a thick carpet of wild grass and berry bushes flush with blooms. Their bodies had tensed, their heads snapping up and turning in the direction of the bus as it growled and creaked its way toward them.

To the deer's credit, in Acharon's opinion, they'd likely decided that nothing so ungainly and bizarre looking could be a threat. They moved farther to the opposite side of the road and returned to grazing.

"Not very smart," Asher said.

"Why?" They seemed smart enough to Acharon just by the fact that they moved out of the way.

"There's a mountain lion in the area. It's pretty big, isn't it, Green?"

"Yes, Ashe, it is," Green said. He stood as fast as he answered and then took the stairwell down to the lower level.

Ashe tracked Green and then turned back with a sour look on his face. "He liked to take late night walks. Something he never bothered to share with me before. He got himself attacked during one of those late-night strolls. If Boone and Jamon hadn't been up and about, they might not have heard him screaming."

Acharon noticed tears in Ashe's eyes.

"Idiot almost got himself killed," Ashe added.

"He's okay now, yes?" Acharon had his own experience being attacked by a mountain lion.

"Physically."

"When did this happen?" Acharon's experience had been a month ago. He'd only had a few nightmares, and they weren't really that bothersome to him.

"Couple weeks ago." Ashe laughed. "A medi-pod can repair a lot, but it can't repair stupid."

Whatever else Ashe might have wanted to say, it was drowned out by the squeal of the brakes and Boone on the speakers.

"Final stop!"

The stop was as rough as the start.

"It's going to fall apart under our feet one day," Ashe said as he moved for the stairs.

Acharon followed, saying, "We'll be gone before that's a problem."

"Gone?" Ashe asked over his shoulder.

"Yeah, Paris. The boat."

Ashe snorted. "Right. The boat."

"Is there a problem with the boat?"

"Hey, Acharon," Boone said. His voice was loud enough, his words quick enough to cut off Asher. Asher shook his head and stepped off the bus where Green was waiting. Boone was grinning at Acharon. "You like the ride?"

"Memorable." He stepped away from the stairs, so the four women, Sena in the lead, Sovelet bringing up the rear, could pass by and exit. Sovelet gave him a gentle squeeze on the arm as she walked past. Boone followed as Acharon asked, "Is there a problem with the boat?"

"It's your first night here, Acharon. We can talk about the boat tomorrow. Come on, everyone's waiting."

Boone moved to the front and led the small group to what looked like a standard Last Wave auto-diner. Except, in this case, someone had gone through the trouble to dress it up. Curtains and fairy lights hung in the windows. The edges of the windows had been frosted with fancy curlicues. The wood door was dressed with metal straps and twisted iron bars over its small window.

Warm light spilled out of the windows making the air appear to glow. Acharon could hear the faint rise and fall rumble of multiple conversations beyond the windows.

Boone had stopped. He turned to Sovelet and Katuva. "Are you ready?"

Feeling left out, Acharon said, "I am."

Sovelet had turned to Katuva. "You don't have to, you know. We can go back to the enclave."

"Nonsense," Green said. He seemed to have recovered his buoyant good humor. "Come along, honey, I'll protect you from the masses."

Without asking, he hooked Katuva's arm with his own and started toward the door. Katuva was dragged forward for several steps and then moved to keep up. Boone had moved to the door and pulled it open.

The volume of noise went up until Katuva and Green stepped over the threshold. Katuva came to a dead stop, slipping her arm out of Green's. To Acharon, it looked like she was going to back up, but Sena and Jaina were too close behind.

What was worse was that every conversation in the restaurant had ceased the moment Katuva had jammed to a halt.

Acharon moved next to Sovelet and said, just for her ears, "This is going to be fun."

14

Acharon had pushed up on his toes to see over everyone's shoulders into the room. There were tables and what looked like a buffet near the back. There were a few clusters of people holding wine glasses and beer mugs while wearing open mouths.

"That's not Sovelet," someone said loud enough for even Acharon to hear.

"Who is that?"

Then, finally, "Green, that can't be Sovelet."

Acharon could only assume Green was grinning. He seemed like the guy who liked the attention, as long as it was good.

"They found someone else," Green said. "In Nebraska!"

The din of noise Acharon had heard before the door opened tripled in volume as everyone in the restaurant voiced their surprise as one, but with different exclamations and questions.

"How'd you survive?"

"Is that possible? In Nebraska?"

"What's your name, dear?"

"Can she speak?"

"She's not an animal, Benen."

"Well, she's not saying anything."

Acharon turned to Sovelet, wondering if she felt the same kind of confusion. He judged from her look that she was feeling scared. He started to move forward, intending to help Katuva. He wasn't sure how, but he knew that Sovelet would want him to no matter his feelings for Katuva.

While he tried to brainstorm a solution, Boone stepped in front of Green, temporarily shielding Katuva.

"Everyone, please." The room went sullenly silent. "This is Katuva. She's been living alone and isolated for quite a few decades. Let's give her a chance to adjust. So let's not pile on the questions and comments. Give her time to eat, maybe drink a little reconstituted wine."

The last suggestion brought laughter and raised glasses.

Boone turned to Katuva. Acharon heard him ask, "Are you going to be okay?"

There was a longer than usual pause to a question before Katuva nodded.

"Great," Asher said. He scooped Katuva's arm and entered, veering left. Green looked caught off guard and hurried to catch up.

"Hey, everyone," Boone said. He waved an arm in Sovelet's direction. "Sovelet and Acharon are here, too. Pile on them!"

More cheers, and Sena and Jaina pushed past Boone and into the throng. Boone waved at Sovelet and Acharon, indicating they should enter ahead of him.

Acharon stepped aside for Sovelet, who was instantly mobbed by friends she'd only communed with digitally for decades. Their conversation, as Acharon slipped past, heading for the food trays, sounded as if they'd been best friends forever.

Several tables had been pushed together. A large number of automated food dishes had been prepared and laid out. There were several pasta salads, some roasted vegetables, meats, mashed potatoes, and a fruit salad. He plated the pasta salads and roasted vegetables and moved down the line.

"Acharon?"

He looked to his left, where a man was standing, holding two beer mugs.

"Yep. You are?"

The man used one of the beer mugs to point at himself. The beer sloshed but didn't spill. "Benen."

"Right." Acharon nodded. "Yes, to answer your earlier question, Katuva can speak."

"Ah, you heard that. Sorry. I was caught off guard. Everyone was, actually. Beer?"

He held out one of the mugs. Acharon took it and carried it with his plate to a table. Still by the door, Sovelet was laughing at something and passing out hugs. It had been a long time since he'd been around so many people at once. Hopefully, no one would jam a penknife in his eye.

"Join me?" He set his plate down and indicated another seat for Benen.

Benen bobbed his head in acquiescence and took the offered seat.

"Can I ask a question?"

"I'm sure you have lots of them." He sipped the beer and was surprised by the flavor. It was the best thing he'd tasted in a long time. "Wow."

"Right? We brewed it ourselves."

Acharon looked at his mug as if he might divine its secrets. "Fresh ingredients?"

"Now." Benen laughed and then paused for a long pull of beer. "We got the idea when we found all these stored grains in a warehouse in Boston. We'd been looking for another ship and found the sealed grain barrels as a happy accident."

"Wait?" Acharon put his mug down. "Another ship? We're taking two?"

"Two, no." He stopped. His mug was halfway to his lips. It slowly drifted down as a thought registered on his face. "No one told you? Oh, man. I'm sorry. I probably should have kept my mouth shut."

Acharon stood. "No. Thank you for saying something."

He looked around and found Boone. When Boone looked in his general direction, he waved frantically. He caught Boone's attention and motioned for him to come to the table. While he waited, he forked several bites of the pasta and a swig of beer. All of it accompanied by Benen's profuse apologies.

"You didn't know." Acharon wiped his lips with a napkin laid out on the table. Boone had arrived. "When were you going to tell me about the boat?"

Boone looked at Benen, who shrugged and pulled into himself.

"How was I to know?" Benen asked.

"Don't blame him," Acharon said. "Just tell me what's going on."

Boone's face lit with a mild smile. "We can deal with logistics tomorrow, Acharon, for now, just enjoy, yeah?"

Acharon set both hands on the table. "How am I supposed to enjoy myself when I know there's a problem?"

"You'll manage," Boone said. He started to turn.

"I think you owe me an explanation," Acharon said. "Sit and give me the short version, so I have an idea. Please."

Boone looked around the room. Acharon looked, too, and could see Katuva bracketed by Green and Asher. At the same time, several other women and another man formed a half-circle in front of them. Katuva had a wine glass in her hand, and she was talking, though she still seemed to have her eyes focused more on the ground than on anyone in particular. Sovelet and her friends had migrated to the food and were spooning dishes in between bursts of laughter.

What Acharon also saw was that Boone had no way out. No one needed him to join their conversation at the moment. He had to sit. Acharon smiled pleasantly while Boone pulled out a seat and slid onto it.

"Well?" Acharon followed his question with a fork full of vegetables. They were a little chewy. Likely their auto-cookers needed adjustments. He could help there.

Boone sighed in a long, this-isn't-going-to-be-easy sort of way. "There was an accident. It caught fire one night. Burned it to the keel. But we have another boat. We're still going to France."

"Unless something happens to it," Benen said. He quickly busied himself with his beer when Boone glared at him.

"Nothing's going to happen."

Acharon looked at Benen who looked elsewhere, and then at Boone, who matched him look for look.

"It wasn't an accident, was it?"

"More beer?" Benen jumped out of his seat and grabbed Acharon's mug. He hurried away without a look back.

"So, that's a yes," Acharon said.

Boone slid his mug back and forth on the table several times. "We can't be sure. But, yeah, it looks like it."

Acharon reached for his own beer and realized it was gone. Benen was at a keg, filling both mugs while having a whispered conversation with someone else.

"Do you know who?"

Boone leaned on the table, speaking in a more hushed tone. "We don't know for sure. A couple of us have our suspicions, but that's all it is. We could be wrong."

"You don't believe that," Acharon said. They wouldn't be so hush-hush about it if they weren't sure.

"No," Boone said. He added a head shake. "We don't believe it's an accident."

"Okay. But you have a second boat."

Boone grinned. "A better one, too. Found it in a warehouse in New Jersey. It was in an old inventory. Not a Last Wave one, but some billionaire from way back. I'm not sure what he was thinking, but it was to our benefit."

Acharon knew what he was thinking. He was thinking he was going to live forever with some miracle drug or other that was coming on the market. Most were fraudulent. People seemed willing to take advantage of each other, even as extinction drew close. The other drugs that he'd likely gotten a hold of, and was disappointed by, only seemed to work in vitro or in the first years of life. Everyone alive right now was alive because of those drugs. Because their parents thought they should have a long life. If they only knew.

"Where's the boat? New Jersey, still?"

"Nope." Boone looked triumphant. "Just down the street. We got it in the water and used an old tugboat to bring it around to the waterfront. We've been working on her. Still just looking for a few more things."

Acharon mulled the information over as Benen slowly returned to the table. He watched Boone as he approached. His attitude became more buoyant after seeing Boone's face.

"Everything good?" He sat and slid Acharon's mug toward him.

"I don't think you're in the dog house if that's what you mean," Acharon said. "So, do we have a launch date? The passage window is closing."

"Another week? Maybe two." Boone looked at Benen, who shrugged.

"Cutting it close," said Acharon.

"I'm sure someone is disappointed with our good luck."

"You keeping watch on the boat? A guard?"

"We can't," Benen said. He pressed his lips together as Boone glared in his direction.

"If we set a guard, people will want to know why," Boone said. "What do we tell them? That a bear might try to break in and steal stuff? Set the boat on fire? No, we've just been keeping those who we think are responsible busy and as far from the ship as we can manage."

"So as long as nothing goes wrong, two weeks at the most."

Benen raised his mug. "What could go wrong?"

Acharon was about to provide a detailed list when he realized that they had been the only ones talking. He looked out across the room. Sovelet's group was looking at Katuva's group. Everyone in Katuva's group had backed up, widening the space between them and her. Everyone except for Green.

"What's going on?" Boone asked.

Acharon had an idea. "Nothing good," he said. "Excuse me."

He rose the same time that Sovelet did. She looked his way, her expression was one of sadness. Yes, he had guessed right. As he and Sovelet approached Katuva's group, a whispered conversation had gained momentum.

"They're not called suicide cults," a woman Acharon hadn't met was saying. "That's a pejorative. They were passage groups."

"It was still suicide. And it's wrong." The person expressing displeasure turned and bumped into Acharon. She glared at him. "Thanks for bringing her."

Acharon watched the woman stomp away in a mixture of shock and anger. It wasn't his idea. He turned back to see that the group around Katuva had changed. Green was still there, as was Ashe, though he looked like he didn't want to be.

There were some women, too. Sena was close in, an arm's reach from Katuva. He recognized Grace from a passing conversation, as well as the woman named Eudora. There were four other women and a couple more men.

Sovelet had arrived, too. She'd wedged herself in between Katuva, who seemed grateful, and Green, who seemed jealous.

"What happened?" Sovelet asked.

Katuva held up the wine glass. It was empty. "It's been a very long time since I had any. And it just slipped out."

"I asked her if she'd belonged," Green said. He seemed a mix of pride and concern. "The midwest was rife with passage groups. It makes me wonder if anyone else is out there."

"No," Katuva said. She looked as if she were trying to read the wine stains at the bottom of her glass. "We were one of the last. I called the other known groups when I missed passage. No one answered."

Great, Acharon thought. More secrets being kept. He took several steps and paused as he moved away from the group. Those around her were making sympathetic noises. But they were also asking pointed questions about how many people had been in the cult. How had it felt, spending her time with people who all planned to take their lives at the same time? Why didn't she make the passage? That last one brought a lot of angry voices to the conversation.

As Acharon was turning away he could hear Katuva coming to the defense of her husband.

"You knew?"

Acharon found himself almost nose-to-nose with Boone.

"Yes."

"Anything else you might feel inclined to reveal at this late date?" Boone had his arms crossed high on his chest.

Acharon didn't like the tone. "Nope," he said. "How about you and the boat?"

The comment seemed to take the angry energy out of Boone. He chewed on his lip and nodded short nods for ten heartbeats.

"Fair enough," he said. "When were you going to tell us?"

Acharon shook his head. "I wasn't. That wasn't my responsibility. And anyway, you know now, don't you? Great party."

Acharon left Boone watching Katuva and the group that had pulled in closer. He went back to the table where his food, beer, and Benen waited. Benen's eyes sparkled with interest. The one thing Acharon didn't want to do was answer a bunch of questions.

He deflected with his own, asking, "This beer we're drinking. Is it still made from long term storage hops and stuff?"

"What?" Benen looked surprised, and that suited Acharon. "The beer? Yes, the beer! No. A couple of us -- Ashe, Beatrix, Harriet, me -- we did some historical research and found old fields where they grew hops and wheat for beers. They'd been allowed to go to seed. I think that's what Harriet said. Anyway. That took us a while and then building a brewery. They wouldn't let us build it in the enclave. So we did it right next door!"

He took a long drink from his mug. "No one complains about it when they drink it."

Unless they lose their appetite, Acharon thought. Out loud, he asked, "Any chance you know what rooms Sovelet and I are staying in?"

"You bet. Tenth floor, southeast corner." He laughed. "If we knocked down all the buildings in between, you could see the ship."

"I'll see it tomorrow." Acharon stood and gathered up his dishes and their unfinished food. His appetite had gone elsewhere. "Reclaimer?"

Benen looked disappointed. He pointed to a small alcove. "In there."

Acharon dumped everything but the beer mug into the chute. He was assuming it was the same as the ones back home and would shred everything, turning it into compost that the recycling trucks no longer collected.

He stepped out of the alcove to find Benen waiting.

"Here," Acharon said. He handed the mug to Benen and started toward the door.

Halfway to the door, he caught Sovelet's attention long enough to mime sleep to her. She nodded and then turned back to the conversation. They all seemed to have gotten tired and pulled chairs into a circle. Someone had refilled Katuva's wine glass.

Acharon was glad Sovelet was with Katuva. At the same time, he was nervous even though she told him hundreds of times she'd never leave him purposefully. That was one-on-one, and it was clear from the popularity and success of the suicide cults that group persuasion had its strengths.

"Hey, Acharon." Benen had followed him to the door.

Acharon did his best not to roll his eyes. "Yeah, Benen?"

"Oh, no questions." He reached behind a maître d's podium and removed a double-barrel shotgun. "I'll walk with you. And we might need this."

"The mountain lion?"

"He's big," said Benen as he pushed the door open and stepped out. He held the door for Acharon. "And he's not all that afraid of us."

"Why should it be?" Acharon gave Katuva's group one last look. Boone was standing on the edge of the group. Acharon hoped that maybe his level-headedness would prevail. He stepped out onto the sidewalk. A sidewalk that had been scraped just clean enough, like the monorail station's stairs.

The waning daylight that had accompanied them to the restaurant was gone, replaced by a star-filled sky. The buildings around them were in dark profile, reaching for the sky as if searching for an answer. Down at street level, working street lights marked the corners of the cross streets all the way down to the Columbus Circle.

"I know. It didn't even know we existed until it came here," Benen said. "That has to be why it attacked Green. Can't believe he was out alone."

"I was told he likes to take walks at night."

They both started walking. Acharon felt that Benen was carrying the shotgun too casually for a person worried about an aggressive mountain lion.

"Sure. I think we all used to," said Benen. He stumbled on the grass hidden curb. "Sorry about that. Seem to have gotten clumsier with age. Anyway. We all did. Talk walks I mean. Most stopped when the cougar was spotted. Some took walks in groups and were armed. But no one but Green was foolish enough to cut the corner on the park, let alone walk on that side of the street."

"Followed the deer," Acharon said. It was a comment meant for himself. He'd watched the predators slowly infiltrate Sausalito, following the deer and rabbits as they populated the area.

"We got some black bear, too." Benen's voice trailed off.

Acharon looked around and didn't see anything to be concerned about. Not that he was any kind of hunter or woodsman. Like all the rest of the remaining Last Wavers, they'd been raised in safe spaces like New York, Chicago, Dallas, San Francisco. Places where technology congregated. They'd all been given lots of classes and training in useful skills. Acharon could fix almost anything. The stuff he couldn't fix, Sovelet had always seemed to find a way. They'd learned to defend themselves, too, because no one knew what the end of the human race held in store for the last actors on the stage.

"Can I ask you about your friend? Katuva?"

So it wasn't the possibility of black bears that had stilled his conversation. Achron doubted the altruism of Benen walking back to the enclave with him as protection. He supposed it was much like an old fashioned bandaid. Sometimes a person had to just grab it and pull fast to get it off.

"I wouldn't say she's my friend, Benen. What do you want to ask?"

They crossed 57th Street at a diagonal, putting them on the east side of 8th Ave.

"She was really out there all alone? All those years?"

"That's what she says," said Acharon. "I have no reason to doubt her. Others have done it, I'm sure."

"Yeah, okay. I guess so. And she really belonged to a suicide – I mean, passage group?"

"Suicide cult, yes, she did." Acharon paused. So many secrets. "At least that's what she said. Again, no reason to not believe her."

"Why's she still alive?"

Acharon used the rest of the walk to Columbus Circle, retelling what he knew about Katuva's failed attempt to be part of the suicide cult's elaborate group death. The idea still angered him, but he kept it tamped down. He didn't want his emotions to be misinterpreted.

They stayed to the right, merging onto 59th Street. Acharon was eager to get into the enclave and put a door between him and Benen. He liked the guy, but he could also use a break from all the questions. He walked a little faster and was glad to see Benen hurry to match his pace.

"So, wow. And her husband goes and dies. That sucks."

Acharon nodded. He was tired from a day's travel, food, beer, and more company than he'd had in decades. Fortunately, Benen had withdrawn mentally, one finger tapping an annoying rhythm on the barrel of the shotgun. So, Acharon was relieved to finally arrive at the enclave and get inside.

"Hey, you want me to show you where your rooms are at?"

Acharon waved him off as he pushed the button for the elevator. "You already told me where it was. Thanks, Benen. See you in the morning."

He stepped inside the elevator as the doors opened and began poking at the button to close the doors the moment the tenth floor lit up. When the elevator started moving, he breathed a sigh of relief. Just as quickly, he cursed at himself. He'd left Sovelet's travel bag in the monorail carriages.

15

Acharon did not hear Sovelet come into their rooms during the night. He did recall rolling over once to find her there. It had been late, he was sure of that. Even as he'd gotten out of bed, she hadn't moved. She hadn't been feigning sleep. He'd checked.

Finding her in bed wasn't as surprising as finding Katuva curled up on the couch, her arms holding a blanket tight to her while she slept. Acharon did not check to see if she was feigning sleep. He did, though, watch long enough to be assured she was breathing.

Then he went looking for breakfast.

Before and after finding Katuva, they'd eaten a lot of emergency rations. Things that may have been beneficial to their health but tasted more like the containers in which they'd been packaged. Last night had been a treat compared to the few days before their arrival.

Maybe they'd have coffee. He pushed the call button for the elevator and stepped in when it arrived.

He didn't expect that they would be growing their own plants. But considering the size of New York City and its easy connectivity to other metropolises, they'd had more warehouses to store things in. There'd been all sorts of strange items stored back in the Berkeley warehouse. The thousand yoga mats always came to mind. And if they'd found all the ingredients for beer, why not the one ingredient for coffee?

The elevator shuddered to a stop, and the doors whispered open. Acharon stepped out into the lobby and suddenly realized he had no idea where the enclave restaurant was. He walked further into the open space. He looked, turning around completely, hoping for a sign. Maybe someone would walk by.

Then he smelled it. Frying potatoes, eggs, and perhaps toast smells danced through the lobby, teasing Acharon with their location. There were three possible doors. He'd start with the middle then the others if he was wrong.

The elevator bell dinged as he reached the door. He paused and waited as several other people stepped out. He recognized Jaina but not the man and woman with her.

"Morning, Acharon."

"Morning, Jaina," he said. When he paused, Jaina laughed.

"I guess you didn't get the full introductions?"

"People seemed too interested in Katuva to bother. I guess."

"Katuva." The man with Jaina made Katuva's name sound like a contagion the way he pronounced it.

Jaina pointed. "This is Aiman. Not a fan. I'm sure you understand."

"I think I do."

"And this is Tadala."

"Also not a fan," Tadala said.

Acharon didn't want to have this conversation. "Is anyone a fan of breakfast?"

His comment earned him three laughs.

Aiman, smiling, said, "If you are, you're going the right way."

"And, yes, Acharon, we're all fans of breakfast," Jaina said.

Acharon nodded and pushed the door aside and stepped into a short hallway.

"One more door," Tadala said.

One more door led Acharon to a spacious room that looked as if it could seat several hundred. In the early days of the enclave, it probably did, just like San Francisco's enclave.

"Acharon!" A waving hand drew his attention to Benen over by a makeshift kitchen.

"Hey, Benen," said Acharon. He looked back at Jaina. "Is the auto-kitchen broken?"

She laughed and then said, "No. Works fine. Benen's been on a do-it-yourself kick since he started brewing his own beer."

"He's got himself a coop full of chickens," Aiman said.

"Makes for good fertilizer if you have a garden," said Acharon.

"Oh, he's got that, too," Tadala said.

They'd reached the front of Benen's kitchen. It looked to Acharon like it had been ripped out of some random cafeteria and dragged here.

Jaina handed him a plate. "Don't be fooled," she said. "Half the people here labor in the garden. Me included. Everyone just likes to act as if they aren't enjoying themselves."

The thought of a garden reminded Acharon of their home back in Sausalito. Their floating island where, as far as he ever knew, Sovelet enjoyed tending to the vegetables that had become a consistent part of their diet. As for himself, Acharon had found pleasure in the digging, planting, weeding that came as part of the responsibility. "To each their own, I guess."

"About right." Benen, a little bleary-eyed, was standing over a steam tray of scrambled eggs. "What do you fancy?"

"Coffee?"

Benen's beaming face dimmed a little. "Just the stuff from the auto-dispenser. We did scour the records for any stored beans. Alas."

"Fortunately, I'm used to it," Acharon said. He pointed at the eggs, potatoes, and fruit salad, which Benen scooped and deposited on a plate, smiling as he offered Acharon the plate.

Acharon considered an empty table but realized it might give the wrong impression. He joined Jaina and the other two early risers at a table near the middle of the big empty room.

While they ate, Jaina and her companions asked Acharon about San Francisco and the journey across the country. He answered most questions with ease but found himself moving from clarity to opacity as the questions drifted into their time with Katuva at her home. They were less curious and more interrogative.

It was clear to Acharon that these three were not fond of Katuva's presence. Acharon could understand their concern, but he had gotten somewhat used to her. Well, mostly. It was clear, even to him, that he was reluctant to have her be in contact with anything he might eat or drink.

Not wanting to continue the interrogation, Acharon shoveled through the remains of his breakfast. As his excuse, he explained that he needed to get things out of the carriages they'd arrived in.

"There's a gun locker at the front desk," Aiman said. "Rounds on the top shelf."

Acharon thanked them, deposited his dishes, waved goodbye to Benen, and found the gun locker in the lobby. Several people exited the elevator while he checked the shotgun and loaded rounds. As they noticed him, they either waved or ignored him. He returned their action in kind, though he wasn't pleased with the general atmosphere.

Locked and loaded, Acharon gladly exited the enclave and turned right, the direction of the monorail station. As he walked, he scanned the street on both sides. Mountain lions liked a good ambush. Bears liked to charge. A stampeding herd of elk would just trample everything in their path. Those were extreme cases, as Acharon knew from experience. If he had paid better attention in those instances, he might not have gotten hurt in the first place.

However, despite the few mistakes, he liked to believe he was good at observation. Especially when it came to people. He wondered how different their reception would have been if Katuva hadn't revealed her past in too much detail. Or, how different the reception would have been if she had not been with them.

Acharon crossed 57th Street. The pavement here had buckled under the unrelenting push of young trees that had found a foothold and were unlikely to surrender it. That was how nature was going to beat humans in Acharon's opinion. She would take her time, but it was just like carving out the Grand Canyon. Slowly, she was going to wear away at everything humanity had done to her. In the end, she would leave nothing to mark the passing of a species. Nothing that could be found without a shovel and a lot of digging.

It took little things to change the course of history. An eager scientist in an aggressive company creates a new GMO. That GMO's chaff dust just happens to render the next generation of sapiens sterile. A woman from a suicide cult enters an enclave. Soon enough, the social dynamic is changed. How would they all fare on a ship, crossing the Atlantic just ahead of the winter storms, if they couldn't all be agreeable now?

Movement across the street, along the edge of Central Park, caught his eye. He stopped walking and brought the butt of the shotgun to his shoulder. Several minutes passed with Acharon holding position. Then, several bucks, five and six-pointers, pushed through the undergrowth, focused on the berries they'd found, giving Acharon several curious glances before ignoring him.

Acharon moved slowly, edging further away from the deer until he felt increasing his speed wouldn't spook the deer. The encounter brought up a common thought that he chewed on at moments like this. How many animals had lost their fear-memory of humans? Any animal that was a favored prey of predators was going to be naturally cautious. Still, he'd had several odd encounters with foxes, water fowl, and several deer. Maybe humans just didn't look threatening.

Acharon decided his last thought was double-edged. On the exterior, the physical aspect of humans definitely didn't look as threatening as something like a wolf or brown bear. But on the interior, the brain, there probably wasn't a more dangerous creature. Dangerous even to its own kind.

The thoughts circled back around to Katuva, which caused Acharon to shake his head in wonder. They'd gotten themselves in quite a jam.

Fortunately, he arrived at the station before his thoughts could spiral back around for a third go.

The station was as he remembered it. The newly cleaned stairs. The paired carriages he, Sovelet, and Katuva had arrived in. The door to the carriage he'd forgotten to shut. There'd been too many distractions with Katuva's appearance on the platform.

That was the kind of mistake he wasn't prone to make. He was supposed to be the cautious one. Over-planned, over-prepared. Those were the words people would use to describe him. That's what Sovelet had said on many occasions while trying not to roll her eyes or laugh.

But this? Something as simple as shutting a door? Something he'd been doing for over a hundred years? Open doors were bad. Nature may abhor a vacuum, but it loved an open door.

Once again, Acharon pushed the rifle butt into his shoulder. He scanned the area around the carriage for any more surprises. There were a few more carriages parked a little further along the rail. The scuffed and trampled weeds gave Acharon the impression they'd recently been moved.

"Knock, knock," he said with a raised voice. He hadn't heard any movement inside the carriage, but maybe something was taking a nap and might wake up grumpy.

Acharon side-stepped to the front carriage. The tip of the shotgun was raised enough to cover the bottom part of the open doorway. He peered into the dim interior, back into the second carriage. Nothing moved.

With quick motions, he turned the shotgun, banging on the carriage exterior with the butt. He re-shouldered the shotgun and stepped back.

A long minute and nothing happened. So, Acharon moved closer to the doorway and took a quick peek to the front of the carriage. Still nothing showed itself or moved. He could also see further into the rear carriage from his new position.

There was clear evidence animals had been inside during the night. The sleeping bags and the bed had been pulled at and torn. The containers on the ground were lying on their sides and open, packets of dehydrated and preserved foods were strewn across the carriage floors. From the smell he was now becoming aware of, some creature had also taken the time to mark the carriages as their territory.

Well, in Acharon's opinion, they were welcome to the carriages, so long as he could find what he came for.

The looking took a little effort. One of Sovelet's bags was missing. He found it a little later, outside, down on the track, one corner nibbled through. With Katuva's bag, his pack, and Sovelet's stuffed computer bag, Acharon was going to have trouble with the shotgun if anything dangerous showed up. On the plus side, whatever it was that attacked would have a hard time getting to him through all the gear.

Before he left, Acharon considered the carriage doors. Should he shut them? Did it even matter? If he did, time would still prevail. Dirt would fill the cracks, weeds would grow and die, creating a deeper loam for larger plants to grow. They'd push their roots deeper, growing wider, forcing deeper cracks in the carriages until they broke through. Water would drip inside, dirt would collect, things would grow in the dim light of the interior. Eventually, a tree might take hold, wrapping around a carriage or tearing through the joint that connected the two. From there, it would only be a matter of time until it would be shattered, buried beneath layers of dirt and second-growth trees.

He left the doors open and exited the platform.

A block back to the concave he had company.

"There you are." Sovelet was with Jaina.

Trailing close behind, Katuva was with Sena and Green. Of the three, only Sena and Green seemed to be in good spirits.

"Here I am," Acharon said. He stopped and dropped the bags on the ground, being sure not to let the computer bag actually hit the earth-coated pavement. He had to juggle the shotgun onto his other shoulder to control the bag's descent. "I could use a little help."

He looked at Green until Green caught on and hurried over to pick up the bags.

"That's mine," Katuva said. She grabbed her bag from Green, clutching it to her like an old lady would have gripped her purse while crossing through a sketchy neighborhood.

"I don't mind," Green said. He held out his hand, his cheery smile still on his face, even after Katuva responded with an emphatic shake of her head.

"Well, you can carry mine," Sovelet said. Though, Acharon noted, she did take her computer bag.

"Why are you all out here?" Acharon shouldered his pack and started walking with the group back in the direction of the enclave.

"Boone was asking about your whereabouts," Jaina said. She'd take one of the handles on Sovelet's computer bag, sharing the load.

"Benen said you'd left the building," Sovelet added. "Since I didn't see my bag in our rooms this morning, I figured you'd be going for it."

"Animals got inside the carriages. Had a party. Thrashed the place." Acharon pointed at Sovelet's bag in Green's hands. "Found yours outside the carriages. Someone liked the taste."

149

"You sure you don't want help with your bag?" Sena was asking Katuva.

"No, thank you."

"I don't mind," Green said.

"I said, no." Her tone was emphatic and final.

Green looked momentarily taken aback. He stumbled on the uneven ground, waving it away with a laugh, and then smiling cheerily again. He started talking about tripping and what incidents were the funniest, to him.

Acharon was glad that Green wanted to ramble. Katuva's last remark had stilled the tongue of everyone else. He understood why Sovelet might want to carry her computer bag. She'd put a lot of work into them and wanted them to remain safe. She wasn't concerned about the other bag. She might not have even cared if the animals had destroyed it. That was just clothes and a few toiletries. Things easily replaced. He'd assumed that was the same case for Katuva. Yet, she seemed awfully protective of it, and that worried Acharon.

The stories Green was bombarding them with, punctuated by his own honking laughter, distracted Acharon just enough that he wasn't able to give Katuva's bag his undivided attention. But, he thought as they reached the front of the enclave, it would have been nice if the animals had carried her bag off instead.

Inside the enclave, Acharon returned the shotgun to the gun locker. He now had Sovelet's bag in his possession. He was standing at the elevator, waiting for it to return to the lobby. Sovelet and Jaina had gone to the dining room. Katuva, despite her insistence that she would be okay on her own, had disappeared into the elevator while Acharon had been stowing the shotgun. Now he was alone and waiting.

The dynamic of the enclave seemed to have shifted with their arrival. Or, to be exact, the arrival of Katuva. Acharon doubted things would have shifted so far if it had only been him and Sovelet.

The ding of the elevator arriving pulled Acharon's attention to the doors. He started forward as they slid open and then just as quickly stepped back.

"Morning, Boone," he said. Boone had emerged from the elevator with several other people. He only stopped when Acharon had called him by name. "I heard you were looking for me?"

"I was?" The rest of the group he'd come to the lobby with stopped several meters away.

"Jaina said you were wondering where I was." Acharon didn't know why, but the conversation felt awkward. It felt like he'd called after someone by name only to have them turn around and be someone else.

Boone laughed and waved the words away. "That. No, I was just wondering if you'd come down for breakfast yet. But it looks like you've been even busier."

Acharon looked at the bags he was carrying. "Yep. Forgot them on the carriages last night. Animals had at them for a bit."

"Well, they're safe now." Boone nodded and turned to join the other people in his group.

"I can put these in our rooms," Acharon said. He had to raise his voice as Boone was moving away. "Then maybe we can go look at the boat?"

Boone waved without looking back. One of those, 'Great, see you then,' kind of waves. A disinterested wave. A wave that concerned Acharon.

He would have considered it more, but the doors to the elevator started sliding shut. A foot into the narrowing gap stopped them, and they opened once more. Acharon stepped in, punching the ten with his elbow. There was no doubt the dynamic had changed.

As the elevator crawled upward, Acharon wondered what would come of it.

16

"It's your first day, Acharon," Boone said. He was leaning back in his chair, one foot up on the empty chair next to him, his left hand curled around a cup of steaming, artificial coffee. "Settle in. We'll get there."

Acharon wasn't sure what he'd said as he walked away. He knew he'd been trying to be polite, despite the frustration gnawing at his gut. He didn't see a need to settle in. They weren't supposed to be staying here. That was the whole point of coming to New York. Get on a boat and go to France. If he was going to settle in, let it be on the boat when they were at sea.

There were seven people still in the dining room. Three sat with Boone. Acharon recognized at least one of them as being part of the group camped around Katuva the night before. A couple sat at a table in a corner, speaking softly but animatedly. That left one more person behind the makeshift kitchen, puttering, looking like they weren't looking in Acharon's direction.

"Hey, Benen," Acharon said.

Benen looked up, appearing as if he hadn't known Acharon was approaching. Acharon found it amusing. At least someone was being pleasant.

"Hey, Acharon. What can I do for you?"

Acharon looked around the room. Boone appeared to be in deep conversation with his table mates, though he also seemed to shift his gaze in Acharon's direction. He lowered his voice and said, "I was hoping to see the boat today. But Boone doesn't seem to be interested."

"And it's all you can think about," Benen said. He was untying a stained apron. "He was late today, for breakfast. Normally, he'd have been down here even earlier than you appeared. You want to see the brewery?"

"No, I want to see the boat."

Louder, Benen said. "Sure, I can show you the brewery."

"That's not what I asked." Acharon was still keeping his voice low.

"Kitchen's closed," Benen said to the room. The couple in the back continued their conversation unaware. "Anyone else want to come to the brewery?"

Several people at Boone's table rolled their eyes.

"We're good, Benen," Boone said. Then, to Acharon, "Enjoy the tour."

Confused, Acharon followed Benen out a side door. Behind it was a bare-walled corridor.

"This way," Benen said. His voice too loud for the enclosed space.

"Did I not speak loud enough before?" Acharon asked. His voice was at an appropriate level for the hallway.

Benen now spoke at the same level. "Yes, I heard you. But Boone's pretty protective of the ship ever since the accident with the first one."

Acharon noticed the air-quotes for the accident.

"So, if I said I was taking you to the boat," Benen continued as they pushed through a fire door, "we might have had company. And I had the feeling that you wouldn't get the good look you'll need."

"Why?"

"Hang on." They were in a narrow alley space. Benen was unbolting a door. "Keeps the wildlife out. Anyway, based on what Sovelet has said on the internet, you're the boat guy. And that might be important."

Benen pulled the door open and waved Acharon to enter. Still confused, Acharon entered. Benen followed behind, pulling the door shut.

"We got to remember to come back to the enclave this way. Or the door won't get bolted."

"And someone might get suspicious."

Benen smiled. "Now you're getting it. This way."

"Is everything okay here? I thought everyone was on board with the ship. With sailing to France."

They were in a space that hadn't been designed for a brewery. However, Benen seemed to have managed well enough. Acharon waited while Benen checked some gauges and meters. After checking readings, Benen flipped open a large ledger and made some notes.

"Okay," said Benen. He slapped the ledger shut, pulled a shotgun off a shelf, and took off in the direction opposite that which they'd come. "So, everyone agreed. But I think it's because no one wanted to look like they disagreed. Sometimes I wonder if Boone even cares. Though, to be fair, he's taken charge with gusto. It was like once he committed to the idea, he made it his own. I don't think we would have tried to look for another boat if it hadn't been for him pushing us to look."

Benen pushed through a door that put them back into an alley.

"So some people have dragged their heels in cooperating with the idea. But Boone has been the catalyst. Maybe he's just taking a moment to catch his breath now that you and Sovelet are here."

"And Katuva," said Acharon.

Benen stopped at the exit to the alley. He turned to look at Acharon. "I don't think Boone likes her."

Acharon had his doubts. "I saw him standing on the edge of her fan circle," he said.

"She's from a suicide cult. Right?" When Acharon nodded agreement, Benen continued. "And you can bet he's concerned. Someone like that has the potential of poisoning the well. That came out wrong. But you get the idea."

They crossed the avenue and continued walking down 57th Street.

"You can bet," Benen continued, "that someone like that, they come here and start preaching the glory of group suicide. Next thing you know, everyone wants to die."

Acharon decided not to relate the story from Katuva's little town where she'd offered Acharon and Sovelet the opportunity to join her in committing the act of suicide. Not that he or Sovelet had taken her up on the offer, but it still might give him the encouragement to continue thinking the way he was thinking.

Once across 8th Ave, it was less than a kilometer to the waterfront. Fortunately for Acharon, Benen kept his one-sided conversation to light subjects. He rattled on about the first attempts to brew their own beer. After laughing at his own mistakes, he bounced over to the chickens. They were wild, and he'd only found them over in New Jersey when they were looking for the first ship. Everyone had said the idea was ridiculous until they had their first fresh-egg omelet. They'd made their way back to New Jersey and trapped the rest of the flock Benen had seen.

The most important part of the conversation was that it never wandered back to Katuva. It was pleasant, that just for a moment, everything didn't revolve around her mysterious appearance.

What everything should have revolved around was the boat. The eagerness to complete it and sail to France, that Sovelet said imbued their emails, was absent. The spearhead of the project, Boone, seemed to be the least passionate.

Perhaps Sovelet had read too much into their enthusiasm. She did want to live instead of just exist. But it would be unlike Sovelet to obfuscate. She would have merely been honest and made him work with that. Which meant that something had changed.

"Here we are," Benen said. It snapped Acharon's attention back to the moment.

He looked around, seeing the wharf and Hudson River. Much was covered with moss, weeds, and small bushes. It was like everyplace else. But here, there was a boat. But he couldn't see it.

"Here we are, where?"

Benen laughed. "The boat."

"I'm sorry," Acharon said. He looked around, still baffled. If it was here, they couldn't easily hide it. Not with the mast sticking up like a towering signpost. "I don't see a ship anywhere."

"Right," Benen said. He started walking onto the wharf. "Come on."

Acharon followed, baffled, trying to understand. Was it on the wharves on the other side of the Hudson? Did they take a skiff across? No, that wouldn't make any sense.

"Now?" Benen had stopped walking.

Acharon looked around, ready to snap at Benen for the excessive practical joke. Then, he realized what he'd been doing wrong. There was a ship. It was a sailing ship. But as it didn't have a mast, his eyes had passed right over it.

He could feel Benen looking at him. He could feel Benen's smile. He had, apparently, understood what had befuddled Acharon.

This ship was in great shape, minus the mast. The cockpit was in the center of the boat, in a raised cabin. That was going to make piloting the boat more comfortable and safe during the inevitable inclement weather

So, if there was a sailboat, there must be a mast. Acharon looked around and finally saw the mast laying in the weeds on the pier. It was not something a person just picked up and dropped into place. Next to the mast was the boom, a long, narrow rectangular tube that tapered near the aft end. He didn't have to inspect it closely to understand it was a furling boom where the mainsail could be rolled into it. Another feature that would make the trip easier.

Acharon turned to Benen, who'd become distracted by a couple squirrels chasing each other through a row of trees growing on the pier.

"Why is the mast not on?"

Benen pulled himself away from the squirrels - one had fallen from a low branch, the other diving after it - and gave Achron a rueful look. "Yeah, that," he said. He waved a hand and started walking. "You have to see it."

They walked back along the pier toward 57th. Instead of starting down 57th, Benen took them to the right. They walked half a block down 12th Ave before he stopped.

"That's the problem," he said.

Acharon assumed that the problem Benen was pointing at was the crane sitting motionless in the middle of the avenue. It was a boom crane. Not the largest Acharon had seen. This one was a three-axle affair. He'd actually used several larger cranes in building the floating island he and Sovelet had lived so comfortably and quietly on. It felt like a lifetime ago.

He walked toward the crane. Off to the side, he heard Benen hurry to catch up. The crane looked in remarkably good shape. The tires had cracks in the rubber, but not deep enough to make them unusable; they still held air.

"What's the problem?" Acharon asked. He walked along the side of the crane, his hand trailing along the surface of it, leaving finger-trails through the thick dust. "Why is this a problem?"

"Power." Benen thumped the side of the crane and half-heartedly kicked at one of the tires. "It worked great when we found it. We didn't push it hard. I mean, look at the tires. If those go, I don't know we can find replacements. So we moved it slowly. When it ran out of power, we ran cables and patched into buildings nearby, using what we could with what remained of the electrical grid."

Acharon went around the crane until he found the access panel for the batteries. It came off easily, and he pulled the battery tray out to examine them. They were old, but if treated kindly, they should still be at least at seventy-five percent capacity. "Problem's not the batteries."

"That was my guess," Benen said. "Several other people, too. But it kept running out of juice every five blocks or so. We tried leaving charging cables hooked to it. It was amusing until we set a building on fire over near 10th and 35th."

"No one ran a diagnostic?" Acharon followed the lines from the battery terminals. They were good batteries. Not the last generation developed, but pretty close to it.

"Well, some of us -- not me, that's for sure -- have computer skills, but no one was sure how to deal with this. They were going to work with Sovelet on it, but then we lost communication with you guys. And then you were on the way, so Boone said it could wait."

"Tell you what," said Acharon. He was opening the cabin door. The smell of grease mixed with dust and aged plastic rolled out like a cloud of bad perfume. Fortunately, Sovelet had never been fond of perfume. He slipped onto the seat. "If you'll go and ask Sovelet to come help, I'll start going through the systems. Maybe I'll get lucky. If not, Sovelet will find it."

Benen looked around. "You sure? I mean, the mountain lion? The other animals?"

"Will you be okay walking back by yourself?" Acharon smiled after his question.

"What? Me? Yeah. I mean, I have the shotgun." He paused as his face registered concerned. "You don't want me to leave it here, do you?"

The concern made Acharon laugh. He climbed out of the cab and clapped Benen on the shoulder. "Of course not. Don't worry about me. If anything shows up, I can take shelter in the cab."

"Well, if you're sure." Benen didn't look sure.

"It's the kind of thing I'm used to, Benen. So, you'll go and see if Sovelet wants to come help?"

Benen nodded and looked around. "Okay. Maybe an hour? Two, if run into trouble."

"See you then."

Acharon looked at Benen, keeping his look gentle until Benen seemed to realize that the time to go was now. Benen raised the shotgun in salute before turning and quickly walking back up 12th. Acharon watched until Benen turned on 57th with a last raise of the shotgun.

Now that he was alone, Acharon took a moment to look around. On the city side, there were buildings. Some were broken with age. A few had the plastic coating. All of them, with no one to tend them, were hugged by ivy tendrils, festooned with moss and grass window sill caps. Young trees pushed up from everywhere. Even on the dock side of 12th Ave, trees grew not just on the docks but also on the U.S.S. Intrepid.

Mother nature didn't care about the history of humans. Except to cover the scar of their existence. Acharon knew, with the historical obelisks in the major cities and floating in space, some future species or intergalactic visitors might discover humanity's existence, giving it life once more as an archeological curiosity. But, at least they would be remembered. That is, until whoever discovered the obelisks faded away, too.

Acharon laughed. He was beginning to wonder if he was safe, alone with his thoughts. He returned to the crane's cab and unscrewed the knobs that held the dash in place. He started there and began tracing wires.

After a half hour of crawling under the crane and wiggling into spaces, he wasn't surprised to discover several things. There were some wires near the batteries, coated with corrosion that closed the circuit where it shouldn't. That was easy enough to clean up.

The thing Acharon thought he might, and was sorry to see, was damage to one of the boards that controlled the charging of the batteries. The scars across it were fresh. A little searching through the toolboxes built into the side panels resulted in him finding a small hand ax. A light layer of rust on the ax head showed minor scrapes where the ax had been used.

Someone didn't want the ship outfitting to continue. But they had to know that he would arrive and could solve a problem like this. So, perhaps what they'd really wanted was to slow the work down. But why?

Acharon mulled over his ideas as he continued a check of the crane. He was just finishing checking on the crane's electric engines when he heard someone shout his name.

Coming down 12th Ave, Benen walked with Sovelet and a small entourage. Acharon waved and wondered to himself if one of the people accompanying Sovelet was responsible for the sabotage.

"So, you need a diagnostic run?" Sovelet asked as she reached Acharon and the crane. She had her computer bag, though it looked less bulky than usual.

"Yes. And then a schematic to work around a control board." Acharon showed Sovelet. He held a finger to his lips when she saw the marks on the board and looked back at him. "I don't think we'll be able to order a replacement."

"I could search the internet," Sovelet said. She pulled her laptop out of her bag. "Might find it in inventory somewhere."

The small group that had come with Sovelet, which included Jaina, Tadala, and Aiman, were gathered around. He wouldn't be able to say everything that was on his mind. "It might be hundreds of miles away," he said to Sovelet. "We're running out of weeks to sail. Unless people want to wait another year."

"We've been talking about this for a decade," Tadala said. The others nodded.

Jaina added, "We had to find the first ship before Boone accepted that it could be done. That was two years ago?"

"About two," Benen said. "And we've been plagued with setbacks ever since."

Sovelet looked at Acharon, her eyebrows arched. She had a look on her face that said she knew how Acharon was going to react. She was right, of course.

"Things will change now," he said.

17

Sovelet had to employ Jaina's skills to finish running the diagnostics. That job and the workaround for the damaged panel were done in three hours. At one point, Benen and Aiman returned to the enclave to pick up some food and water.

They returned down 46th, which surprised Acharon. He'd been watching down 12th street.

"Sorry," Benen said. He slid a pack off his back. "Someone was watching us."

"Watching?" Acharon scanned the area, seeing nothing but the city and the river. "'Watching,' like spying? Or did someone just look your way, and you thought they were watching?"

"No, we were definitely being watched," Aiman said. He had a pack, too, and was unloading aluminum water bottles. Tadala grabbed three and walked around to the crane cab. "I thought it was Green. But I also thought I'd seen him talking with Katuva and Grace over coffee. So I'm not sure."

"Could have been anyone," said Benen. "Which is why we took a more circuitous route." He pulled a container from his pack. Inside it was a dozen sandwiches hastily wrapped in some wrinkled butcher paper.

"Don't tell me you also bake bread," said Acharon as he accepted one of the sandwiches. It was stuffed with tomatoes, cucumbers, lettuce, mustard, and some thinly sliced protein loaf. It tasted better than it looked.

Benen grinned and then said, "All right. I won't tell you."

"You're head chef on this voyage," Acharon said. He took the container of sandwiches around to the other side of the crane.

Sovelet was just putting the cap on her water bottle. Her lips still shone with water. "Hey," she said. "Almost done."

"Good. I rigged the board with a couple of jumps. Should hold up. Sandwich?"

"Sandwich?" Sovelet took one from the container and opened it. She stepped back as tomato seeds and juice dripped to the ground. She looked even more dubious than Acharon until she took a bite. She nodded appreciatively. "That's good."

"I told him he's head chef on the cruise."

"Cruise?" Sovelet seemed more dubious of that than the sandwich, if Acharon had to guess.

"All done." Jaina was unplugging the laptop from the crane's computer system behind the dash panel. "It should distribute the power as needed. And we should be able to monitor the charge here, on the laptop."

Benen, who had wandered around the crane, was wiping his lip with the back of his hand, erasing a streak of mustard. "It's good to go?"

Acharon nodded, as did Sovelet and Jaina.

"Great," said Benen as he crumpled up the paper from his sandwich. "Now, all we got to do is charge it."

Charging the crane required a series of cables. Fortunately, those had been left behind, several blocks down the road. Aiman and Acharon had to do some splicing as the plug had been destroyed in the building fire. One of the buildings near the crane had a solar grid. The output was low. It would take several days unless something was done.

For Acharon, this was déjà vu all over again. He'd done this at the waterfront warehouse in San Francisco. Then he'd done something similar at the hospital. Several times in the journey to New York, he'd also found himself on top of a building, cleaning panels, encouraging wind turbines to turn. The only difference was those times he'd either had an elevator or a short ladder or series of steps to climb.

The panels here were atop a twelve-story building. The elevator didn't work. Acharon had rummaged together a few cleaning supplies, and with Tadala for company, they climbed thirteen flights of stairs.

Once on the roof and after a short recovery break, Acharon and Tadala got to work. They scrubbed the panels with hard bristle brushes to break up the guano and dirt. After breaking it up, they brushed the panels off with push brooms they'd found in a custodial locker on the lobby level. There was no water to give a good rinse, and the sky, bright blue, didn't look like it was going to help with rain any time soon.

After twenty minutes of sweaty labor, Acharon shouted down to the rest of the group. "How about now?"

"Stand by." Benen's voice echoed off the nearby buildings.

"I wonder how Boone's going to take this," Tadala said. She'd swept a section of the ground clear and was sitting with her back against the short wall that capped the building.

"I'd think he'd be glad we were doing this. Now we can get back to work."

"I don't know." Tadala paused to drain the last of the water from her bottle. "He seemed okay with giving up after someone burned the first ship."

Acharon turned to look at her. "So, you believe it was on purpose?"

Tadala laughed. "Everyone believes it. They - we, I guess - just act like it was an accident. That way, no one has to accuse someone else of being a traitor."

"Looks great!"

Down below, Benen and Sovelet were both giving a thumbs up.

"Do you suspect someone?" Acharon asked.

Tadala climbed to her feet and then waved at the people by the crane. "No," she said. "I mean, there are several, but I just don't see them desperate enough to take that kind of action."

"So, not Boone?" Acharon held the door open for Tadala.

"Boone? No." She started down the stairs. Acharon was several steps behind her. "I mean, he was reluctant to start and okay with giving up when it happened, but when we were working on it, he was really into it. He actually looked pretty downcast when he got the news."

"And he wasn't all that keen to start again?"

Tadala took the turn on the fifth floor. "Seemed that way. It was Asher and Benen who found the other ship. They've always been good at finding stuff."

"Beer. Chickens," Acharon said. He liked those kinds of people. There'd been a few at the San Francisco enclave. They were fun to be around.

"And all the ingredients for bread, the seeds for the gardens. When they get something in their head, they work hard to make it happen. I think Green was jealous of Benen, even though Benen is hetero."

They stepped out of the stairwell into the lobby. Acharon said, "I would think Asher would be jealous of the way Green hangs around Katuva."

"Yeah, that's kinda weird. Green's never showed that much interest in anyone but Asher." She paused as they stepped out of the building. "I don't know a lot about Green, even after fifty years living in the same place together. Maybe he's trying to live vicariously through her? Small town stuff? I don't know."

Acharon didn't expect her to have all the answers, or any. But, it was even clearer that everyone in the enclave wasn't on the same page. And the one person who he thought was eager to make the voyage, Boone, seemed to be reluctant. Oddly, it was Benen who appeared to have the drive to do something.

"Ten hours," Aiman said as Acharon and Tadala joined the rest of the group, gathered around the crane's cab door.

"Ten hours?" Acharon leaned in to peek at the panel. Someone had already remounted it.

"Nine point seven five hours," Benen said. "If you want to split hairs."

"Ten. Nine and three quarters," Sovelet said. "Either way, it's not going to be ready until well after midnight, depending on the building's batteries, too. So, tomorrow afternoon?"

"No matter which way," Jaina said. "We're done doing all we can until tomorrow."

"Back to the enclave?" Acharon asked.

"Back to the enclave," said Tadala.

"The tomatoes need harvesting," Benen said. He seemed quite pleased with the information. It raised a good-natured chuckle from the rest of the group.

"All right," said Tadala. "Let's go pluck some tomatoes."

With six people working, harvesting the tomatoes took less than a quarter-hour. Another forty-five minutes was spent listening to Benen explain the garden's system for watering and detailed explanations on the building of the garden. The others added information to either clarify or minimize Benen's slight tendency to exaggerate.

What was true, though, was that the enclave had built their garden on the terraces of the building. Benen had spearheaded the project, recruiting nearly everyone to help bring barrels of dirt and compost out of Central Park and up the elevators.

Before dinner, Acharon and Sovelet returned to their rooms for the first time that day. They had planned to clean up and join the same people in the dining room. Benen was excited to share some ale he'd been bottling before Acharon and Sovelet arrived.

They entered to find themselves already with company. Katuva, who'd been sitting, balled up on the couch, started to stand when she realized they were home.

"No, no," Sovelet said. She hurried over to Katuva. "Is everything okay?"

"Yeah, I guess." She looked in Acharon's direction, smiling a weak smile at him. "I didn't have any place else to go where I could be alone. I'm not used to so much attention."

"Well, of course you can stay here," Sovelet said. She looked at Acharon. "Right? It's okay?"

Like he would say anything to disappoint his wife, even if he felt differently. "Right. It's completely okay. Besides, we're only going to be here for a few more days. Things are really going to be crowded then."

Katuva looked surprised. "I heard we weren't going anywhere for another year."

Acharon and Sovelet exchanged looks. Sovelet asked Katuva, "Where did you hear that?"

"I don't remember who said it." She looked down at the floor.

Acharon wasn't buying it, but what was he going to do?

"Well, maybe they misunderstood," Sovelet said.

"I guess. I remember other people being surprised, too."

A solid, repetitive thumping reverberated off the door. At the sound, Acharon noticed Katuva's face pale. She and Sovelet looked at Acharon. He left the living area and went down the short hall, opening the door.

"Hey, Boone," Acharon said. He stepped aside. "Come on in."

"Thanks, Acharon. Sovelet in?"

Acharon indicated the direction to the living room with his arm. "In the living room. Go ahead."

Boone started down the hall. Acharon took a quick peek down the central hallway. All the other doors were shut. He closed and locked the door.

Down the hall, he heard Boone. "Ah, Katuva. People were wondering where you'd disappeared to."

Acharon moved through the short distance at a quick pace.

"She's not used to so many people at once," Sovelet was saying.

"Right," Boone said. He was by the windows, turning to look past the curtains. "Good view of the park."

"Fortuitous," Acharon said. He wanted to sit, it had been a busy morning. But he wasn't inclined to do so as long as Boone was standing. He didn't feel threatened. He just liked the playing field even. Not being aware had cost him an eye before.

Boone turned back around, facing the room. "I hear you got the boom crane working?"

"We got the batteries working," Acharon said. "There was some damage that we were able to repair. It's on a charge right now. We'll know better tomorrow."

"I'm just curious," Boone said. He put his hands in his pockets and leaned against the window frame. "Why didn't you come and tell me what you were about?"

Acharon held his hands out. What can you do? "It was serendipity, really. We were looking at the boat."

"You and Benen," Boone said. It was snapped out, like one of the old court dramas Acharon and Sovelet used to watch back on their island. The prosecutor trying to trip up the defendant.

"Yes," Acharon said. He spoke deliberately. "He answered the questions I asked. He seemed more interested in returning to the enclave, though. Something about beer."

"And yet, he was there all day." Boone scanned the room, passing over Katuva as if she didn't exist. "And then he brought reinforcements? Sovelet?"

"Did we do something wrong?" Sovelet asked.

Acharon had to resist the natural urge to smile when someone made the mistake of thinking they could intimidate her. They'd been married for more than a hundred years, known each other since they were toddlers. He knew anyone who tried to force the upper hand on her did not stay her friend.

It really was a shame. He'd liked Boone initially. Now, he had serious doubts.

"Did you do something wrong?" Boone smiled. "If you got the boom crane working, I'd have to say you did something right. I just wish you had kept me in the loop."

Sovelet was about to say something. Acharon didn't think it would be encouraging, so he beat her to it. "We were caught up in the moment, Boone. I'll be sure to let you know if we decide to do anything else."

He could feel the heated glare from Sovelet, but he had to ignore it.

"That's all I can ask," Boone said. He started to leave and then stopped. "Oh, almost forgot. In consideration of Katuva's preference for some space, we've prepared a private apartment for her. See you all at dinner."

Without waiting, Boone left the apartment. Before the door had swung shut, someone else was knocking at the door.

"It's open," said Acharon. He remained in the living room, watching the door.

"Evening, Acharon." It was Green. He was closely followed by a grim-faced Asher.

"Acharon," Asher said.

"Green. Asher," Acharon said. "We're in here." He wasn't sure what he expected from Katuva. He'd seen her look happy when they'd first met her. He'd also seen the look on her face when he and Sovelet had rejected her offer of collective suicide. He had never seen the defeated look she was wearing now.

Sovelet must have recognized it, too, she was huddled with Katuva. She'd moved to sit on the edge of the coffee table, her head close to Katuva's. Acharon could see Sovelet was talking in a whisper. Katuva was shaking her head to whatever Sovelet was saying.

"Heard you got the crane fixed," Asher said. There was a shine of hope in his eyes.

"We'll know tomorrow," said Acharon. "Great news, right, Green?"

"Yeah, great." His smile, hollow, carried him past Acharon into the room where he seemed to grow at the sight of Katuva. "Katuva! Did you hear the wonderful news?"

He went and sat next to her, sliding his hand between Sovelet's and Katuva's, pulling Katuva's hand to his lap.

"We fixed you up a nice new apartment," he said. Acharon noticed he hadn't even acknowledged Sovelet. "And it's right across the hall from mine and Ashe's.

Katuva looked up at Acharon and then over to Sovelet. "Sounds great."

Green stood, pulling Katuva with her. Acharon couldn't understand why she looked so unhappy. They seemed to accept her and trust her, something that Acharon had a difficult time doing. Sovelet trusted her, though, and that was what mattered to him.

"Hold up," Acharon said. He stepped further into the living room. "We have no problem with Katuva staying here with us. So I think that should be her decision."

"Nonsense," Green said. He laughed to smooth the rough edge of his retort. "She'll be much happier in her own place."

Sovelet had moved back away from Green, her hands holding each other enough to turn them white where they held each other. "We really would love it if you'd stay."

"Katuva?" Green's voice was wheedling.

There was a long moment of silence. Katuva's head came up, her eyes nearly made contact with Sovelet's before sliding away. "It's okay," she finally said. "It doesn't matter."

"There you go," Green said. He started for the hall, pulling Katuva along. "You're going to love it. And we can visit whenever you want."

He kept chattering as they exited the apartment and disappeared down the hall. Ashe paused at the threshold. Acharon felt like he wanted to say something. Instead, Ashe waved a weak good-bye and left.

"There's something going on," Sovelet said. She pressed close to Acharon. He slipped his hand around her shoulders.

"Ashe and Green's apartment is on this floor," Acharon said. "She's not that far away."

"I know. I just feel like she's being pressured."

"What kind of pressure? Ashe and Green are partners. I can't imagine seeing Katuva has somehow changed Green. That seems unlikely to the point of being ridiculous."

"I didn't mean that. Just something."

"Suicide?"

Sovelet froze in Acharon's arms. A moment later, she relaxed. "I don't think so. I think that would put her in good spirits if someone wanted to join her. I don't know."

Acharon gave her a kiss on the head. "Well, we can't do anything until we know what the problem is. For now, we have to clean up. We have a fresh salad and questionable beer to drink."

"I'll need a few minutes." Sovelet headed into the bedroom.

Acharon went and shut the door and turned the lock. Maybe things would be different when the departure date for France was definite. Maybe they should have just stayed in California.

18

Acharon was pretty sure it was the wine. He'd stuck to beer while Sovelet had poured liberally from the wine carafe for her, Jaina, and Tadala. They'd all stayed up late, but gone to bed at the same time. So, it had to be the wine.

He shut the apartment door, letting it touch gently against the jamb. It had been a night reminiscent of the days back in San Francisco before Thyme had gotten greedy for power and control. Everyone in little groups around the club sitting areas debating in genial ways, telling jokes, ribbing each other, enjoying the company.

In the hallway to the elevator, Acharon could hear some voices beyond several of the doors. Aiman and Tadala were awake. At least one of them. For a moment, he considered knocking on their door. He barely paused at the thought before continuing to the elevator. This was his third day and he didn't know other people's peculiarities. They might have a morning routine, and he didn't think it necessary to ruin it. They would be down later. As would Sovelet.

The elevator ground its way to the lobby without a single stop along the way. Clearly, there weren't a lot, but he knew that people occupied some of the other floors. Boone, if he recalled from a conversation, was on the second floor. Most of the others were on six, seven, and ten. It was a big empty building in a big empty city.

The lobby was equally as deserted.

That was not the case for the dining room. Acharon was surprised to see a small group around a table to the far left of the room. He was surprised to see Katuva among them and not surprised to see Green by her side.

Katuva was talking quietly but animatedly. Her head moved as she seemed to make contact with the other six people at the table. Her hands alternated between chopping the air and locked together like a religious person at fervent prayer.

Next to Green, Sena looked in Acharon's direction. Without looking away, she reached out and tapped Katuva's forearm. Katuva's head snapped around, also seeing Acharon.

It was an odd mix of emotions. Hope had been there at first but disappeared behind a blush of embarrassment that weighed her face, tilting her head down, breaking eye contact.

Green's look was that of someone who was displeased with an interruption.

Acharon raised a hand. "Morning," he said. He continued toward Benen's makeshift kitchen. Acharon was unsurprised by the lack of returned greetings.

Benen was a different matter.

"Good morning, Acharon," Benen said. He'd already grabbed a plate and was dishing it with eggs, potatoes, and cinnamon swirl toast. He held the plate out for Acharon. "Trust you slept well?"

Benen had drunk more beer than Acharon. Aiman had tried to match him, but when he missed his chair, returning to the table, he'd decided he'd had enough. Acharon hadn't even tried to keep up. Benen could handle his beer.

"Yes, thank you." Acharon took the plate and walked to the end of the service counter and punched buttons to order a cup of coffee with light sweetener. Coffee was a liberal term when applied to the instant stuff developed for the auto-cafes and restaurants. "Did you even sleep, Benen?"

Acharon took a table next to the kitchen. Benen ordered his own coffee and then joined him.

"Like a baby. Always do. What did they call it? 'Sleep of the just,' or something? Sovelet still sleeping off the wine?"

"Seems that way." Acharon wiped some egg off his lip with a napkin and then nodded in Katuva's direction. "How long have they been there?"

Benen, to his credit, took a casual just-looking-around-the-room look. "They weren't here when I came in. They were when I'd come in from the coop with the eggs. Lost a chicken last night. There's a fox somewhere. Anyway, they'd already gotten drinks and were deep in some conversation. When the volume started to rise, I'd hear a 'shush,' and then half of them would look in my direction before their conversation continued."

He took a sip of coffee. "I'll tell you this, Acharon. There's always been little cliques here. But they've been fluid. Sometimes I'd be close with someone for a decade. Then they, or I, would develop another interest that would draw us in different directions. Some years might pass, and we'd be back with a new or old interest, carrying on like old times. But this." He used his mug to indicate the direction of Katuva's group. "This is different. They've been closing themselves off from everyone else since yesterday morning. Ashe and Green had a blistering argument last night, coming off the elevator. Katuva was backed into a corner, trying to be invisible. They saw me and suddenly lost the ability to talk."

Acharon nodded. He was tearing the toast into smaller pieces, feeding them into his mouth. He paused to ask, "Do you think she's trying to recruit them?"

"Recruit them?" Benen looked confused for a ten count. Then the look on his face changed. "You mean, 'recruit,' as in suicide cult. That's what you mean?"

That's what Acharon meant. He nodded.

"Excuse me." Benen went and ordered a refill for his coffee. Acharon knew he was thinking. When he returned, he nursed a few steaming sips of coffee. Finally, "I don't know a lot about the suicide cults, the passage cults. Maybe you do? Anyway, I thought they didn't recruit or coerce. That was part of their unspoken code of honor, or whatever."

Acharon nodded. He didn't know as much as Sovelet, but that had been one point she tended to hammer home whenever they got in this discussion.

"So, maybe they are talking about suicide and the cult stuff," Benen said. "It's difficult for some people to wrap their head around the idea of voluntary mass suicide. I don't get it. I mean, I get it, but I don't 'get it.'"

"Right, I'm sort of in the same boat," Acharon said. His coffee had grown cold, but so had his appetite. "But I don't 'get it,' and I don't 'get it.' Sovelet does."

"Right, so maybe they're just curious," Benen said. He stood. Acharon realized people had entered the dining hall. "Maybe they're just trying to understand, too. And, maybe they just like her company. Excuse me."

Benen returned to the kitchen. Acharon looked at Katuva's group. He realized that the people who'd just entered the dining hall were Sovelet, Jaina, and Ashe. Behind them, Boone had also entered, but he'd stopped just inside the door, watching Katuva's group.

"Morning, dear." Acharon shifted his attention from Boone to Sovelet. She seemed in good spirits if a little red in the eyes. He gave her a hug. "How are you feeling?"

"Been better." She returned the hug. "You?"

"Good. You want me to get you something?" He indicated the serving line.

She patted his arm. "I'm okay. Besides, you have company."

Acharon didn't understand what she meant until he turned around to see Boone approaching.

"Acharon," Boone said. He'd reached the table where Acharon remained standing, his coffee cooling in the mug he still held.

"Morning, Boone." He didn't sit until Boone took a chair. "Can I do something for you?"

"You're going to move the crane today?"

"Morning, Boone." Benen appeared at the table, a steaming mug of the coffee in hand. He set it in front of Boone before hurrying back to the kitchen and the people scooping up eggs.

"That's the plan," said Acharon. He scraped the remains of his eggs with the tines of his fork. "Assuming that it has enough battery power to move. We'll take it all the way to the dock if we can. Did we need to check with you first?"

Boone laughed, waved a hand. "Don't overthink it, Acharon. You're going to need a few extra people to handle lines when the mast goes up. If we don't know what you're up to, we won't know when to help."

"Right, sorry." Acharon knew he was feeling defensive. He just wasn't sure if it wasn't uncalled for. "We can let you know when we get it to the dock."

"Sure, sure. Looking forward to it."

Boone stood, saluting with his coffee cup and left. Acharon watched Boone leave. Boone slowed as he passed Katuva's group. Katuva went silent as he passed. Several others found things on the table to look at until he passed.

"What was that about?" Sovelet was sitting down next to Acharon. She pushed one of two coffee cups she'd brought to the table in his direction.

"Boone wants to know what our plans are. So he can help."

Sovelet speared a lump of egg with her fork. "Let's hope that's what it is."

The group walking to the boom crane had grown by two with the inclusion of Thaddeus and Harriet.

Thaddeus was more of a bookworm, spending his time reading in the enclave library. Benen had said in an awed voice that Thaddeus had read every book in the library, including the dictionary.

Harriet was, according to Benen, bored, and just wanted to be included in something. As one of the first of the Last Wave born, she was nearing one hundred seventy-five years of age. Her parents had been biochemists in a pharmaceutical company. She'd received most of the same treatments the end of the Last Wave received.

Both had expressed eager interest in the voyage to France and seeing Paris. Thaddeus even pulled a pocket English-French dictionary out to show he'd been preparing. When Acharon had mentioned that everyone in the French enclave spoke English, Thaddeus responded, with all the delight of a kid getting ready to take a trip to the toy store, that he was learning French for the library in Paris.

"They said the Bibliotheque Nationale is in a wonderfully preserved state," Thaddeus said. He was pacing Acharon, slapping his translation dictionary against the palm of his left hand. "And that it was in a remarkably preserved state. Most of the twenty million books are still there. Twenty million!"

"That'll keep you busy," Acharon said. Someone nudged his other shoulder. He looked to see Jaina pointing to Sovelet, who was mouthing the words, be nice, at him. Acharon made an expression of annoyance. He thought that was what he was doing.

Before Acharon could retort, Benen pushed forward, pointing.

"The charge cable, look!" He broke into a trot that Acharon felt obliged to reproduce.

The rest of the group hurried, but Benen and Acharon reached the cable ahead of the rest. The cable was actually a series of cables. They'd been scavenged by the enclave when they first located the boom crane. Even though a loose knot had been tied with the cables to keep them from accidentally coming unplugged, that was precisely what happened.

"How?" Benen asked. "Did a deer trip over it?"

"Unlikely," Acharon said.

"So sabotage, then," said Benen.

Acharon turned to the approaching group. "Sovie, can you check the charge on the batteries?"

Sovelet and Jaina turned away from the rest of the group, hurrying to the crane.

"It came unplugged?" Thaddeus asked.

"Not without help," Benen said. He was looking around as if he might see the culprit lurking nearby.

"But you can't know that for sure," said Tadala. "If the plugs fit together loosely, they could have slipped apart by even the lightest touch."

"Lightest touch, Tadala?"

"Yes, Benen, a pig nosing along could have pushed just enough to knock it loose."

"Whose side are you on?"

"Tadala is just suggesting a possibility," Aiman said. "We shouldn't always assume the worst."

"I heard someone in the elevator early this morning," Harriet said. "It was just after dawn. I was doing my yoga when I heard it come up and then go back down."

"Hang on," Acharon said. He'd been listening to the conversation, but he'd been watching Sovelet and Jaina at the cab of the crane. They had just come back around. "How's it look?"

"Ninety percent," Sovelet said.

"Then we're good," Acharon said. "Benen, could you and Tadala roll up the cables and bring them, just in case?"

"How did we get such a full charge?" asked Benen. He started untying the unplugged cables.

"The charging was done before dawn," Acharon said. "Whoever did this just didn't know. Even if they had, I'd bet Sovelet exaggerated on the charge time. Just to be on the safe side. Now, let's see if we can get this thing rolling."

Rolling had been a concern. Acharon had worried about it off and on through the night and morning. The tires had weathered the century plus they'd been on the crane. Someone had the foresight to raise it up on its jacks before walking away for the last time. But while it might take rubber tires thousands of years to break down completely, they could still dry out and fall apart long before.

Acharon decided that they would take their time even though the crane was capable of freeway speeds. There was no reason to encourage the tires to fall apart any faster than necessary. Once they knew they had enough power and it was going to hold, Acharon set Benen in the driver's seat.

"It's an easy drive," he said.

Benen smiled. "I got it this far."

"Sorry, Benen." Acharon smiled a further apology. "I'm glad, then, that you're the one at the wheel. No donuts."

"No donuts."

"See you on the dock, then." Acharon shut the door.

"We're going to work on the boat?" Harriet asked.

"Yes," Acharon said. He started walking. Everyone else trailed after him and Harriet. "At the least, we can get the mast up. Assuming we have everything."

"We have everything," Aiman said. "We have those cables to keep the mast up."

"The stays," Thaddeus said. "And spreaders, and sheets, and halyards. I think. I've only read about them."

Acharon gave Thaddeus and comradely pat on the shoulder. "That about covers it."

Achron found Thaddeus's grin to be contagious. He knew that Thaddeus was reacting to having his knowledge confirmed. For Acharon, it felt more like an acknowledgment that this was a thing that was going to happen.

They walked faster than Benen drove the boom crane, arriving at the dock with enough time to clear away the weeds from around the mast. They worked in pairs to attach the stays and then as a group to muscle the boom into place.

Acharon noticed that the sails weren't in sight. No crates or containers marked with the appropriate stencils. Everyone seemed to be in good spirits, and he didn't want to derail that. He could always do that later.

"Should someone go for lunch?" Acharon asked.

"I'm not sure anyone wants to miss the raising of the mast," Thaddeus said.

Acharon could see them all looking at each other before their eyes settled on him. "We'll need all hands on deck when the mast goes up. The most we'll be able to do is to get the boom crane into position and hook its cable to the top of the mast."

When no one said anything, Sovelet started moving. "I'll go."

"I'll help," Jaina said. She joined Sovelet. "If Sovie's going, Acharon wouldn't dare put that mast up without her."

Jaina's comment raised a good laugh from the group. Benen gave Sovelet the shotgun he'd been carrying. That still left the shotguns Acharon and Aiman had in their possession. Tadala decided at the last minute to join Sovelet and Jaina. The three hurried off, waving to Benen in the boom crane.

Benen had finally arrived. The front of the boom crane was limping on a flat tire that was slowly shredding itself as the vehicle continued to move. As it took a wide turn onto the dock, there was a dull popping noise, and the vehicle shuddered.

"Sounds like another tire," Aiman said.

"We can run it on rims, now, if we have to," said Acharon.

However, the rest of the tires remained intact and inflated as Benen brought it down the dock, parallel to the boat.

With Harriet and Thaddeus supervising, Acharon, Benen, and Aiman positioned the stabilizers. They would keep the vehicle from tipping over while the boom moved, doing its job. The stabilizers made the entire vehicle look like some giant metal bug with its four legs reaching out to either side of the body, ready to take flight or scurry for cover.

When the outriggers had settled, and the crane leveled, Acharon jumped into the operator's cab on the top, near the counterweight. The crane groaned disagreeably with a lack of use. Slowly, though, Acharon convinced the telescoping boom to extend and then swing out, bringing the hoist mechanism over the masthead.

He lowered the hoist, allowing Aiman and Benen to run a loop of thick rope just under where the shrouds and stays were connected to the mast.

Acharon jumped out to inspect their work.

"Looks great."

"Just in time," Harriet said. "The ladies are back with lunch."

Acharon turned. It wasn't Sovelet and the other two women. "Katuva, Green, afternoon. Is that Sena with you, too?"

"Yes, I am," Sena said. "This is Carwyn. Not sure if you got the official introduction."

"Carwyn," said Acharon. He hadn't been introduced, but he'd seen Carwyn huddled in the same group as Green and Katuva. "Come to help?"

"I was told you had enough help already," Green said. "We just wanted to see how things were going. Having trouble with the mast?"

"Nope, mast looks great," Benen said. "Just waiting for lunch. You didn't happen to see Jaina? She was with Sovelet."

At the mention of Sovelet's name, Acharon noticed Katuva's head come up. After a quick look around, she returned to examining the ground a couple meters ahead of her feet.

"Haven't seen them," Sena said. "I thought they were out here with you."

"They were," Acharon said. He was wondering if Boone had sent Green and the others to check on Acharon's activities, but he kept that thought to himself. Out loud, he added, "They've gone back to the enclave to pick up some lunch."

"And now they're back," Benen said.

Benen was looking past Green. Acharon followed and saw Sovelet, Jaina, and Tadala, each with a plastic basket in their arms. Sovelet had her shotgun hanging by its gun strap over her shoulders. He'd have to remember to say something about that later.

Green turned and looked, too. His pleasant demeanor seemed to fade with the sight of Sovelet and the other women. He turned back, "Well, we don't want to get in your way. We just thought we'd come out and say hello. So, 'hello.'"

His hand was firm on Katuva's, and he almost knocked her over as he started to walk away. Sena was caught off guard and jogged to catch up.

"Hi, Katuva," Sovelet said as the two groups passed.

Acharon didn't hear Katuva's response, but he did see Sovelet's face go from cheerful to concerned. Katuva was older than he and Sovelet. She could make her own choices when it came to what company to keep. He just wished the others would think twice about keeping her close.

Benen and Aiman helped with the baskets. The women had put together a small but pleasurable picnic with vegetables from the gardens and hot pasta dishes from the automated kitchen. Everyone dished out what they liked and then sat on one of the old benches along the pier, looking out across the Hudson to New Jersey.

Some of them were engaged in little conversations that Acharon wasn't lending much attention to. He was cataloging items they would need for the sailboat before they could set sail. Supposedly it had almost everything. So it was just a matter of filling in the gaps.

However, Acharon couldn't shake the worry that if someone was willing to burn the last ship, what else might they have sabotaged.

19

If Acharon hadn't stood, the rest of the group on the end of the pier might have sat there until the setting sun pushed their shadows far across the Hudson. There was an initial reluctance to move. They might have won the stubborn contests, but Sovelet followed Acharon to his feet. The rest gave in good-naturedly, packing up the leftovers and trash.

Raising the mast went easier than even Acharon could hope. With one person on each shroud and stay, they had the mast in its collar on the first try. Benen and Acharon started bolting the mast to the tabernacle.

"Ow!" Benen dropped his ratchet and cradled his right hand in his left. "Caught my knuckles."

Acharon took Benen's hand. He'd smacked it against the boat deck, scraping the skin off of two knuckles. "Do we have gloves anywhere?"

"I can look down below," Harriet said. "If someone can tell me where to look."

"I'll be fine," Benen said. He pulled his hand away, flexing and turning it front and back. "It's just a couple scratches."

"That's fine." Acharon picked up the ratchet and handed it back to Benen. "But when we get back to the enclave, you get checked out in the medi-pod."

"Right. Promise." Benen started again at tightening a bolt. On the second pull, it slipped again. His knuckles banged the deck once more. "Dang it!"

"Benen?" Sovelet started back to the mast.

Benen jumped to his feet, shoving his hand under his other arm. He hissed when he pressed it tight and then said, "I'm fine. I'm fine. I'm just going to walk this off."

Sovelet smiled with a small shake of her head and returned to the forestay she'd been tightening. Acharon watched her bend back to work and then turned to follow Benen's progress to the pier only to see him slip as the boat moved under him. He hit the deck with his hip and shoulder.

"I'm all right," said Benen. He climbed to his feet, grumbling. It was clear to Acharon that Benen's pride had taken the most abuse.

"Benen," Acharon said. "One hand for you, one hand for the boat."

"I know, I know." Benen limped down the pier.

Acharon went back to tightening the bolts at the base of the mast.

"How's Benen?"

Acharon looked up at Sovelet, after tightening down the last bolt. "I'm not sure if he's clumsy or just eager to get the boat done. He's fine. Though I'm not sure if we should let him use a knife once we're under sail."

"He'll settle down," Sovelet said. She handed Acharon a bottle of water, from which he took a long drink. "I think the people who want to go are just eager to make it happen."

"And concerned that someone might try and stop them." Acharon stood, stretching his back. "I was under the impression everyone was eager to head to Paris."

"That makes two of us, dear. Now come and check my work on the forestay."

Sovelet's tensioning of the forestay needed only the most minor of adjustments. He continued around to the port shrouds and the aftstay when Benen returned.

"Hey, Acharon." He waved at Acharon, and then conspicuously pointed to the land end of the pier. "Company."

Acharon crossed the boat to reach the pier. He looked toward 12th Ave and saw a single person coming along the pier. Boone.

"Right," said Acharon. "I'll talk to him."

He stepped onto the pier and began walking in Boone's direction. It wasn't lost on him that Green had been here first, and now Boone was making his appearance.

Boone pointed at the mast behind Acharon. "I see you got it up."

"Went up pretty easily." He turned so that he could see the sailboat and Boone. "Would have let you know, personally, but I figured you'd have heard from Green."

"I did."

"And as we had enough people to do the job, I figured why wait?"

"You figured a lot." Boone paused. Acharon waited to hear where the conversation was going. "Did you figure out if the mast will be okay over the winter? Maybe it would have been better to leave it down until next summer?"

That confused Acharon. "Next summer. Are you suggesting we should stay here another year?"

"What's a year?" Boone laughed. It lacked energy in Acharon's opinion. "We've been working on the whole boat thing for a decade. One more year wouldn't hurt."

"Or not even go at all." Acharon meant it facetiously.

"It's something to consider. There are other options."

Acharon pointed at the people on the sailboat. "Those people seem eager to go. I'd assumed this was the general consensus."

"Used to be," said Boone. "Used to be. But that's really a moot point. Without an engine, you won't be able to get the boat out of Manhattan."

"There's no engine?" Acharon was confused. "I thought there was an engine, and that was how you got it here from New Jersey."

"Barely got it here." Boone rolled his eyes. "The amount of ozone you could smell and heat and noise. I think everyone's been afraid to test it since then. Kind of the Schrodinger's cat conundrum. People could keep believing this was possible as long as they thought the engine would work and get them out to the ocean."

The problem with this news, as Acharon considered it, was that it could be absolutely true or complete fiction meant to dissuade people from trying. It was the kind of thing Thyme would have done back in

San Francisco as he consolidated his control over the enclave. Though Thyme was less subtle.

"I'm sorry, Boone, but I was under the impression that you were on board with this idea, too."

"Who doesn't get enthusiastic about a new idea after decades of just hanging around? Everyone was excited. It gave everyone something to talk about for months. Perhaps if there'd been a boat to jump into at that moment and sail to France, everyone would have done it. But with time comes reflection."

"And the second boat?" asked Acharon?

"There are still some that like to keep busy with their idea." He pointed to where Benen was gingerly stepping aboard the sailboat. Acharon was glad to see him holding onto the shrouds for support. "He's built a brewery, a hen house, and a rooftop garden. People are just finding ways to keep their minds busy. Even if it's a daydream."

Benen's work didn't seem like daydreaming to Acharon. It seemed like a person putting thought to action. A maker and a doer.

"And what if we get this to work? The sailboat. And we ca get it out of here and to sea? What then?"

For an answer, Boone gave Acharon's shoulder a friendly squeeze. "I guess we'll talk about that if it happens. Anyway, have fun."

Boone waved goodbye to anyone on the ship looking in his and Acharon's direction before turning and walking back toward the city. He left behind some whiffs of uncertainty that disturbed Acharon. His mind inhaled the idea that maybe all of this with the boat and going to Paris might just be a silly fantasy.

Acharon didn't like that idea and shook it out of his head. Doubt like that was poisonous and slowed a person's actions. No, Acharon thought, we can do this. He hurried back to the boat.

"Benen, what do you know about the engine?" Acharon had seen it, recognized the brand and style. They weren't common and unlikely to be lying around in a Last Wave warehouse waiting to be plucked.

Benen turned, using the mast for support. "What do you mean? It's electric. Pulls energy from a battery bank, which is charged by the solar panels built into the deck and sails."

"Good, but does it work?"

The light came on in Benen's expression. "Right. That. It was a little hesitant when we used it. A little grinding noise that came and went. Why? What did Boone tell you?"

Using a shroud for his own handhold, Acharon stepped onto the boat and then down to the covered center cockpit. "He made it sound worse than you did. I'm going to go take a look. Stay here in case I need help."

Acharon took the stairs at the hatch down into the boat's cabin. The cockpit sat right above the engine room. To the port side were storage and the navigation room. The starboard side was the galley. To aft were two bunk rooms, a small sitting area, and the hatch to the engine room.

The first time he'd seen it, he'd felt pretty confident that this wasn't the original engine. The boat was young enough that it likely always had an electrical one. But looking at the fittings and brackets, there'd been modifications made to accommodate an engine substantially larger than the room was designed for.

There was just enough room to squeeze past the bulk of the engine. On the forward side of the engine, Acharon unlatched the access panel. It was one of four that allowed for maintenance and repair of the engine.

Acharon didn't swear much or often. But for several seconds, he cussed up a small storm. The bushings were not only fried, but they'd also been overheated. They were now permanently damaged.

The other three access panels only made the situation worse. The engine wasn't going to turn no matter how much energy they threw at it. No one had sabotaged it, but whoever installed the engine should have been keelhauled.

By habit, as he thought, he reset the access panels. There was a time when ships didn't have engines. Ships larger than this one. They'd had square sails and multiple masts. They'd used currents and winds not only to cross the oceans but to get in and out of harbors.

Acharon had always had the use of a motor to assist with docking and mooring. He could do this.

His pep talk was disrupted by a loud boom as something struck the boat's deck. The noise was followed by a cry of pain.

"Benen?" Acharon squeezed back around the engine that was good for nothing more than ballast and hurried topside.

He found everyone who'd been working on the boat gathered in the cockpit. As a testament to the size of the cockpit, there was still plenty of room in the space. Everyone was clumped together on the aft end of the u-shaped bench. Acharon quickly recognized everyone but didn't see Benen.

"Acharon." Sovelet's head appeared above the group. "It's Benen. He's hurt."

Acharon joined the group and found Benen in the middle, lying prone on the bench. His shirt was off, wrapped around his right forearm. His stomach and the front of his pants were soaked in blood. Rivulets of it ran down to his elbow, slowly dripping on the cockpit floor.

"What happened?"

"I forgot one hand for the boat." Benen grimaced more than smiled at his joke.

"He cut his arm," Aiman said. "It's bad."

"He slipped," said Harriet. "I saw him. Tumbled in here."

Acharon looked around and noticed the pole for the cockpit table. There wasn't any blood there, but just past it, the blood trail started.

"Sorry, Acharon."

"No need, Benen."

Tadala, who was cradling Benen's head, said, "He needs to go to the medi-pod."

Everyone agreed, including Acharon.

"I'll take him," Acharon said. He felt responsible for Benen as he had pushed Benen into helping him. Benen might disagree, but Acharon felt that way, and that was enough. "You all can finish up with stays?"

"We'll be fine," Sovelet said. "Everyone? Let's get him up and on the pier."

"This time, Benen," said Acharon. He guided been across the deck. "Don't worry about a hand for the boat."

"Thanks," Benen said.

The others hoisted him onto his feet and helped him onto the boat deck and then across to the pier.

"We'll take care of the blood, too," Jaina said. She'd paused on the boat deck next to Acharon. She put a hand on his shoulder. "He'll be okay."

"Right." Acharon stepped onto the pier. Benen was waiting, standing on his own feet, Aiman and Thaddeus stood next to him, their hands holding onto his upper arms. "Can you walk, Benen? Or should I find a car?"

"There's no car around here. We've used them all up." He pulled himself free of the other two men and stepped toward Acharon. "I can walk."

"You're sure?" When Benen nodded emphatically, Acharon looked around and asked, "Where's Benen's shotgun?"

It took a couple seconds to find it. He'd left it on the benches they'd used during their lunch. Everyone gave Benen a hug. Acharon got a couple, too. They waved goodbye one last time and then started the walk back to the enclave.

The walk was awkward for Acharon. The few other times he'd walked with Benen, Benen had kept up a primarily one-sided conversation. Now it was Acharon's turn. He found he was terrible at it.

Fortunately, Benen seemed to be in too much pain to notice Acharon's awkward attempts at conversation. By the time they crossed 8th Ave on 57th Street, Acharon had stopped talking. By the time they turned on 8th, Acharon had slipped a hand under Benen's shoulder.

"I'm fine, really," Benen said after he stumbled on a mossy hump on the sidewalk.

"I know you are," said Acharon. He caught Benen on another stumble. "This just makes me feel useful."

"If I didn't know how good the medi-pods were, I might be inclined to lay down and take myself a nap."

"Keep walking, Benen, I'm not carrying you."

"It's just another block." They'd already turned onto 56th.

The banter died as quickly as it rose. At the steps to the enclave, Benen was taking full advantage of Acharon's assistance.

There was no one in the lobby as they crossed to the elevator. The elevator doors opened on an empty box. They turned together as Acharon knuckled the second-floor button. As the doors slid closed, Acharon noticed the dribbling trail of blood that marked their passage through the lobby.

Acharon looked down and saw that Benen's side was striped with blood drops. "Almost there," he said. "Hang in there."

Benen cleared his throat and said, "That for me? Or is that for you?"

"Both of us."

The elevator dinged, the doors slid open. Acharon started forward with more urgency than he'd bothered with before. Out of the elevator, Acharon had to look around for the medi-fac. He hadn't received a tour of the enclave other than the gardens on the roofs. The only reason he knew that medical was on this floor was the red cross in a white circle next to the floor button in the elevator.

Just as he saw it, Benen said, "It's over there on the right." Perhaps he should have asked Benen sooner. It didn't matter now. He guided Benen towards the medi-fac door.

Like most enclave medi-facs, there was a variety of medi-pods for increased requirements. Any of them could give a basic physical and print out medicines from aspirin to cancer treatments. Others could do sutures, set bones, treat burns. The big ones could do what they'd done for Acharon, replace a penknife-punctured eye, or print new lungs as had been done for Sovelet.

Benen only needed a half-dozen sutures and a blood treatment. Hopefully, that was all.

Acharon helped Benen to the third medi-pod in the room. He leaned Benen against the pod's transparent, plastic wall and tapped the data screen to wake it. When the screen came to life, he typed in Benen's name and got lucky. It recognized the name, meaning that Acharon wouldn't have to pester Benen for more information.

The lights in the medi-pod came on. The door glided open.

"Here we go," Acharon said to Benen.

It took a few minutes, but Acharon finally had Benen on the table. He stepped out of the pod and tapped the medical response button that told the machine to go to work. The door shut, and the clear plastic went opaque on the bottom two-thirds. Acharon could see the mechanical arms reaching out to tend Benen. Acharon recognized the needle arm that would deliver an effective pain killer. He'd been glad to see that a couple times when he was the patient in the medi-pod.

Now was the rough part. Although the medi-pods had decades of successful development, even the best tech could glitch. Or someone could steal the bio-cartridges. But even when running correctly, it still required time. Which meant Acharon would have to wait.

There was a couch by the door. Maybe he could take a little nap. He sat down and then stood right back up. He'd heard a noise. It wasn't the hum of the medi-pod looking after Benen. It was the sound of another human. A grunt, like someone would make when shifting from one uncomfortable position to another.

"Hello?"

When no one answered, Acharon started down the aisle between the two rows of pods. Behind the second one on the right, he found a woman sitting on the floor.

"Hi," Acharon said. "It's Grace, yes? You're Grace?"

"Yes. Help me up, please?"

Acharon held out a hand and pulled Grace to her feet. "Were you trying to get a pod to look at your knee?"

"No. Excuse me." She slipped past Acharon and started for the door.

Something on the ground caught Acharon's eye. He looked to see several printed pill packets on the ground. "Hang on, Grace." Acharon picked the packets up. He could feel a single round pill in each one. "Did you drop these?"

When Grace looked at Acharon's hand, her eyes went wide. She hurried back to Acharon and snatched the packets, shoving them into her pocket.

"Yes, thank you." She turned and started toward the door again.

Acharon followed. "Everything okay, Grace?"

Grace turned at the door, her hand on the knob. "Yes. It's fine. I have-- I'm sick. Cancer. Listen, Acharon, my husband, Jamon. He doesn't know. I don't want him to know. He'll just worry. So please, don't say anything. Okay? Thanks."

Her words had come in a staccato rush. Acharon hadn't even responded before she was out of the medi-fac, the door clicking shut in her wake.

"That was peculiar," Acharon said to Benen, even though he knew Benen couldn't hear or respond.

Acharon took a seat on the couch. When he'd seen Grace on the ground, she'd been rubbing one knee. It reminded him of times when he was squatting to fix something or dig something. His knee would get stiff from the position, and he would rub it for a few moments after slowly standing up.

Had Grace actually been hiding? Was she that concerned about being seen in the medi-fac? That was odd. The medi-pods had been effective in keeping them all alive this long.

And what about those pills she'd taken back so quickly? Acharon had known many people over the near century and a half he'd been alive. Some of them had developed cancer. Unlike the olden days of chemotherapy and radiation, pills with targeted treatments had been designed. He'd seen those pills. Grace's pills weren't for cancer.

More lies. Acharon closed his eyes and tried to think of something pleasant, like sailing away from this place and never coming back.

20

"Hey, Acharon."

Achron pulled himself from sleep. He felt momentarily disoriented. He'd fallen asleep when Sovelet had gone into the medi-pod to fix her hand. And while he knew this wasn't that moment, he still had to shake off the feeling.

"Benen. How you feeling?"

Benen flashed his forearm. The synthetic skin patch stretched from wrist to elbow. Barely visible under the patch, the perfectly spaced stitches were barely visible. Over time, as the wound healed, the stitches would dissolve. Then the synthetic skin would do the same.

"I'm feeling good," Benen said. "But I could probably use a shower and some new clothes. Pity, this. I've had that shirt for thirty years. One of my favorites."

"Could probably find another one just like it," said Acharon. "If we checked through the warehouses."

"Wouldn't be the same. I got a couple other shirts that are almost as good." He started toward the door, stopping when he had his hand on the knob. "You staying here?"

Acharon started. "Me? No. No, I'm up." He stood and followed Benen out the door

They rode in silence up to the sixth floor.

"See you in the dining room," said Benen. He stepped out of the elevator and turned down the hall. Acharon watched after him until the doors shut and the elevator began climbing to the tenth floor.

As Acharon exited the elevator, he noticed Green coming out of Katuva's apartments. Acharon nodded and turned in the other direction toward his.

"Acharon, wait."

Acharon waited as Green quickstepped his way to Acharon. The usual smile covered his mouth. "Have you seen Katuva?"

"She's not in her apartment?" That seemed odd to Acharon as Green had just been in there.

Green looked back the way he'd come as if Katuva was going to appear at her apartment door. "No, she wasn't in. Do you know where she is?"

What makes him think I would know, Acharon thought. Out loud, he said, "I haven't seen her since the pier. And she was with you."

"Right. Right." Green looked nervous in Acharon's opinion. "Maybe she's visiting with Sena. I'll check with Sena." Green stepped over to the stairwell door. "Thanks."

"You're welcome?" Acharon said as the stairwell door swung shut. To himself, he added, "Too many secrets."

He continued to his and Sovelet's apartment uninterrupted. As he opened the door, he thought he heard someone sobbing. "Sovie?"

"Living room."

Acharon shut the door, engaging the deadbolt, and went to find Sovelet in the living room. She was not alone. She was not the one doing the crying.

"Everything okay?"

Sovelet sat on the edge of the couch seat, one hand rubbing back and forth across Katuva's shoulders. As she continued the sympathetic rub, Sovelet looked at Acharon and shook her head. "I don't know."

"Okay," Acharon said. He was at a loss for what to do. If it was Sovelet, she would tell him the problem, and he would do his damnedest to fix it. "Green was asking after Katuva."

Katuva sat up straight, causing Sovelet to sit back, pulling slightly away. Katuva's voice was wet with tears. "You didn't tell him I was here?"

"How could I?" Acharon held his hands out, elbows bent. "I didn't even know you were here. He went to ask Sena."

"Thank you," said Katuva. She wiped at her face and nose with the sleeve of the oversized sweater she was wearing. "I just needed a little time to myself."

"You should try locking the door to your apartments," Acharon said. He earned a scowl from Sovelet for his comment. In his defense, he added, "I saw Green coming out of your place."

"I know," Katuva said. She pulled a handkerchief from a pocket of the sweater and took a second to clear her nose. She folded it and slipped it away, saying, "Sorry."

"You don't have to be sorry, dear," Sovelet said. "But why were you crying?" She turned to Acharon. "I'd only just gotten here. The boat looks great, by the way."

Katuva's focus shifted from Sovelet to Acharon and back to Sovelet. "I can't. I shouldn't talk about it. I'm sorry."

She stood, and Sovelet followed her to her feet.

"I need to get cleaned up," said Katuva. "I'm sorry for bothering you."

"You aren't bothering us," Sovelet said. "You know you can stay here."

"I know." Katuva moved around the coffee table. "But then they'd just come here looking for me. I'll be okay. I just needed some time to myself."

"To cry?"

"Acharon!"

Acharon shrugged. Katuva seemed to be crying a lot and doing it in their apartment.

"I know." Katuva moved to the hallway, her hand resting on the end of the wall. "I'm sorry about everything. It's not like it was back at home. In the town."

"Hold on," Acharon said. He went to the kitchen and returned with a key. He held it out to Katuva. "In case you need to hide out again."

Katuva looked to Sovelet, who nodded.

"Thank you." Katuva took the key and walked to the door. Acharon and Sovelet followed halfway and waited while Katuva unbolted the door and opened it. She turned and looked at them for a few silent heartbeats before saying, "You should have left me there."

The door closed before Sovelet could get her own words out. "What did she mean?" she asked Acharon instead.

"Like I would know." He went back to the kitchen and closed the drawer where he'd pulled the extra key from.

Sovelet followed him. "This place is fractured."

"I thought we already agreed on that?" Acharon was pouring water from a bottle into a glass. "That and the basket of secrets that everyone keeps moving around."

He took an ice tray and added ice to his water. The systems in place for the Last Wavers had held out longer than intended, but not as long as the last people who needed them. Tap water wasn't safe to drink unless boiled and filtered. He'd learned from Benen that they'd rigged several filtration systems for the enclave over the last couple of decades. None of them fed into the taps.

"Do you have any ideas?" asked Sovelet.

"I was going to say suicide," said Acharon. "But if that were the case, why would Katuva be so sad? That's exactly what she wanted. Water?"

"I don't think that's it," Sovelet said. She took a sip of water and handed it back to Acharon. "And I have my doubts about Katuva wanting to die."

"She asked us to do it with her!" Water sloshed as Acharon set the glass onto the counter too hard. "She held out the pills right there at the table."

"She also didn't look too upset when you vociferously denounced the idea."

"I wouldn't know," Acharon said. "I wasn't exactly focused on her emotions."

"You weren't, that's true. But there's more to Katuva's story than she'd told us. Maybe more than she knows. Anyway. Benen. How's he doing?"

"He's good." Acharon picked up the glass and licked the water off the outside. "Medi-pod fixed him up just fine."

"Good." Sovelet walked back to the living room. Acharon followed.

"He said he'll miss his favorite shirt."

"Hm." Sovelet started straightening the couch. "That's too bad."

Acharon read the signs and knew Sovelet didn't want to talk right this moment. Likely, she wanted to think, to mull over Katuva and the people who glommed onto her.

"Well, I'm going to get cleaned up."

"Uh, huh," Sovelet said.

Acharon knew she was already deep in thought. He left her and went to the bedroom to change and clean up. Perhaps when she was done with the problem of Katuva, they could talk about the boat. He still had to figure a way to get it away from the dock and out of the harbor.

Sovelet was more herself by the time they left the apartment. She updated Acharon on the mast and stays as they rode the elevator down to the lobby. She even managed to keep a positive conversation going about the boat and Benen's situation as they entered the dining room to see Katuva already surrounded by a table of people.

Katuva smiled briefly as she looked in their direction. But then, Green put his hand on hers, and she quickly lost the shine in her expression.

Benen, much to Acharon's surprise, was already at the kitchen, tossing up a large metal bowl full of green lettuce, bright shavings of carrots, and half-moons of cherry tomatoes. It would make an excellent addition to the auto-kitchen's spaghetti and garlic bread.

He waved to Benen when he caught his eye and got a chin-raised greeting with an infectious grin in return.

"Acharon. Sovelet. Over here."

Acharon turned his attention and found Jaina waving at them. She was sitting with everyone who'd been with them at the pier. They were seated at a table near the kitchen but on the opposite side of the room from Katuva's gathering.

"Why are you sitting way over here?" Sovelet asked. She looked in Katuva's direction to add meaning.

"We were here first," Tadala said. "Green and Grace came in after us and barely waved."

"Did they even bother?" asked Thaddeus. He had a book open on the table but looked up during the conversation. "It seemed to me they turned away before anyone here could acknowledge their presence. But I was reading Shakespeare's Othello. Quite riveting."

"I'd like to think they waved," said Tadala. She eyed Thaddeus, waiting for a retort, but he didn't seem to notice as his eyes scanned the words in his book.

"Hey, folks." Benen put the bowl of freshly tossed salad in the middle of the table. "Enjoy. I have to make another bowl for table one hundred."

Acharon didn't think there were a hundred tables in the room, but the meaning was clear. He turned to Sovelet. "Spaghetti?"

"Yes, please." She was already dishing up salad as she sat.

At the food line, Acharon found Benen once again tossing a big bowl of salad, dribbling in vinegar and oil as he went along.

"You sure you weren't a chef in another life?"

Benen chuckled. "I couldn't boil water without burning it. But that was over a hundred years ago." He paused in action and words. Then, "Seems strange, doesn't it. Our parents would have said, twenty, maybe thirty years ago. They marked their life's progress in decades. Look at us, marking life in centuries."

Acharon hadn't thought a lot about his family. His parents had died when he was just turning fifty. His older siblings - there had been two - died when he was in his eighties. They'd almost made it to a century. The people he thought of tended to be the ones most recently in contact with. That went back to the people of the San Francisco enclave. Though, if pressed, he might have a hard time naming most of them.

"I don't know if it's strange," he said. "It's the only life I know."

"Good point," said Benen. He was adding more carrot shavings and stopped. He pointed with his chin. "Oh, this'll get interesting."

A lone figure had entered the dining room. He looked around, stopping when he reached Katuva's group.

"Who is that?"

"Grace's husband, Jamon," Benen said. "I don't think he likes it that Grace is mingling with that group."

"Does Jamon want to go to France?"

"Yeah, he does." Benen began tossing the salad again. "He thinks the adventure would give Grace more to look forward to."

Acharon looked back at Benen. "So, he does know she has cancer?"

"Has?" Benen shook his head and set the bowl on the counter. "She had cancer. About twenty years ago. Jamon pushed her to take the treatments. She's always seemed a little less of herself since then. She used to be an amazing ballroom dancer. Be right back."

Benen took the salad bowl and started toward Katuva's table. Jamon had also approached the table. Acharon didn't hear him say anything, but he recognized Grace when she stood up.

Grace left the table and went to Jamon. Everyone at Katuva's table looked like they were trying not to watch. Rather than sit, Jamon and Grace stood in the middle of the dining room, having a whisper-quiet argument. Jamon appeared to have lost the argument because moments after coming over to him, Grace turned and rejoined Katuva's table. Jamon started a slow walk to the kitchen area.

Benen had slowed his approach when Grace moved. Upon her return, he set the bowl down and quickly retreated.

"Evening," Acharon said.

"Yeah." Jamon picked up a plate and spooned a small pile of spaghetti on his plate.

Benen had returned and pulled a third bowl of tossed salad out of a small fridge. He used tongs and laid a small pile on Jamon's plate.

"More?" Benen asked.

Jamon shook his head and turned away. For a moment, it looked like he was going to join the table with Jaina and Sovelet and the others. Instead, he nodded to them and continued by, taking a table equidistant from both groups.

Acharon looked to Benen. "Awkward?"

"Terribly," said Benen. He pointed with his chin in the direction over Acharon's shoulder. "And it just keeps getting better."

Turning again, Acharon saw Boone enter the room. Like Jamon, he stopped and appeared to be surveying the space. He nodded in Acharon and Benen's direction before turning to walk to Katuva's table.

"I'm going to sit before Sovelet's spaghetti gets cold," Acharon said.

"Later."

Acharon returned to the table, setting a plate before Sovelet. She had seated herself between Jaina and Harriet. He took a seat that gave him the worst view of the room, but he figured that might not be such a bad thing.

"How's the salad?"

"Amazing," Sovelet said. "Reminds me of home."

Acharon harrumphed. "It's the only thing that does."

"Wait," Aiman said. "I thought you liked sailboats, too."

A smile caught the side of Acharon's mouth. "Good point, Aiman. Anyone want to talk about what to do tomorrow on the boat? If someone knows where the sails are, maybe we could get them on and wired."

"Tomorrow might not be a good day."

Everyone at the table turned in the direction of Boone, who was approaching the table with his plate.

"What's wrong with tomorrow?" Acharon asked.

"Storm's coming through," said Boone. Jaina had pulled out the chair next to her, but Boone shook his head. "Should hit around midnight. May go through the day."

"Is it a bad storm?" Harriet asked.

"Possibly," Sovelet said. Acharon looked at her, surprised he hadn't expected her to know, too. "The models are old. We've lost a few satellites. But it could be a drizzle, or it could be a full-on downpour with some lightning thrown in for fun."

"Either way," Boone said, "not exactly the safest weather for raising sails. Yes?" No one answered as Boone scanned the people around the table, stopping at Acharon. He added, "Wouldn't want anyone to wind up like Benen. Or worse. So relax. Take a day off."

Boone turned and walked into the small sea of empty tables. He paused to say something to Jamon that Acharon couldn't hear before leaving the dining room with his plate in hand.

"I'm not in trouble, am I?" Benen had appeared at the table, causing Jaina and Harriet to yelp in surprise. "Sorry. I heard my name. Just wanted to make sure I wasn't singled out."

"Boone said not to let you die," said Aiman. "At least not until the next batch of ale is done."

"Oh, okay. Good to know."

"That's not what he really said," said Sovelet.

"That's good to know, too," Benen said. "Anyone want cake? We've chocolate?"

The cake was from the auto-kitchen. As everyone but Acharon and Sovelet hadn't had an actual homemade cake in decades, they were all pleased with how it came out. While the cake lacked the moistness of Katuva's, he felt more comfortable eating it. He grimaced at the thought of how he'd acted in Katuva's home when she'd told him she was part of a suicide cult. Maybe he'd overreacted, but he'd also never been face-to-face with someone so willing to take their own life. Even Sovelet would have let her disease progress naturally until the pain was unbearable.

"You going to finish that?" Sovelet was tapping Acharon's plate with her fork.

Acharon looked at his plate, then at Sovelet. She was smiling, and he was sure she knew he'd been thinking deeply. He pushed the plate in her direction, letting her have the last few bites.

Benen returned to the table, a cup of hot tea cupped in his hands. He'd been running back and forth, taking plates to the other group and then out to Jamon. Several times Acharon rose from his chair with the intent of helping, only to have Benen shoo him back to the table. Now, though, he was done and joined them at the table.

The conversations were mostly superficial. Stories about people's youth, favorite experiences. After a time, they were joined by three other people, Jahzara, Marianne, and Dorothy, who'd been absent for most of the meal but made sure to show up for cake.

After a time, people began to leave. They left in groups or alone. Acharon wanted to stay and help Benen, but Benen insisted he liked the time alone.

Together, Acharon and Sovelet returned to their room. They paused long enough to see the light under Katuva's door and the flickering shadows of more than one person present.

In their own apartments, Acharon paused to look out into the darkness of the city. The sky was blanketed by thick clouds. Raindrops began to tap against the windows. The storm had come.

21

When Acharon woke the next morning, he wasn't quite sure if he hadn't woken in the middle of the night instead. The sky was still dark. Rain raced itself down the windows in wide rivulets. Today was definitely not the day for working on the boat's sails.

Sovelet was still asleep. Acharon took the time to heat a pot of water for instant coffee. Someone had said in some passing conversation that Paris still had beans in hermetically sealed cans. A real espresso at a cafe along the Seine sounded nice. Especially if the skies were clear.

Of course, they had to get there first. And Acharon was beginning to wonder if going was to be a battle of wills. He also wondered if some were going to elect to stay behind. There certainly seemed to be a considerable lack of will to get involved.

Clearly, there were two camps. The dividing line wasn't vague, though there did seem to be at least two people standing outside of them.

Movement in the bedroom attracted Acharon's attention. A cough and the ruffle of sheets. He poured a little hot water into a second cup that he prepared along with his and swirled the contents before topping off with more hot water.

"That mine?"

"Yep." Acharon handed Sovelet the cup of instant coffee.

Sovelet was wearing flannel pajamas recently unsealed. It had taken two days to air out the smells of the preservatives from the packaging that had protected them for close to two hundred years.

"Not going anywhere today," Sovelet said. She pointed with a head tilt toward the windows.

The sky had lightened a little, no longer dark gray by one or two shades. Rain still coated the windows in running sheets of water. While they both stood looking out into the wet gloom, a lightning bolt reached down and tapped the top of one of the buildings on the west side of Central Park. It lit the sky. Acharon turned his head away, blinking away the image of the lightning bolt.

"Definitely not going anywhere today." He deserted the window and sat on the couch, watching the dull day from a distance.

Sovelet followed, slowly, nestling in beside him, her coffee cup resting on the side of her knee. "So, what do we do today?"

"If we were back on our island, we'd do just this." Acharon chuckled. "Though you'd soon be in the office, messing with the computers."

She elbowed him gently. "First of all, it wasn't 'messing.' Second, we're not there."

"We used to wander through the other buildings, looking for interesting treasures."

Sovelet shook her head and followed with a sip of coffee before saying, "That was something like forty years ago."

"We could get drunk? Benen has some ales and a stout that is supposed to not only be ready, but drinkable."

"The last time you got drunk, you were thirty. You remember?" Sovelet sat up and leaned back on the couch. She stared at him. "I remember. You really want to repeat that?"

"Right. Maybe not."

Sovelet settled back against Acharon. "So, realistically, what do you want to do today?"

Someone knocked on the door.

"I could start by answering the door."

Sovelet moved aside as Acharon levered himself up onto his feet. He left the coffee cup on the table.

At the door, he found a grinning Benen with a covered tray. Behind him, Jaina and one more person whose name Acharon couldn't immediately recall.

"Morning," he said.

Benen nodded. "Morning, Acharon. You remember Marianne? Last to the table yesterday evening?"

"Yes. Morning Marianne, Jaina. Come on in." Acharon stepped back and waved them through. "Company, Sovie."

Benen turned right into the kitchen space. Jaina and Marianne followed Sovelet's voice into the living room. As they made their good mornings, Acharon turned into the kitchen.

Benen was searching the cupboards, finding and pulling down plates and glasses. Without looking in Acharon's direction, he asked, "Can you start some hot water?"

Acharon filled the pot he'd been using the last couple of days with more water and set it on the stove.

"I found a great use for canned bread," Benen said. He pulled the cover off the pans he was carrying to reveal several containers of reconstituted orange juice. Beneath, separated by a metal tray, was a pan of something baked.

"Overnight French toast?"

"Overnight French toast. I had the eggs, and there was a lot of this bread, so I thought I'd give it a try. That was a couple of weeks ago. I've been perfecting my recipe since then." He waved at the pan of cubed French toast. "This is the culmination of my short time experimenting with it."

Acharon started setting out plates along the counter. "So, your conclusion is that it's safe for others to eat?"

Benen laughed. "And then some. This is just like the grandmother you probably don't remember would have made."

For a second, Acharon thought he had forgotten. Then he had a vague image of an older woman who would take him to the park down the street and watch as he played with the other children. Many of those kids would live normal lives as their parents had decided not to have extended-life treatments for their children.

He'd met a few of them when they were all getting into their nineties. Their bitter jealousy made it difficult to stay among them. Their short lives were not Acharon's fault.

To be fair, he'd also met quite a few Last Wavers who resented their parents for the very opposite. They were often prime candidates for the suicide cults.

Acharon shook off the trail of tangent thoughts. "Actually," he said, "I do remember my grandmother. She never made French toast that I recall."

"Then I got her beat." Benen clapped Acharon on the shoulder as he chuckled cheerfully.

Together, they served out the overnight French toast, drizzled maple-flavored syrup across them, and portioned out the orange juice. Acharon carried three plates, Benen brought the juice and coffee.

"Prepared to be amazed," Benen said.

He and Acharon paraded into the room. Sovelet and the others made the appropriate appreciative noises while plates and cups were served out. Benen quickly left the room and returned with his and Acharon's plates.

Minutes of silent eating and hand-over-mouth compliments followed. Acharon was glad that Benen brought plenty. Fortunately, he didn't have to feel like he was taking advantage of the opportunity. Everyone, Sovelet included, had seconds.

"So, here's a question," Acharon said. It had been ten minutes since he'd had his last bit of French toast. He was now on the rare third cup of coffee. "You don't normally seem to desert your kitchen during meals. Why are you really here?"

Benen, Jaina, and Marianne laughed the embarrassed you-caught-us laugh.

"I'm here," said Benen, "to ask you something Jaina wanted me to ask you."

Jaina shrugged, pursed her lips, and then said, "I asked Benen because Marianne asked me."

"Wait? What?" Sovelet looked at the three and then to Acharon, adding, "I'm so confused."

"You're not alone," said Acharon. "Marianne?"

"I asked Jaina to help me because I, Dorothy, and Jahzara had an idea. And we wanted your opinion."

"We're sort of outsiders, Marianne," said Sovelet. "Is it something you should talk to the enclave about?"

Jaina leaned forward. "In case it's not obvious, we haven't been a cohesive group for several decades. We have Benen's kitchen, henhouse, and brewery, only because a small group of us were willing to help out. Most didn't want to be bothered."

"But they gladly benefit from it," Marianne added.

Benen smiled. "I don't mind sharing. Too many eggs, you know?"

"Okay, so what did you want to ask us about?"

Marianne acknowledged Acharon's question by turning to him. "The three of us want to host a bon voyage party."

"That's it?" Acharon looked at Sovelet. "Want to have a party?"

"Sure. Can I help?"

"Anyone can help," Marianne said. "That's not the issue. Nor is a lack of participants. We just don't know what night to have it. Would seem kind of lame to have it a week before we sail."

"I don't think we'll be here another week," Benen said. He looked at Acharon. "That right?"

"That's what we hope." Someone knocked on the door softly enough that Acharon almost missed it. He stood. "I'll get that."

Marianne shifted her attention to Sovelet. "Will you or Acharon be able to give us a firm date? So we can plan?"

Acharon heard Sovelet agreeing as he opened the door. Thaddeus was pressed close to the door, stumbling as it opened.

"Thaddeus?" Acharon helped him recover his balance. And though he doubted it, he asked, "Everything okay?"

"I'm not sure," Thaddeus said. He followed Acharon's waved hand across the threshold. "That's why I came up here. Oh, you have company?"

"Come on," said Acharon. He led the way back into the living room. "Thaddeus, everyone."

A chorus of hellos greeted Thaddeus.

"Sorry," Benen added. "We ran out of French toast."

"That's okay." He paused and took a deep breath. "I don't know if it's important, but I was looking outside, down in my rooms. I'm on the fourth floor. Right above the entrance, so it's a good view.

"Sorry," he said. "I get distracted easily. But you know that. I think it's because of all the reading. Or not. Maybe it's something else."

"Thaddeus," Sovelet said. She grinned and nodded at him. "You were looking out the window. Is that important?"

"The window? Yes. Very. That's when I saw a small group of people leave the enclave."

"Leaving?" Jaina asked. "Leaving where?"

"No idea," said Thaddeus. "But they went left."

"Same direction as the pier," Benen said. He twisted in his seat, facing Acharon. "You don't think?"

"I don't know," Acharon said.

"We should go check," said Benen. He stood and began collecting dishes.

"It's raining," said Sovelet. She was looking at the window. Rain was still washing down it in slow sheets.

Jaina had started to help Benen with the dishes. She said, "There's a coat room in the lobby. More than a hundred raincoats."

Benen stopped and looked around, stopping when he found Acharon. "We should go?"

"If they do anything," Thaddeus said, "we might not be able to fix it or find replacements."

"Okay," said Acharon. "We'll go. Everyone or maybe just me and Benen?"

"I'm going," Sovelet said. Acharon knew it wasn't a point for discussion.

Everyone else in the room followed Sovelet's lead.

"All right. Let's get to the lobby and find some raincoats."

"Wait," Benen said. "Dishes? Please?"

The number of raincoats was closer to two hundred in Acharon's frustrated opinion. Even with hurrying, every person for themselves, it still took ten minutes to get everyone in a raincoat. Acharon kept adding the minutes together. Counting the dishes and elevator ride, they were approaching twenty minutes when Thaddeus tapped him on the shoulder.

"You don't have a raincoat?" Acharon asked. He recalled giving one to Thaddeus, but maybe that was wishful thinking.

"No, it's the gun locker."

Acharon followed Thaddeus over to the gun locker, where Jaina was standing, leaning on the locker door. When she saw him, she waved a hand into the open locker.

"Behold," she said. "All the shotguns are gone."

Not only were the shotguns missing, but Acharon noticed that every box of ammo was also absent.

"Why would they take all the weapons?" Thaddeus asked.

Acharon doubted they did take them all. The missing ammunition implied another reason for the empty locker.

"What's going on?" Benen approached, snapping his raincoat closed.

"No one wants us to go out," Acharon said. "They've taken all the shotguns and ammunition."

Benen peeked into the locker and nodded. "That's okay."

"You really want to go out there without protection?"

"I got protection." Benen patted his raincoat.

"You know what I meant," Jaina said.

"I do," said Benen. "There's two of them over where I brew the beer."

"Why are they over there?" Sovelet asked from halfway across the lobby.

"More importantly," Acharon said, "do you have enough ammo?"

Benen moved out from behind the lobby counter. "Sometimes, when I come into the other building, I leave the shotgun there since I don't need it for the walk between the buildings. And I may have forgotten one or two of them over the years."

"Right," said Acharon. "And ammo?"

Benen grinned. "You know, I think there may be a box or two over there as well."

"How long have you been paranoid?"

"Not sure." Benen started walking with Acharon toward the dining room. "Maybe I've always been? Comes in handy."

"This way, everyone," Acharon said.

"We're walking, we're walking," said Jaina. She pulled a laugh from everyone as they entered the dining room.

In the room with the brewing rig, Benen located three shotguns and an ammo box with six boxes of shells.

"Forgetful, huh?" Jaina said. She held a shotgun out to Thaddeus, who gently pushed it back in her direction.

At the door leading out to the street, they stood as a pack, watching the rain pour down.

"We ready for this?" Acharon asked. Someone nudged him in the back, compelling him to step forward, into the rain. "I take it that's a yes."

He scanned the street as he walked across the sidewalk and onto the road. Immediately his foot sank into the water-saturated dirt built up along the curb. If he was lucky, that would be the worst thing that happened on this outing.

Except for the tapping of the rain on his plastic raincoat and the squelching of everyone's feet around him, the city was silent. It was also empty. Acharon knew everyone was watching the streets and buildings, just as he was. He was also sure they saw nothing as well.

Even though he'd only been in the city for two days, he'd gotten used to seeing deer, skunks and rabbits, and a lone coyote. He hadn't seen the cougar and was okay if that event never occurred.

By the time they were in sight of the pier, the rain had begun to let up. What had been a steady downpour had become a tired drizzle. In the distance, the clouds were beginning to look like the whipped edge of an old flag too long on the pole.

Along with the absence of wildlife, there was also an absence of other people. Acharon knew they could have come and gone already.

"The rain seems to be dying out," he said. "So let's keep everyone on the pier. Sovelet? Could you check the stays and lines? Benen? Keep me company?"

Acharon gave his shotgun to Marianne and stepped onto the deck and then into the cockpit. He turned and watched Benen copy him with one hand for the boat.

The hatch to the cabin was closed. Acharon saw that as a good sign. If someone was intent on sabotaging the boat, he doubted they would be kind enough to close up after themselves. Acharon opened the hatch, and after a few seconds of peering into the cabin gloom, he stepped inside.

The examination didn't take long. By the time Acharon and Benen had verified that nothing in the cabin, engine room, or navigation station had been damaged, the rain had given up. The flat cloud cover had fragmented, allowing rays of sunlight to slip through and dapple the city and the river with spots of warmth.

"Stays look the same as yesterday," Sovelet said. "How about below?"

"No damage," Benen said. He continued to show caution as he crossed the deck and stepped onto the pier.

"It doesn't look like anyone was below," Acharon said. He was still standing in the cockpit. "No physical signs of tampering."

"I don't think they came here," Jaina said from the pier.

"I really did see people leave the enclave," said Thaddeus. "I promise it's not my imagination."

"No one doubts you," Sovelet said.

Marianne gave Thaddeus a quick rub across the shoulder blades.

Benen looked around. "So where could they have gone?"

"Don't know," Acharon said. "But, as they haven't damaged the boat, I'm not really all that interested."

There was a moment of silence. It seemed to Acharon that everyone was waiting for someone else to say something. Anything, or something specific.

Finally, "Should we go back home, then?"

Acharon acknowledged Benen's question with a nod. "Seems like we might as well. Maybe go through the brewery? Leave the coats and shotguns there?"

"Might not be a bad idea," Jaina said. "Especially if someone is trying to control our movements."

"All right." Acharon stepped off the boat. "Let's go back."

"Or."

Acharon turned to Sovelet. The only person who hadn't moved. "Or?"

"Since we're here," she answered, "we could do the system updates and inventory."

"You wouldn't need everyone, would you?" asked Thaddeus.

"No," Sovelet said. "Just a couple of us. Me, Acharon, Jaina. Benen, if he wants to stay and help."

"That would leave Marianne and Thaddeus to return home by themselves."

"We're not helpless," Marianne said.

"You want to go back, Benen?" asked Acharon.

Benen smiled, pulling his head down into his shoulders. "Truth is," he said, "I got a lot of rain down the back of my coat. It's cold and wet, and I'd like warm clothes. We probably will be fine with the one shotgun."

"Seems like dry clothes would be a good idea," Acharon said. "And that would split the groups evenly. You want the second shotgun?"

"You keep it," Thaddeus said. "We'll be fine with Benen along."

"Then, we'll see you after a while."

"Right." Benen turned to Marianne and Thaddeus. "Shall we?"

"A second," Sovelet said. "Marianne, could you spread the word for a meeting. So we can discuss the date we're leaving?"

"And pick the party time. Yes, I will."

Everyone waved goodbye. Benen's group started walking off the pier.

"Okay," Sovelet said. She stepped onto the boat and looked back at Jaina and Acharon. "Let's get to work."

22

Acharon and Sovelet had different strengths. So when she'd stepped on the boat and said, "Let's get to work," he knew what that meant. Besides meaning the boat systems getting updated, it meant this was a thing she was in charge of.

He'd never balked when she took the lead. Sometimes it was fun. Sometimes, like in San Francisco, it had saved his life. And while he could access programs in a system to run them, he was not as competent at manipulating them. Sovelet, on the other hand, had a talent, several degrees, and over a hundred years of experience.

So she was the leader. He just needed to stay out of the way and not interrupt. In his attempt, he did a quick survey of food, water, the batteries, and auxiliary equipment for the boat.

When he checked in with Sovelet, he got hushed by her and Jaina. Over their shoulders, he could see lines of code sliding up the monitor screen. He decided to go topside.

The clouds had surrendered the sky to the sun. Acharon would admit to anyone that asked, that the heat of the sun felt good. It was almost enough to burn off the mental chill he'd been suffering since the first dinner here in New York.

Rather than dwell on the enclave, Acharon looked around, hoping to find a distraction. Sovelet had already checked the stays and lines, so his inspection was quick. When he was along the starboard side of the boat, where it was tied off to the pier, he noticed the large cleats that dotted the edge of the pier at regular intervals. His brain glided into slipstream of memories. Some were his own. Others were from books, movies, stories told to him by other sailors.

The important part was that he knew how he was going to get the boat away from the dock and into the river without an engine. He just didn't know when. However, he did know someone who could find that answer for him.

He went to the hatchway. "Sovie," he said. "Are there tide charts for the present day?"

"The old models should still work, why?"

He hurried down the steps, keeping a hand on the hatchway until he was safely on the cabin floor. "'Why?' So we can set sail, of course."

Acharon, Sovelet, and Jaina arrived back at the enclave several hours after Acharon had his epiphany. He was still in high spirits as they returned the shotguns to Benen's brewery.

Benen was present.

"Thought I'd check on my tanks and fermentors while I waited for you," he said.

After throwing on a raincoat, Benen led them around to the front entrance of the enclave. They put away their dripping raincoats and entered the dining area, their feet still wet from the adventure. Acharon was surprised by the smell of something fresh and warm. He could tell by everyone else's reaction they were surprised, too. Benen more than anyone else.

Then a voice startled him.

"There you are!"

They turned as a group to see Harriet coming out from the door of the auto-kitchen. She had a pie in her hands, it was steaming.

"The kitchen made it." She smiled at Benen. "I know it's an affront to your skills, dear, but I thought you all might like something to eat, with some coffee."

She said the word 'coffee' the same way Acharon thought it. It wasn't real coffee. That was a rare find.

"As long as no one tries to give me credit," Benen said. "And I'll be happy to help eat it. I've eaten that stuff for decades, and I'm still alive."

"A testament to the abilities of the medi-pods," Jaina said.

Benen laughed. "True. True. I'll get cups."

Acharon fetched plates and forks while Harriet set the pie on the table. They all settled around, Acharon doling out the plates and forks. Benen made two trips for the 'coffee' before taking his own seat.

"All's well?" Harriet asked.

Acharon nodded. Harriet had pulled an old server's trick and asked just as he'd clamped his mouth around a forkful of pie. The pie was hot, and it was a few seconds before he dared to swallow it without choking.

Sovelet spoke for him. "Everything looks good. Acharon has even found us a launch date and time."

"Wonderful," Harriet said. She clapped her hands for emphasis. "Marianne and the other girls are going to be very excited."

"We still have to bring it before the entire enclave," said Acharon. That was how they'd done it in San Francisco. From the few conversations he'd had over the decades, it was how other enclaves did it, too. There was no leader. Everything was set up commune-style. Everyone had a say so. A vote was the decider. Simple majority.

"Yes, yes," Harriet said. "Thaddeus went to talk to Boone as soon as we got back."

"Where is he now?" Sovelet asked.

"Can't say. Maybe a book ambushed him? He'll be here--. Oh. There he is."

Everyone but Harriet, who'd been facing the dining room's main entrance, turned to see Thaddeus entering. He waved. Acharon assumed he wanted them to know where he was. Old habits.

As he drew near, Acharon asked him, "Did you get an enclave meeting set up?"

"I think so. Is that pie?" There was a pause as Harriet served him a slice of pie and Benen fetched him a hot tea. After a bite and a nod of appreciation, he continued. "I talked to Boone. He didn't seem to think anyone would want to, but I asked him to check. So we went door to door and asked everyone to meet down here before dinner."

"Everyone agreed?" Benen asked.

There was a slight hesitation before Thaddeus answered. "They did. It wasn't easy. Boone seemed pretty intent on scuttling the effort. He kept telling people they shouldn't feel compelled if they weren't interested. He said it was doubtful we'd even set out this year anyway."

Sovelet leaned forward. "Did he stop by Katuva's room?"

"Oh, yeah." Thaddeus's eyes went wide. "We found a bunch of people there. They didn't look too pleased to have an interruption. Most of them were against going to a meeting. But then, Katuva said yes and that they all should go and hear Acharon out."

"That changed their minds?" Sovelet asked.

"Reluctantly, I think. Greene argued the longest against. But Katuva, she was fiery adamant."

"Interesting," said Sovelet. She returned her attention to her pie.

"So, everyone will be here for dinner?" Benen asked.

"Seems like it," answered Thaddeus.

Benen stood, gathering his plate and cup. "Sounds like I need to get to the garden. And the hen house. Anyone ever had a souffle?"

No one nodded yes. Acharon had seen one in a video on a cooking site, but that was the closest for him.

The lack of an answer seemed to please Benen. "Great. No one will know if I mess it up. See you all at dinner."

"We should probably get cleaned up?" Jaina asked.

Sovelet was scraping the last of the apple pie filling off her plate with the edge of her fork. "Sounds like a good idea." She finished her sentence by mouthing the last of her pie.

There was a steady stream of people into the elevator as it dropped from the tenth floor to the lobby. Some of those present greeted Acharon and Sovelet merrily. Others seemed to not see them or were sorry they did. They turned away from them, facing the front of the elevator, seemingly interested in watching the doors closed. Sovelet looked his way several times, arching her eyebrows.

Being first on, they were last off the elevator. Acharon had to catch the door with his hand to stop it from closing. When they were off, the elevator climbed again. Presumably, there were still people on their way down.

In the dining room, the two camps were again squared off. Katuva was in a group off to the left. Sovelet waved at her and received a small waggle of fingers and a furtive look. Others in her group, facing the entrance, returned blank looks or dagger-shooting eyes.

"Charming group," Acharon said. His voice was a low mumble.

"Hush," said Sovelet. She took his arm in her hands and walked to the farther corner of the room, near Benen's kitchen.

Harriet, Thaddeus, and Aiman were already present. They waved with more enthusiasm. A half-empty pitcher of beer was in the center of the table.

"Started without us?" Acharon asked. He accepted a cup of beer poured by Aiman.

"Just trying to keep busy," Aiman said.

A chattering of voices drew Acharon's attention back to the doors. Marianne, Tadala, and Jahzara entered, talking animatedly, punctuating words with laughter. They waved cheerily to the crowd surrounding Katuva and didn't seem put off by the lack of response.

"Hi, everyone," Marianne said as they approached the table where Acharon and the others sat. "We are so excited for this party. Just don't tell us it's tonight."

"It's not," Sovelet said.

"Oh, good," said Tadala. "We're not that ready."

"Personally," Harriet said, "I can't wait to go. We haven't had an adventure like this since we went looking for the first boat."

There was a general consensus among the New Yorkers. Acharon was glad to see they were excited. He chanced a look at Katuva's group. They seemed in good spirits, though more restrained. Perhaps some of them would have a change of heart now that the idea of sailing to Paris was a reality. Or it would be, in two days time.

Benen came to the table. He used his chin to point toward the doors as his hands were full, carrying a large bowl of salad in one hand and small plates in the other. "Looks like we've got a full house."

Another glance at the back of the room showed the last three straggling in. Jamon stopped just inside the door. His head moved from side to side and then stopped. He started to raise his hand, gave up on that, and continued into the room.

Fast on his heels was Asher. Asher didn't spare a look for Katuva's table. It seemed his interest in Katuva had evaporated about as fast as

Green's had increased. He took a table to himself at the front of the room, opposite where Acharon's group was sitting.

The doors closed behind Boone, bumping up against him as they did. He looked at Katuva's group and then across to Acharon's group before taking a seat at a table roughly halfway between the two groups.

"Salad," Benen said. He set the bowl on the table and then the plates. "I went all out on this one. Not much left in the garden, so eat up."

He returned to the kitchen.

"Hello," Sovelet said.

Acharon looked over his shoulder to see Jamon standing close by. "May I join you?" he asked.

"Of course," said Thaddeus. He stood, pulling out the seat next to him. "Beer?"

"Yes, please," Jamon said, pulling in his own seat.

Thaddeus poured him a beer. Sovelet served him salad before serving everyone else.

They ate in silence for several bites. Acharon observed Benen taking another bowl of salad to Katuva's table. He arrived cheerily but left with a more stern look. He then took individual salad plates to Asher and Boone.

"So, the boat's a go?"

Acharon turned to Jamon. He had a little bit of beer foam on his top lip. His eyes were red-rimmed.

"It is," Acharon said. "Its stocked, and the charts and tables are updated. We put the sails in tomorrow. That's it."

"When did you want to sail?"

Acharon looked at the rest of the table. When his eyes met Sovelet's, she nodded.

"Day after tomorrow. Around noon, as the ebb tide starts."

Marianne and the other party planners whooped with excitement.

"Are you going to tell the others?" Tadala asked.

"Not yet." Acharon shook his head and looked to the kitchen. "I want to enjoy my meal first."

Benen brought out several serving pans and set them in the warmers. He looked at Acharon, a question on his face, and gave a thumbs up. Acharon returned the thumbs up.

"Everyone. Attention," Benen said. His voice carried across the room, hushing the whispered conversations at the far table. "Dinner's served. We've got synth-beef and chicken cutlets, breaded, fried. I let the kitchen do that. Scalloped potatoes, also from the kitchen. And finally, corn on the cob from the garden. I did that. So, dig in. Tonight should be a night of celebration."

"Oh, no," Marianne said. Her voice was hushed. "Tomorrow is going to be a night of celebration."

"Well? Dig in, people," Benen said.

Acharon's table paused until it was clear Katuva's table wasn't moving. Then, they rose and lined up, taking plates, and dishing food. Out of the corner of his eye, Acharon saw Asher rise and take up the end of the line. Boone was slowly making his way, too.

Several times someone at Katuva's table started to rise. A harsh whisper from Green put them back in their seat. Only when the rest of the enclave, Benen included, had filled their plates and left the serving line, did the other table rise and make their way over.

Unlike the rest of the enclave, who'd chattered and laughed their way through the line, Katuva's table had all the spirit of a funeral procession. But, not talking was a more efficient way to get through the line it seemed. They were back at their table in less than five minutes. They ate with the same solemnity with which they'd served themselves.

The talk around Acharon's table evolved, moving from memories, ideas for Paris, plans for a party. Benen was silent, eating through his meal before anyone else.

"I have to check on the ice cream," he said when someone asked him why he was eating so fast.

"Do we make the announcement before or after dessert?" Acharon asked.

"Before," Jaina said. "No one misses out on dessert, especially if Benen got the ice cream machine to work."

Benen was on his feet, gathering his dishes. "You can do it now. I know what's going on, and I'm already on board."

After he left, Acharon looked to Sovelet and received a nod. He hated public speaking. It was one thing when giving directions on a job. But, speaking to a group, trying to sell them on an idea, he'd rather try and make it through San Francisco again.

He took a deep breath and then stood, excusing himself from the table. Everyone there was watching him. As he turned, he saw that Boone and Asher were also keeping an eye on him. Acharon moved up the room, away from tables where people were sitting.

"Excuse me," he said. "If I could have everyone's attention? Thank you."

The people at Katuva's table who had their backs to him didn't turn around. He could tell by the way they held themselves, though, that they were paying attention. Those facing him avoided looking in his direction. Everyone but Katuva who gave a quick half-smile when they made eye contact.

"As you know," he said, "Sovelet and I came here from San Francisco to join you on a crossing to France. To join the rest of who's left at the Paris enclave."

He paused and looked around. Thaddeus flashed a thumb's up.

"There'd been some troubles with the first boat. And there seemed to be troubles with the second boat. However, with the help of Sovelet, Jaina, and a few others, we got that all sorted out. We only have to mount the sails. Then the boat is ready to go."

"You forgot the engine," Boone said. He leaned back in his chair, arms crossed. "That boat isn't going to move without an engine, not being on the inland side of the pier."

There was a hushed rattle of whispers at Katuva's table.

"Actually," Acharon said. He reminded himself not to smile. "We got that solved, too. Using the tides, we'll be able to turn the boat and then launch. Turn on the flood, launch on the ebb. Once free of the pier, all we need is sails."

"So, the boat is seaworthy?"

Acharon turned to Jamon at the table he'd been sitting. "Yes. Seaworthy. As they used to say, Bristol fashion."

"When did you want to sail?" Asher asked. His voice was flat, refusing to betray any emotion.

"Day after tomorrow," said Acharon

There was a small cheer from his table. Katuva's table was a huddle of whispers, heads bent toward each other across the table. Boone looked surprised.

"Now, I don't know how it works here," Acharon said. "But in San Francisco, we took votes on this. So I'd like to see a vote for sailing in two days."

"What if people vote against?" Boone asked.

"Then we'll need to vote on a day."

"So, you're saying the boat sails no matter what?"

"That's what I'm saying, Jamon."

"So this is really a formality, then," said Asher.

Acharon shrugged. "Well, I guess. But if someone really needed another day or two, maybe the launch date could be put back."

"Heck, no!" Jaina was on her feet. "I vote 'yes' to two days."

"Wait, wait." Boone slowly rose to his feet. "You're forgetting the weather. It's the beginning of the winter storm season. Think of the rainstorm we just had. The smart thing would be to wait until next spring."

There was a murmur of agreement from Katuva's table. Green had his arms crossed, his emotions shut off.

"Put it to a vote," said Jamon. He, too, had stood. "'Yes', we go; 'No', we wait."

Acharon looked at Boone. After looking around the room, Boone shrugged. "Take the vote."

"All right," said Acharon. "Those in favor of sailing in two days, please stand."

As expected, everyone at Acharon's table stood. Not to his surprise, Asher stood, too. But, and he almost gasped in surprise, Katuva stood, shaking off Green's hand as he pulled on her. Several seats down, Sena stood, too. That was more than half the enclave. There wasn't any need to ask for the second count.

"Looks like an overwhelming majority," Benen said. "Desert, anyone?"

23

The new day, though filled with the energy of anticipation, could not shake away the last tendrils of doubt from the previous evening. It had ended about the way Acharon had expected. There'd been a few surprises, he had to admit, like the shouting match on Katuva's side of the room that sent Sena from the dining room, crying. Katuva had barked something at Green and followed her. Their entire group looked uncomfortable, and then Jamon's wife spent some whispered moments with him before they left together.

Everyone at the table where Acharon was sitting tried to keep the good mood going, but it had been of little effect, and soon they'd broken up. Marianne and her two friends went to do some last-minute planning. The others, after helping clear tables for Benen, left for their own rooms.

Breakfast had brought some lifting of spirits. But it was when Acharon was on the pier that he felt the mood rise by several degrees. It was like seeing the first wink of a sunray through the clouds after a particularly miserable stormy night. There was a promise of improvement.

For himself, Acharon was surprised and pleased to see that everyone who'd voted to sail on the ebb tide tomorrow was present to help with the sails. He was even more amazed when the last one appeared.

"Sena, morning."

Sena's eyes were bloodshot and underscored by dark bags. "Hey," she said.

"You sure you want to be out here right now?"

She looked straight at him, making eye contact. "Why wouldn't I be?"

Acharon took a mental step back. "Right. Well, good. We'll start soon. Benen brought several carafes of the coffee stuff." He pointed to where Benen had set up a makeshift serving table. Then he pointed in another direction and said, "I'm just going to check in with Sovelet."

Quickly, but not so quick to seem like flight, Acharon went over to the end of the pier. Sovelet was there, talking with Marianne and Tadala. He motioned for her attention.

"Something wrong?" she asked after separating herself from the other conversation.

Acharon looked in Sena's direction. He felt Sovelet do the same. "I'm glad Sena's here, but she looks pretty defeated."

"She'll be okay," Sovelet said. "She just got ousted from her group and needs time to find her own place."

"Well, maybe you can keep her with you." When Sovelet started to scowl, Acharon quickly raised a hand. "We have more people than we need for fixing the sails. I was going to ask if you could find jobs for some of them, anyway. You know, so they feel like they're contributing."

The scowl eased, and Acharon relaxed with it. His opinions of Katuva had and sometimes still were a sore point.

"Yes, I can keep her and some of the others busy. There's still some stuff to rearrange below. Can people be on deck? The cockpit?"

Acharon paused to look at the boat. The boom hung across the cockpit, nearly reaching the aft of the boat. "Let us get the mainsail loaded into the boom. Then, when we're working on the foresail, you can put people to work on the deck."

Sovelet stepped back. Acharon could see the glint in her eye that forewarned mischievous coming. He was proven right as she raised a salute and said, "Aye, aye, captain."

"Funny."

"Isn't it?" She smiled and squeezed his hand as she turned away and called for Sena. "Dear? I need your help."

She left Acharon and met Sena halfway, wrapping her in a hug that was reciprocated with emotion. They walked toward Acharon. Sovelet had an arm around Sena's shoulders. She gave Acharon a wink as they passed. He turned to watch as they reached Marianne and Tadala. Each took a turn hugging Sena, who now started to show the beginnings of a smile.

Acharon turned away, leaving them to bring Sena into the group their way. He found Aiman approaching, a mug of something hot in one hand, a half-eaten slice of cinnamon toast in the other.

"You ready to get started?" Aiman asked.

"The real question," Acharon said, "is, are you ready?"

With so many hands to assist, Acharon found it took longer than if he'd rigged the sails alone. Granted, they were some of the largest sails he'd put on rollers. Still, it seemed that people spent more time apologizing for stepping on each other's toes than actually doing work.

It was with a sigh of relief that Acharon finally tied off the foresail sheets to their respective winches. Like everything else on the boat, they were automatic and would work in tandem to control the foresail when underway.

The crew, as they'd begun to refer to themselves, had all retreated to the pier. Benen had somehow produced several large plates of sandwiches and pitchers of water with cucumber slices bobbing among cubes of ice. When some of the 'crew' turned toward Acharon, they smiled and raised glasses of cucumber water. Acharon wasn't sure if it was a toast or a taunt. He waved, leaving it to them to decipher what he meant by that.

Movement in the cockpit distracted him from thoughts of cool ice water. Sovelet and Sena were coming up from the cabin. Sovelet looked in his direction and smiled.

"All done up here?"

"Yep. All done down there?"

Sovelet nodded. "Have been for a while. I was just showing Sena how the nav station worked."

Acharon wasn't sure that he liked that idea. Sena had just come over from a group that seemed more interested in them not sailing.

However, as much as he might feel concerned, he also knew to trust Sovelet.

"It would be good for more than one or two people to understand how the systems work. Just in case."

"Good idea," Acharon said. He understood that she was trying to waylay his concern. Not that he would stop being concerned. That was partly how they'd survived so long. He noticed people missing. "Where are Marianne and the others?"

"Them." Sovelet laughed, causing Sena to smile. "They were so focused on this party, they were about useless below. So I sent them on ahead to make their preparations."

"This isn't going to be just a dinner, is it?"

"It's not."

Acharon turned to look at Benen. "You're in on this, too?"

Benen held his arms out benevolently. "Who else has kegs of beer and has reconstituted several cases of wine? Not to mention a bon voyage cake I started this morning."

"And I suppose you want to get rolling, too?"

Benen looked over his shoulder at the plates, few sandwiches remained, and the pitchers of cucumber-infused water were nearly empty.

"We'll clean up," Sovelet said. Acharon nodded in agreement.

"Right, then." Benen smacked his hands together, rubbing them vigorously. "See you at the party."

Benen trotted off to talk to a few people and pick up his shotgun before walking quickly in the direction of the enclave.

"They're pulling out all the stops."

"Yes, dear," Sovelet said. She rubbed his back. "It's the last time they'll have a party here. They plan on making the most of it."

Was everyone, Acharon wondered. "What's going to happen tomorrow?"

"Do you mean, will those who voted 'no', show up?"

Acharon shrugged. He wasn't sure what he really meant. He wasn't sure what to expect. "I can't imagine anyone would choose to stay if everyone else was going."

"Everyone isn't like you, Ach."

"No one's like me."

Sovelet laughed. "Thank goodness." She gave him a peck on the cheek and then said, "If we're done here?"

"We are." Acharon smiled and pulled Sovelet in for a hug. Almost a hundred and fifty years, and he still got teary when he thought of how much she meant to him. When he released her, he added, "I'll just close up the boat. Then we can go."

"I'll deal with the plates and pitchers."

"Make Thaddeus help," Acharon said as he walked away. "Tell him to pull some weight."

Closing up the boat and getting everyone back to the enclave took longer than Acharon had believed possible. Everyone's moods were elevated, so there was a lot of joking and chatter that interfered with cleaning up around the pier, gathering Benen's plates, cups, and pitchers. Finally, though, they'd all made it back to the enclave and disappeared off the elevator onto several floors on the way up to the tenth.

Acharon had let Sovelet clean up first before taking his turn. He was feeling tired but satisfied that everything was going to work out. For those who'd voted not to sail tomorrow, he could only hope they came around.

"Ready?" Acharon asked. His shirt and pants had the creases of decades in a sealed, plastic envelope pressed into them. Fortunately, it was no longer a thing to judge people by. At least, that's what Sovelet always told him.

"Ready." Sovelet came into the living room. She had a flowery skirt and a plain blouse. Acharon didn't point out that her clothes lacked the creases he couldn't banish.

They walked to the elevator. Acharon pushed the call button when they stopped before the doors. Below, he could hear the elevator grinding its way up to their floor. Just before it dinged its announcement of arrival, Sovelet put a hand on his shoulder.

"You go ahead, okay? I'm going to check on Katuva."

"You want me to wait?" Acharon asked. He wanted to wait. Just to reassure himself.

"I'll be fine." She pushed him towards the opening doors of the elevator. "I'll be along soon enough. Go."

"Okay." Acharon turned inside the elevator and pressed the lobby button. "Don't make me come look for you."

"You won't have to."

The doors closed, leaving Acharon alone. The isolation lasted one floor. Then, the doors opened, revealing his companion for the rest of the ride.

"Hey, Acharon."

"Hey, Aiman."

They both stood back as the doors shut. The elevator shook as it slid down two floors and let several more people, Tadala, Harriet, and Thaddeus, come aboard. By the time the doors opened in the lobby, the elevator box had become crowded with the addition of Asher, Jaina, and a withdrawn Jamon.

As they filed out into the lobby, Acharon noticed that those who had voted against sailing tomorrow were coldly absent.

Tadala seemed to notice this, too. She asked, "Has anyone seen Katuva or anyone that wasn't happy with the vote?"

"No." Jamon pushed past everyone else, creating a barrier of separation with him in the front.

"I'm sorry," Tadala said.

Aiman put a hand on her shoulder. "Don't let it get to you. He's worried about Grace. They haven't really been seeing eye to eye since…. Well, you know."

"Since Sovelet and I arrived," Acharon said. Jamon was already through the doors to the dining room. "And Katuva. I think that's the real point."

"Kind of hard to deny, Acharon," said Harriet. "And no offense meant, I'm sure."

"That's right," Aiman said. He held out a hand.

Acharon shook Aiman's. "None taken."

Acharon was well aware that the enclave was fractured before they'd arrived with Katuva. She'd just been a sledgehammer to the fracture, widening it. Now it threatened to cleave in two.

"Where's Sovelet?" asked Harriet as Acharon held the door to the dining room open.

"Checking on Katuva. They'll be along."

"Wow," said Thaddeus.

Acharon hadn't taken in the dining room until Thaddeus spoke. Wow was the precise word for it. Fairy lights and holiday lights draped the walls in long dipping arcs. Plastic globes glowed on every table, now covered with mismatching table cloths. Cups and wine glasses were set on every table even though there weren't enough people alive in all of New York to fill every seat.

"Look up," Aiman said.

Overhead, a disco ball, short a few mirror squares, turned, lighting the ceiling overhead with hundreds of moving dots of light.

"Welcome!"

"Oh, I didn't know we could dress fancy," said Harriet. She sounded disappointed.

Dorothy, who had bellowed the greeting, was walking their way. She had on a shiny ball gown that glittered as much as the ceiling. Her hair was curled and up, held in place by a tiara. She gave everyone a hug and a buss on the cheek.

"Glad you're all here. We were beginning to worry."

"Where else would we go?" Tadala asked.

Dorothy shrugged. "I don't know. We thought you were going to come in earlier. Heard everyone out in the lobby and then, nothing. Benen said not to worry, but, you know Benen."

Everyone muttered a humorous agreement. Acharon turned toward the door. The group he'd come in with had been relatively quiet in the lobby. Maybe someone else also went out for fancy clothes and had been returning. Maybe it was wishful thinking.

"We're here now," he said.

"I know!" Dorothy grinned and then grabbed Tadala's hand, pulling. "Come see the cake. Come have some food. Come have fun!"

With Dorothy dragging Tadala, the rest followed. Thaddeus and Acharon were the tail end.

Benen greeted them at the serving line. "I pulled out all the stops," he said. He was dressed from the waist up in a tuxedo shirt and jacket, his apron serving as a poor disguise for his regular khaki pants. "And I pulled up all the vegetables, too. So there's lots of salad, spaghetti, and faux-meatballs. The parmesan is fake, too, but it tastes good. Rehydrated fruit salad, mashed sweet potatoes. Last, this big cake the women made me make."

"Lies." Marianne, in a cocktail dress and waving a wine glass, had come from somewhere that Acharon hadn't seen. "You wanted to make the cake that big. We just said, make a nice cake, Benen. This is all you. Wine anyone?"

From the way Marianne weaved while walking to the nearest table, it seemed to Acharon that she'd already been sampling the wine for some time.

"I'll have some," Jaina said. "Might as well join the party."

She sat with Marianne, who slopped a little of the wine intended for Jaina's glass.

"That's the spirit," Benen said. He seemed to be enjoying himself. "Dish up, people. I'll get us a couple pitchers of beer."

Everyone but Marianne dished up plates with food and gathered at one of the larger tables. Marianne joined them with some small effort.

"You should eat," Harriet said.

Marianne laughed. "I'm having grapes!"

The laughter rolled around the table, generating small conversations that bounced around the table like a bee stuck in a car. Acharon had conversations about sailing with Thaddeus and about gardening with Benen and Harriet.

During the conversations, Beatrix had arrived, receiving an off-balance hug from Marianne. Asher appeared shortly after. He was quiet but did join the table after dodging a Marianne hug but accepting a glass of wine.

Jahzara wandered off. A few seconds later, music started, piped in through speakers in the ceiling. She returned and teased Thaddeus into a dance. There was some applause and then some laughter when Marianne had attempted to join them.

At some point, Jamon had excused himself with a muttered apology and left the dining room. Acharon assumed it was to check on Grace. Before he could ask anyone, he was hit with a general conversation about San Francisco. It wasn't until he was in a discussion with Dorothy about the museums in France that he wondered about Sovelet. Acharon hadn't kept track of the time.

"Hey," he said to Benen, who'd been leaning back in his chair, one hand tapping the rhythm of the song coming through the speakers.

"What's up, Acharon? Need a refill?"

Acharon noticed his cup was empty. "Not now. Where's everyone else?"

Benen opened his mouth as if to answer as his eyes scanned the room. His mouth slowly shut as he leaned forward. "I don't know. Where's Sovelet?"

"I don't know." Acharon pushed his chair back and stood. The music had changed songs four or five times. Jahzara was dancing with a reluctant Asher while Jaina danced with Dorothy. "I'll be back."

He was halfway across the room when the doors opened and Jamon appeared. His face was wet with tears. In one fist, he gripped a sheet of paper. When he looked up and made eye contact with Acharon, his face changed from a look of deep sorrow to rage.

"This is your fault," he said. He shoved the paper at Acharon, forcing Acharon to step backward. "You brought her here. Now they're all dead!"

24

Jamon's angry shout pulled the attention of the room to him and Acharon like a noisy vacuum. There was movement behind Acharon, but he was too intent on the paper that Jamon had pressed against him. It was a plain white paper with no lines. There were only a few carefully printed lines of words. Some of the words were smudged, diffused by tears, and barely readable. Even without them, the message was clear enough.

"What's going on?"

Acharon looked around the way he might have had he drifted off to sleep for a second and was woken by a sharp sound. He did a double-take between Benen and the note.

"Has no one seen Sovelet?" Acharon asked. He could feel the pressure of panic building in his chest. "Anyone? Please?"

Jaina startled Acharon with a hand to his shoulder. "I'm sure she's fine. What do you have? Why does Jamon think someone's dead?"

Jamon snatched the paper back, tearing it. "Because of that bitch, Katuva. She's talked them all into committing suicide with her."

"No," Acharon said. The panic wasn't letting up. "She said she wouldn't."

"Well, she did." Jamon was crumpling the paper into a ball with one hand. His tears were trickling down his face once more.

"We should check on everyone," Thaddeus said."See who's still in the building."

"You won't find anyone." Asher had come over with everyone from the table. He had a hold of Marianne, who seemed to be sobering rapidly.

"Why wouldn't we find anyone?" Thaddeus turned to Asher. "Do you know where they are?"

"Are you part of this, Asher?" Jamon threw the paper ball, but it fell to the floor before reaching Asher. "Damn you!"

Asher's eyes were wet. "No, I'm not part of it. Green asked me not to say anything. It was their choice."

Acharon turned on Asher. He was breathing deep, trying to stay calm. He put a hand on Asher's shoulder. "Do you know where they went? Do you know where they are?"

It was imperative to Acharon that Asher knew. There still might be time. Instead, Asher shook his head, pulling more of the life from Acharon.

"He wouldn't tell me," Asher said. "They didn't want anyone to interfere."

"Anyone have an idea where they would have gone?" Acharon asked. He looked at each person in the room. All of them returned the same teary-eyed shake of their head. No one knew.

How could he get there before it was too late if he didn't know where to go? It had always been his job to solve the problem. He'd made them an island home so they were safe. When Sovelet's lungs were failing, he'd gotten them safely to the medi-fac in San Francisco and at least gotten her safely back to the warehouse. He'd fixed solar panels and monorail carriages. He'd fixed the boat so they could go to Paris.

Maybe he could fix this. But the panic was rising. He let some of it out with an angry yell. "How can none of you have a clue!"

In the silence, the scratch of the dining room door opening drew everyone's attention. They all turned with the sharpness of worried deer. The door slowly opened. Sena stepped through the opening. Her eyes were also red and wet, tear stains dappled the front of her shirt.

"They said they were going to wait," she said. Her voice was choked with phlegm. "They said they were going to stay behind and wait."

"Well, they didn't." Jamon held out his hand to Sena before realizing it was empty. His focus shifted away as he scrambled for the balled up paper.

"They lied to me," Sena said. She looked nearly as confused as Acharon was feeling.

Jamon had his paper and was pulling it open, tearing it more in different sections as he pushed toward Sena. He shoved the wrinkled paper at her. "They didn't wait. They're dead."

"They might not be," Benen said. Acharon noticed that Benen seemed in control of himself. It was something he should be as well, but he was in the middle of his worst nightmare. Benen asked Sena, "Do you know where they planned to make passage?"

Sena nodded. Jamon started to reach for her, an angry reaction on his face. Three of the women grabbed hold of him. His grief had sapped his strength, and he was easily held.

"Where, Sena?" asked Benen. "Where?"

Sena took two shuddering breaths that seemed to bite off a sob. She sniffled and then nodded as she wiped a run of snot coming down her lip. In a whispered voice, she said, "The restaurant."

That was all Acharon needed. He shoved past everyone and ran. He shoved the dining room door open hard enough that it banged against the wall. His footsteps thundered across the lobby floor, echoed by others. As he reached the outer door, he could see in the reflection of the glass more people running after him. If they were going to stop him, they would have to tackle him.

Outside, Acharon stumbled down the steps, almost falling before he caught himself. His feet slid on the sidewalk with its layer of dirt and weeds. When he had traction, he started running again, heading toward 8th Ave.

As he ran, Acharon replayed all the times Sovelet had told him that she wouldn't leave him. He remembered all the times they argued about the suicide cults. Her always justifying their legitimacy and then just as quickly promising she would never take her own life.

Acharon barreled around the corner at Columbus Circle, stumbling off the sidewalk and onto the street. A small herd of deer scattered ahead of him as he came into view. For a brief moment, he wondered about the mountain lion and then pushed it aside. Being attacked by a mountain lion again wasn't important anymore. He only needed to reach the restaurant before it was too late.

The three blocks up 8th Ave, he ran as if it were the last thing he would ever do. His head pounded, his lungs ached, but he didn't let himself stop until he skidded to a stop at the front of the restaurant.

The lights were dim but on inside the building. He grabbed the door handle and pulled.

"No!"

The door was locked. Acharon yanked on it until his left shoulder exploded in pain. Then he started pounding on the door with both fists.

"Sovelet!"

Someone grabbed his shoulder from behind. He jerked away and continued trying to beat the door into giving up.

"Acharon! Back away."

The voice was loud enough to penetrate his grief for a second. He paused and allowed several hands to pull him back. Benen stepped forward and shoved the barrel end of the shotgun he carried into the crease between the door jamb and the door bolt. The night echoed back the boom of the shotgun shell. The door shook in its frame.

Benen grabbed the handle and pulled the door open, its bolt tearing away the last of the door jamb wood. Acharon pulled free and slipped past the door, catching his left shoulder against the door frame. The pain staggered him, pain points sparked across his vision.

The room had been rearranged. Four square tables had been pushed together in the center of the room. The other tables were stacked off to one side, the extra chairs stacked next to them. Like the dining room at the enclave, the four tables here had been set with table cloths, dishes, and silverware. Two candelabras, their candles flickering in the breeze from the open door, were centered on the middle two tables.

In chairs around the tables, ten bodies slumped forward, their heads either resting on their arms or the table cloth.

"Sovie?" Acharon began rushing around the table. He grabbed each person by the shoulders, pulling them back to see their face before releasing them and moving to the next one.

"Acharon!"

Let them yell, he thought. Their wife wasn't here. He continued pulling at the lifeless bodies until he, in turn, was pulled from behind.

"Let go!" He fought them, trying to break free. His shoulder hurt, sapping his energy.

"She's not here," someone whispered in his ear. "Sovelet's not here."

Achron ceased resisting. "What?"

Benen came into his narrowed vision. His face was red and slick with sweat. His tuxedo shirt was torn. Achron wondered if that was his fault. He should apologize later.

"Sovelet's not here, Acharon."

He was confused. "She's not? Where is she?"

Benen smiled. "I don't know, man. She's just not here."

"Okay. Okay." Acharon nodded and kept nodding. "Okay. Okay, good."

"Katuva isn't either," Benen said. He'd put a hand against Acharon's head. It helped him stop nodding.

"She's not here, either?" Acharon leaned to the side to look around Benen at the table. Jamon was standing near one of the bodies. Acharon vaguely recognized it as Jamon's wife, Grace. He was cradling her head against him. He rocked slowly. Aiman and Tadala stood with him, hands on his shoulders.

At one end of the table, Asher was standing next to Green's body. Asher was whispering something to Green while stroking his hair. Marianne and Dorothy were standing behind him, their faces streaked tears. Around the table, others stood next to friends now gone.

Acharon hadn't gotten to know them all. He'd recognized Green and Carwyn. He tried to place the other still faces to names but couldn't. Not until he came to the other end of the table. He moved, and Benen stepped aside.

"Boone?" Acharon looked back at Benen.

Benen shrugged. "Who knew."

"I thought he was against this kind of thing."

"I don't think he ever said." Harriet had joined them, her hand rubbing gently on Boone's shoulder.

"I thought he was behind the trip to Paris?"

"Maybe he thought it would never happen," Benen said. He bent down and looked in Boone's unresponsive face. "Maybe he thought it was just something to keep us all busy until we came around to his way of thinking."

"Maybe that's why he didn't want Sovelet and me to come?"

Harriet kissed the top of Boone's head. "Maybe he was afraid you'd give everyone false hope."

"Maybe it wouldn't have been false hope." Jamon stood. His face was as splotchy as his emotions seemed to be. "Maybe if you hadn't brought that woman here, Grace would still be alive. Maybe we'd all be on the boat tomorrow instead of none of us."

"None of us?" Thaddeus put down an unfolded piece of paper. "Just because they made a different choice doesn't mean we shouldn't keep to ours."

"What's the point in going now?" Jamon started crying again, hugging himself.

"He needs time," Harriet said. She went and stood next to Jamon, putting a hand on his back, saying nothing.

"It still doesn't answer where Sovelet is," Jaina said.

"Anyone?" Acharon said. "Anyone have any idea?"

Someone coughed by the door. "I'm right here," Sovelet said. She stepped into the restaurant. Her hair was tangled, her skirt torn, blood soaked part of her blouse. In her right hand, she was holding a shotgun by its barrel.

"Sovelet." Acharon walked to her like the air was wet concrete. He wanted to run, but his legs felt as if they might give way at any moment. "Oh, Sovelet."

When he reached her, he wrapped his arms around her and pulled tight until his left shoulder sparkled with pain. Still, he held onto her.

"I thought…."

Sovelet rubbed his back with her left hand. "I know, honey. I know."

Acharon backed off his hug so he could see her face. He looked in her eyes before kissing her forehead. "I'm sorry. I know I shouldn't have doubted."

Her smile was gentle. "I understand. It's okay."

"Sovelet."

She looked past Acharon. "Yes, Jaina?"

"Are you okay?" Jaina pointed at the blood and the shotgun.

Sovelet laughed. "Just a couple of cuts, a little visit to the medi-pod, and I'll be fine. I would have come right away, but Katuva needed some help getting back to the enclave and up to medi-fac."

"She's in a medi-pod?" Acharon asked. He stepped back to look at Sovelet's wounds. They looked familiar. "What happened?"

"Attacked by the mountain lion in the park." Sovelet held up the shotgun. "I had this, but it turns out it wasn't loaded. I had to convince the cat to go away."

"It looks like it took a lot of convincing," Acharon said. "You look like it got you, too."

"A couple times. But I think it got fed up with me hitting it with the butt of the gun and finally left. What happened to you?"

"He tried to pull the door off the hinges," Marianne said. "I bet he tore something."

"Ach?"

"Yeah, I'm in a lot of pain, but that's not important."

"Why were you in the park?" Asher asked. "I mean, why did Katuva go into the park?"

"I think she should tell you that," Sovelet said. "But I think first we need to get Acharon fixed. Maybe me. And there's this to attend to. Katuva will be out for a while."

25

The departure date for France was pushed back. There was a lot that suddenly needed dealing with in the enclave.

Acharon had torn muscles in his shoulder and his bicep. Both required some minor surgery, which required several hours in a medi-pod. Sovelet's wounds had required some sutures and synth-skin. She was out of her medi-pod in less than half an hour.

Katuva's situation was different. Sovelet had said when she got to Katuva, there was already a lot of blood. The big cat had been worrying at Katuva's arm before Sovelet had laid into it with the butt end of the shotgun. When she'd taken a few swats from the cat's deadly claws, Katuva had helped by pelting the cat with whatever large rocks she could pick up with her good arm.

The cat had gotten ahold of Katuva in several places. Her scalp had been torn along with the side of her face. Her left arm had been lacerated to the bone in several areas. The calf of her leg had a large piece torn out.

There wasn't much time for rest. Acharon would like to have slept for a day. He'd been through an emotional wringer, and there was little the medi-pods could do for that except a sedative.

Instead, he felt the need to help. There was a cemetery in New Jersey the enclave used until roughly forty years back. They switched to the golf course in Central Park after that. Acharon wanted to ask why they hadn't been using the body disposal system like they had in San Francisco. After talking with Sovelet about it, he figured right now wasn't the smartest time.

Ten bodies were a lot to deal with. Acharon argued for sealing up the restaurant, much like he'd done for Murphy in his home. Asher felt that it was an acceptable solution. It was Jamon that was dead set against it. The compromise was that Grace was transported to the burial ground at the golf course. The nine others were sealed inside the restaurant forever at the table where they'd shared their last meal.

Acharon had thought that with the burial of Grace performed and done, everything was finished and they could plan for the new departure date. Sovelet had warned him it wouldn't be that simple. Usually, he listened.

Someone knocked on the door to their apartment. Acharon was prone on the couch, watching the clouds slide past the city. Sovelet was seeing to Katuva in her apartment. Someone had to answer the door.

Acharon chose the shortcut and yelled, "It's open!"

He heard the door open and then shut. Footsteps approached. "Hey," said Benen as he peeked around the corner.

"Hey." Acharon waved at the empty chairs. "Have a seat?"

Benen grimaced. "Can't. I agreed to pass Jamon's message."

Achron found himself sitting up. "Message? About what?"

"Enclave meeting."

"About what?"

Benen threw up his hands. "He didn't say. But I think it might have to do with Katuva."

Acharon slouched back into the couch. "What's he want, a trial? Involuntary manslaughter or something?" No matter what it was, as far as he was concerned, it was all ridiculous.

"Again," Benen said, "I don't know because he didn't say."

"All right." Acharon stood. "I'll go tell Sovelet and Katuva."

Benen waved Acharon back. "Don't worry, I already told them. We're meeting in the dining room. See you there."

He was gone before Acharon could voice any kind of concern or frustration. Acharon didn't blame Jamon for being angry. He would have been angry, too. But, unlike Jamon, who was lashing out, Acharon's anger would have been turned inward. People didn't just take their life because other people were doing it and it seemed like a good idea at the time. They did it because, no matter how short-sighted Acharon found it, they believed it was the right thing to do.

What Jamon had in mind, Acharon didn't know. Perhaps he just needed to blow off some steam.

The enclave had felt empty before. Now it felt like a ghost town as Acharon walked the hallway to the elevator. Even when he hadn't seen anyone, he'd heard sounds under the doors. Music or voices always seemed to drift into the hallway. Now there was ear-aching silence. The whir of the elevator car was a welcome distraction from the isolation.

When he arrived at the lobby, Acharon was no longer alone. Just outside the doors to the dining hall, he found Sovelet waiting with Katuva. Katuva was wringing her hands. Her short-sleeve shirt left the synth-skin strips on her arm exposed. Her face was better, a thin strip of synth-skin ran from her chin to her hairline. The red of her eyes had nothing to do with the wounds.

"She's afraid to go in," Sovelet said. "We came down last. But when Katuva didn't see you, she didn't want to go in."

Acharon thought that was odd. "Well, I'm here now?"

Sovelet looked at Katuva, who looked at Acharon before nodding to Sovelet. Achron pushed open the door. When Katuva hesitated, Sovelet arched her eyebrows. With a sigh, Acharon stepped into the dining room ahead of the two women. They followed several slow steps behind.

The room was still the same as when they'd all charged out the night before. Now they were approaching another night. The holiday lights on the walls and the slow turning disco ball above seemed to mock the severity of the moment.

Everyone was sitting at two tables, occupying one side of each, so everyone faced into the center of the room. They looked a cocktail mix of tired, concerned, and annoyed.

The only person who seemed to be distilled down to a single emotion was Jamon. "Good," he said. "Let's get this over with."

"Yes," said Sovelet. "Let's. Start by telling us why we're all here like this?"

Jamon jabbed a finger in Katuva's direction. "Her. She was a poison introduced to the enclave. It's because of her that ten good people are dead."

"I didn't do it," Katuva said. Her voice was sorrowful. "I told them not to. I begged them not to."

"Liar! You couldn't get Acharon and Sovelet to do it with you," Jamon said. He stepped towards Katuva but stopped when Acharon stepped partially in front. "So, you came here and found other people to trick into doing it."

"Excuse me." Harriet had her hand up. "I'm sorry, but if she wanted to find other people to make passage with, why is she still alive?"

Jamon's face twisted with a sneer. "Because she's a coward. A coward twice over."

"No!" The bark of Katuva's voice startled, even Acharon. "It's true I was a coward the first time. But not this time. I told them I wasn't going to do it. That I was wrong before."

"Wrong before?" Sovelet asked. She stroked Katuva's good arm. "With me and Acharon?"

Katuva shook her head. "No. When Carter tricked me into missing passage. He told me he was afraid. That he'd changed his mind. But, I think that the truth was that he knew I didn't really want to."

"So, he did it for you?" It was Jaina speaking, drawing Katuva's attention to her. "But he let you blame him?"

Katuva sniffed hard, and Acharon realized she was crying.

"He let me be mad at him for years. And then, before I could even bring myself to thank him, he slipped on the ladder and died. I could have gone someplace else. San Francisco was still open. Here. Chicago, Atlanta. But I was afraid."

"It was us who should have been afraid," Jamon said. He was still angry as far as Acharon could see, but the fires were diminished.

"Oh, hush," said Jaina.

"Then," Katuva continued. Acharon felt she was talking more for herself than anyone else. "Acharon and Sovelet came by. I thought I could do it then if I had people with me. Prove that I hadn't been afraid before. So I – I'm sorry – I destroyed the monorail, so they'd have to stop."

"And almost got me killed." Acharon hadn't meant to say it out loud. Fortunately, it had dribbled out as an angry muttering. Sovelet heard enough to glare at him.

Katuva continued, saying, "But when I made them dinner and showed them the pills and made the offer, Acharon refused."

"You're darn right."

"What I didn't say," said Katuva, turning just enough to make eye contact with Acharon, "was that I was relieved to hear it."

"Then why did you come here and convince all these people -- my wife, included! -- into taking this damn passage by death crap?" Jamon's anger was back.

Katuva matched him with her own anger. "I didn't convince them. They were already convinced."

The mutterings of surprise bubbled for several seconds.

"They were already planning it?" Benen asked.

"Yes. But they didn't know the protocol to request the pills from the medi-pods. They didn't know the ceremony. They wanted me to lead them. I wouldn't. And last night, when I realized they'd gone already, I got scared. I wanted to go home, and I just ran."

"I'd seen her from her room window," Sovelet said. "I didn't know where she was going. I didn't think I had time to tell anyone. So, I ran after her, remembering to grab a shotgun. I didn't know it was empty."

"I taught you better than that."

"Oh, hush, Acharon."

"They lied to us both, Katuva." Sena stood and came around the table to give Katuva a hug. She turned to the group. "They told us they were going to refuse to go. Then, after you all had left, they were going to have the dinner and the ceremony. I think they were afraid we might stop them."

"You should have!"

"Easy, Jamon," said Benen.

"No. No." Jamon wagged his finger at everyone. His eyes were wet with future tears. "I will not get on that boat with her. She is a sickness. She infects the people around her."

"Now hang on," Sovelet said. "She told you that she asked them not to. It had nothing to do with her."

"She's lying."

Acharon had a gut feeling that Jamon didn't believe his own words at this point. But he was too hurt and too far gone with his anger to step back. Clearing his throat, Acharon stepped forward.

"I will admit that I have not trusted Katuva," Acharon said. "Not since I first learned why she was there in the town all alone. But I think we need to trust her now. Her words have been corroborated by Sena, by Sovelet. And I don't think we should leave anyone behind. Not if they want to go."

"She should stay." Jamon's anger was rising again.

Acharon was tired and wanted an end to all of it. He wanted some food, he wanted to go and get some sleep. "I'll make it simple for everyone," he said. "If you make Katuva stay, I'm staying. And if I stay, I'm pretty sure Sovelet will stay."

"I will," said Sovelet.

"And me," Sena said. She hugged Katuva, bathing her in a companionable smile.

"Well, if Acharon stays, I don't see a reason to go," said Benen.

The rest of the people nodded and said enough that it was clear they weren't going to go without Katuva.

Jamon looked at them, his anger muffled by a sadness. He shook his head and finally said, "I won't get on that boat with that woman on it." He turned and walked out of the room, his head bent low.

"Should someone go and be with him?" Asher asked.

"I don't think it will help," said Thaddeus. "He may feel differently tomorrow."

There was a general mumble of agreement.

Benen stood. Everyone looked at him. "I don't mean to sound callous, but I saved the leftovers from last night. If anyone's hungry?"

26

"Ach? Tides starting to turn."

Acharon, who'd been standing on the pier, his hands shoved into his pants pockets, looked over at Sovelet, and smiled.

"Thank you," he said. "We can wait a little bit longer."

Sovelet smiled back and then disappeared into the cabin. She, Katuva, and Jaina were in the nav station. They were monitoring the time and weather while catching Katuva up on the boat's systems.

Everyone else was topside, sitting in the cockpit or standing in pairs fore and aft. They were all engaged in conversations filled with nervous energy. None of them, except for Sovelet, had ever sailed before. He'd joked that they might need some extra buckets for the first few days. Benen had taken it seriously and disappeared for thirty minutes to return with a stack of plastic pails.

They were only missing one person now. Acharon had a feeling Jamon wasn't going to show, but he was going to hope and hold out as long as he could.

The night had been long, even after Jamon had stormed out of the dining room. The conversations for the rest of them had been centered mostly around Katuva and Sena's involvement with the group. A group that everyone, including Asher, had thought Green was leading. It was with hindsight that Asher recalled seeing Boone and Green in conversations in the hallway or the lobby since Katuva had shown up with Acharon and Sovelet.

Benen admitted in the conversation that he'd been led by Boone to suspect Green was the one responsible for torching the first boat. Acharon had thought Asher would deny and defend angrily for his partner's honor. Instead, he reluctantly admitted that he had had the same concerns as well. All of them, through the conversation, came to the realization that they'd been fed the idea by the same person. Boone.

The emotional roller coaster they all went through over coffee and slightly stale cake was almost as tough as the night before, stepping into the restaurant with the ten dead at their passage dinner. Even Acharon had slept in the next morning.

They'd delayed another day, the start of their own passage. They'd searched for Jamon when it was clear he wasn't in his apartments. They'd checked every room in the enclave, the nearest museums, Grace's grave.

Jamon had said he wouldn't go. Not with Katuva on board. It was clear to Acharon that he meant it. The proclamation weighed heaviest on Katuva.

"Benen," Acharon said. He was still scanning the streets at the end of the pier.

"Yep, Acharon?"

"Let's get ready to move the boat."

Acharon could hear the grin in Benen's response. "Aye, aye, captain."

As Acharon listened with one ear to Benen giving instructions, he watched a little longer. A fox had trotted by, scattering a small warren of rabbits. Deer grazed on Pier 84. Nothing resembling a broken-spirited human appeared.

"We're ready when you are," Benen said from the boat. He had one hand on a shroud, maintaining his balance.

Acharon pulled his hands from his pockets and clapped them against the outsides of his thighs. "Right. Let's get going, then."

The day of the dance, Acharon, with help from some of the others, had used the flood tide and ingenuity to turn the boat. The bow now faced the Hudson and New Jersey. They'd run a series of lines based on his plan. They now used those lines, letting them out aft, hauling them in at the bow, crawling the boat along the pier.

When the boat was about a third of the way into the river, Acharon had everyone tie off. Two more lines were run out to the pier cleats and back to the boat.

Acharon delayed one more time before stepping aboard the boat. Still no Jamon.

"Okay, Benen," he said. "Let's get the teams on the lines."

While Acharon set himself behind the wheel, Benen got the teams on the lines they'd be pulling on command.

Sovelet appeared at the bottom of the cabin steps. "Still, no?"

"Still, no," said Acharon. "And we need to go."

"I'm sorry."

Acharon nodded. "Me, too."

Sovelet disappeared into the nav station. Acharon turned to find Benen standing nearby. He gave Acharon a nod.

"Let's do it," Acharon said. "Toss the aft line and get the teams pulling."

Benen saluted and worked his way aft. Acharon was reassured to see Benen always finding a handhold. There wasn't a medi-pod on the boat. There wasn't going to be one until they reached France. Even then, they had no idea if the facilities at Le Havre, where the Seine entered the English Channel, were still working.

The boat jerked forward. Someone below yelped in surprise. Laughter bubbled up from below.

"Easy on the lines," Acharon said to the teams on deck. "Strong but steady."

The boat moved further off the edge of the pier and began to turn downriver.

"Throw off the lines!"

There was a jumble of chatter from the people on the deck as they attempted to push rope. Fortunately, no one was holding the lines as the boat moved further in the river, guided by Acharon at the helm. They allowed the last of the ropes to slither over the side.

Cheers and applause filled the air. They were finally off.

"Lines are clear, captain." Benen was grinning again. "How much rope do I give the dinghy?"

"Fifty meters, for now," Acharon said. He still had a wild hope that Jamon would appear. They couldn't stop the ship from moving with the current if he did. But they could trail the dinghy as far back as a hundred meters. If needed, they could also drop the sails to slow their progress.

"Fifty meters. Got ya." Benen moved aft once more.

Acharon turned his attention to the sails and their heading. The man who had commissioned the boat nearly two hundred years ago had planned well for single-handed sailing. All of the lines, the halyards, and roller controls for the sails were readily at hand and clearly labeled. Acharon was able to adjust the sails himself, getting the best trim for moving slowly down the Hudson while still maintaining rudder control.

They sailed slowly past the south end of Manhattan, the skyscrapers looming quietly in the late afternoon light. Someone at the front of the boat had noticed harbor dolphins. Now the boat's crew was sitting along the rails, feet dangling as they laughed and pointed.

Sometime later, as they neared Battery Park, Katuva had come topside with a tray of paper wrapped sandwiches. The very last of Benen's lettuce and tomatoes with a protein spread he'd made tasty with spices and rehydrated pickles.

When she returned to the cockpit, there were still several sandwiches on the tray.

"Do you want one?" she asked Acharon. "I didn't touch them."

Acharon paused. He wasn't sure if Katuva was teasing him or worried that he still did not trust her.

"Yes, please," he said. He took a sandwich and set it on the cabin top in front of him. "And if you don't mind, would you pour me a cup of coffee? The carafe is behind you on the table."

It was Katuva's turn to pause. She slowly set the tray down and moved to the table. Acharon turned his attention back to the wheel and the compass. He did an eye inspection of the sails while he waited. He only turned his attention back to Katuva when she put a thermos cup in the holder by his side.

"Thank you," he said.

"Thank you, Acharon."

She took the tray and disappeared below. Acharon took the cup and sipped the coffee, glad for the heat it sent through him. As he set the cup back in the holder, he looked around at the passing city. It was too late now for Jamon to catch them. Even if he was aware of their departure.

It saddened Acharon to think that someone was staying here, alone and angry. But, he wasn't sure he wouldn't have done the same thing if Sovelet had died, too. Maybe Jamon would find peace, maybe he wouldn't. Only he could decide.

As for the rest of them, they had made a different decision.

"Hey, Benen."

"Yeah?" Benen was on the aft end of the boat, watching where they'd been.

"Let the dingy go."

Benen reached for the line, wrapped around a cleat, and began to unwind it.

"Time to go to Paris?"

Acharon responded by pushing a button that pulled the boom closer to the centerline of the boat. The wind pushed harder against the sail, causing the boat to heel over several degrees as it leapt forward, like a lunging cat.

Shouts of surprise and laughter came from the fore of the boat where Thaddeus, Marianne, and Sena had been sitting with their legs over the leeward side. With several shouts of mock anger for the pilot, they moved to the higher windward side. Everyone seemed in good spirits for the trip.

Acharon nodded to himself. "Time to go to Paris."

The End

ABOUT THE AUTHOR

Earl T. Roske is a San Francisco Bay Area writer who juggles writing with childcare, housecleaning, cooking, and dog walking. Despite all that, he still continues to not only write, but to enjoy the process as well.

If you enjoyed this book, consider leaving a review online. It helps readers choose a book and it helps the author, too.

If you're interested in new work by the author, or just want to drop him a line, try the following.

Follow on Facebook:
www.facebook.com/EarlTRoske/

Follow on Amazon to be notified of future releases:
www.amazon.com/Earl-T.-Roske/e/B006GD53XE

Follow on Twitter:
twitter.com/earltroske

And, of course:
www.earltroske.com

Finally:
earltroske@earltroske.com